For all those individuals throughout my life, whether they knew they were teaching or telling stories or just saying out loud what they know, thank you for sharing your knowledge. I have learned so much.

The Cactus Plot

ISBN: 9781932926835 (paperback)
9781932926842 (e-book)
LCCN: 2019942116

Artemesia Publishing
9 Mockingbird Hill Rd
Tijeras, New Mexico 87059
info@artemesiapublishing.com
www.apbooks.net

The Cactus Plot

Murder in the High Desert

By

Vicky Ramakka

Artemesia Publishing
Albuquerque

1. High Desert

In the Southwestern outback, women were expected to shed the prissy helplessness acceptable back east and pull their own weight, whether on top of a horse or alongside it, through dust storms, thunder, lightning, pouring rain, pounding hail, burning heat, or howling snowstorms at high noon or in the dead dark of night.
—Lesley Poling-Kempes, *Ladies Of The Canyons*

Desert sun glowed red through Millie Whitehall's closed eyelids. She pushed herself upright in the seat of her beat-up Ford Explorer and opened her eyes. A huge red and yellow sign, Welcome to the Land of Enchantment, stood at the edge of the truck stop parking lot along Interstate 40.

She fumbled for the day-old coffee in the cup-holder, took a big gulp and opened the door. Stepping out, Millie breathed in New Mexico's cool, morning air. A clump of cholla grew in the sand just beyond the parking lot. "Wow, cholla, genuine cholla cactus." Millie grinned. "I made it."

She hit the restaurant for a trucker's breakfast and a coffee refill. Back on I-40, Millie pushed the old Ford to just a little over the 75 mile per hour speed limit. Every few miles, exit ramps dropped onto empty roads that disappeared into distant blue hills. A cluster of signs sent tourists toward Santa Fe, the "City Different," according to her New Mexico guidebook. A few miles before entering the yellow haze hanging over Albuquerque, New Mexico's largest city, the GPS spoke a command to take the next exit. Millie veered off the interstate and followed arrows guiding travelers toward the Four Corners. "No more polluted city air for me. I feel like a pioneer heading to unknown territory. At least it's all new for me."

She saw another sign that added to her anticipation– Rio Grande River. Muddy water fanned out across the sandy bottom. It was no wider than the Lawrence Brook that flowed through Milltown, New Jersey, which had been her whole world until three days ago.

Siri's voice broke in, "Continue on route for one-hundred and sixty miles." She was gaining on her destination–Wellstown, New Mexico–where she would inventory threatened and endangered plants. Her first real job. She'd be working in the southeast portion of the Colorado Plateau, in high desert, the area's plant species remarkable for their adaptation to extreme temperatures ranging from above 100 degrees in summer to below zero in winter. She'd be among those unique plants, adapted to survive on ten inches, or less, of moisture a year, and most of that coming from winter rain and snow.

Near noon, Millie tapped her phone awake and asked for directions to the nearest gas station. Twenty miles. A quick glance at the state highway map at her elbow showed Cuba as the next town. "Cuba? Siri, are you pulling my leg?"

Approaching the edge of town, Millie leaned over the steering wheel and twisted to peer up at the steep hills edging the east side of the community. Even though it was late March, patches of snow shaded by tall ponderosa pines still covered much of the ground. She bypassed struggling businesses lining both sides of the highway: a Dollar Store, feed store, and a soft serve ice cream place in what appeared to be a former gas station. Half were boarded up, the remainder surviving on providing essentials to local residents who could not or did not want to drive sixty miles to the next closest town.

Finally, something familiar. The golden arches pulled her like a magnet. The combination fast food, convenience store, and gas station was jammed with cars, pickups, motor homes, and tractor-trailer trucks. She maneuvered to the first available gas pump and stepped out into a cold breeze. She shivered and reached for a windbreaker. *High desert, all right.*

Millie watched the pump's gauge roll to astronomical numbers to feed the Explorer's tank and deplete her credit card. She clasped her hands over her head and stretched upward until her heels left the ground. Her lanky 5' 10" body ached from being cooped up for three days on the road. She pulled off the elastic band at the nape of her neck, letting her shoulder-length hair swing back and forth.

The gas hose clunked to a stop. Millie twisted the gas cap back on and patted the Explorer's roof. "Hang on, Rust Bucket. You and I have a lot of exploring to do." She hoped the trusty vehicle would hold up for a little while longer, until she could earn enough to get a newer model with better gas mileage, maybe even something a little sporty. When Millie received her acceptance letter to Rutgers University, the rusted 2010 Explorer was the best choice on the used car lot. It was the most "practical," her father assured her. It would get her back and forth to Rutgers for classes. It was a route he knew well, having worked the night shift in the university's mail room for nearly 32 years. The real selling point for her father was that it had plenty of room for loading supplies for the family's custodial business. *Practical* was always the overriding consideration in Millie's family. At least, its sangria red color made it stand out from the other mediocre choices.

Little did Millie know at the time that she and Rust Bucket would become explorers together, traveling west 2,000 miles. The day after she finished graduate school, she had the vehicle packed and ready to leave. Tears rolled down her cheeks when she waved goodbye to the family and pulled away from the home where she grew up. The tired, conflicted look on her mother's face hurt even more.

Millie shook her head, trying to push away that scene which kept surfacing at least once for every state line she had passed. *They were so proud at graduation. They'd both worked so hard to put Bobby, then me, through college. They had to know I was going to leave.*

There had been few words spoken among them after Millie's announcement that she planned to take a job with the Bureau of Land Management in New Mexico. "That's crazy," her mother said, "how am I supposed to take on cleaning for that new office complex if you run off and study plants at the edge of civilization." *They never said a word about Bobby joining the Army after he graduated. Being the oldest, I guess, made it okay for him.*

She moved Rust Bucket to a parking spot next to the store. The mini-mecca for travelers offered a stunning array of junk food choices. Next to the drink dispensers, desiccated hot dogs rolled endlessly under a heat lamp. Millie grabbed two granola bars, filled her coffee mug, and went to the counter.

The woman at the cash register shifted her eyes from her cell phone just long enough to take in Millie's purchases, and mumbled, "Two thirty-seven."

A newspaper rack next to the counter offered the *Cuba*

News, the *Wellstown Chronicle*, and *Navajo Times*. Millie placed two more quarters on the counter and picked up the Wellstown edition. She said "thanks," and backed out the door with purchases in each hand.

A headline on the bottom of the front page caught her eye. "Body Found On BLM Piñon Resource Area Still A Mystery." *Wait a minute—that's where I'll be working.* She skimmed the three-paragraph article. An archaeologist employed by the Bureau of Indian Affairs fell to his death from a cliff. His body was found by an oil and gas field hand. To date no additional information was being provided by the Medical Investigator's Office.

Millie stopped in mid-stride and read the article again. *That was just a week ago.* She jumped at the beep of a car horn and hustled out of the way. She tossed the newspaper onto the back seat. *I may be a city kid, but at least I know enough not to walk off a cliff.*

Back on the highway, Millie sang out, "Happy Trails to me, happy trails to meeee." Would they be happy trails? Had it been foolish to respond to that flyer on the bulletin board in the Plant Sciences Building about seasonal jobs in federal agencies? The flyer's words flashed in her mind, "Get real world experience in your chosen career." Chosen career—that was the question. Following her heart into botanical research as her professors assumed she would do, or being the good daughter trapped into managing the family's custodial business, like her mother expected. She stepped on the gas pedal, distancing herself from making that decision.

Not a wisp of cloud marred the crystal-clear sky. The landscape sometimes ran for ten miles with little evidence of human occupation except for the dilapidated barbed wire fences to discourage cattle from wandering onto the highway. She marveled at rock cliffs of red, orange, and gray layers and rubbernecked from side to side to take in the sparse vegetation leading to hills dotted with juniper trees and sagebrush.

Finally, the road dropped down into the San Juan River valley. Millie heaved a tired sigh. "Well, here it is, my future lies below." Wellstown's streetlights outlined the strip of homes and businesses along the river. She drove along Main Street, both sides bordered by fast-food restaurants and auto dealerships, their lots mainly featuring gleaming new pick-up trucks. Siri's voice guided her left and right until she reached the small rental house on Rio Camino Lane.

She had picked it from a list of rentals on the internet and scraped together a two-month deposit. All the rentals sounded pretty much alike, "two-bedroom, one-bath, eat-in kitchen," but she liked this one's picture showing an inviting front porch shaded by a giant cottonwood tree.

She spotted the big cottonwood, confirmed the street number and pulled into the driveway. Millie looked up and down the quiet street and gave her back a good stretch after the long drive. She found the front door unlocked, just as the landlord had e-mailed it would be. She surveyed the drab living room, with its worn furniture and ratty shag carpet. *Looks like this place hasn't been updated since before I was born.* Millie nodded. *It'll do.* She was on her own at last, away from peering into microscopes in chemical-smelling labs, away from lugging mop buckets and working until midnight. *I'll be outdoors, doing what I love.*

On Sunday morning, Millie drove to a grocery store to stock up on granola bars and quick-fix meal supplies. In daylight, she determined that the sprawling community was nothing like the images on the state's tourism website. There were no charming adobe casitas with dogs sleeping in the street. Instead, Wellstown's residential neighborhoods mingled with businesses related to oil and gas extraction—machine shops, pipe yards, welding supply stores, and heavy equipment dealers. Big-box stores were prominent—Wellstown being the primary shopping center in a 100-mile radius. She drove past SAM's Club, Walmart, Target and a half dozen dollar stores.

"OMG, how can anybody live here? Milltown may be an old industrial town, but at least people had grass lawns and trees." Millie's gut twisted with an urge to turn around, pack up, and head back East, leaving the unappealing town and scummy little rental house behind. She grasped the steering wheel tighter; that's what her mother expected—that she would retreat back into the family fold. "One season, a few months, I can stick it out."

She steered west and found the Bureau of Land Management office, a boxy, nondescript cinder block building. Millie pulled into the empty parking lot and stopped to read the hours of operation stenciled on the front door. She would be ready to report Monday morning for her new job. She had to know if there was a future for her as Millie-the-botanist, instead of just one of the invisible night workers cleaning other people's fancy offices.

2. Be Careful Out There

Next to the federal government as a whole, the Bureau of Land Management (BLM) is the nation's largest landlord.
—James R. Skillen, *The Nation's Largest Landlord*

Millie arrived at the BLM office a half hour before opening time. Two cars and a pickup truck already occupied the choice spots closest to the front door. Millie lined her SUV up next to them, ensuring it was parallel to the dividing lines.

"Well, you must be the new seasonal botanist," a portly woman with short, wavy hair called out when Millie came through the door. Wiggling out of a heavy sweater and muttering about cold spring weather, the woman maneuvered out from behind the reception area counter. She wrapped an arm around Millie's shoulders, "Welcome to Piñon Resource Area. My name's Agrippina, but everybody calls me Momma Agnes. Let's get you settled into your office."

"I'm Millie Whitehall. Thanks for the welcome, I'm glad to be here." Millie felt so relieved, she wanted to laugh and cry at the same time. A hug and a friendly welcome. And an office. They wanted her here.

Momma Agnes walked with a seesawing gait that nearly filled the hallway. Millie followed through a maze of office cubicles, labeled with the names and titles of the occupants of each workspace—archaeologist, geologist, recreation specialist, range conservationist, civil engineer—specialists doing work in professions that she had only heard of as majors in college.

Her guide pointed to the last cubicle. "This is where you'll be for the summer. Herb Thompson was the botanist here before. He retired four months ago. He celebrated with a trip along the West Coast, said he wanted to swim in the ocean and see real trees. He called his office the 'Herbarium.' Get it?" She winked. "If you wanted to see Herb, just go to the herbarium. That position probably won't be filled until next fall, so make yourself at home."

She looked at her watch. "Ay, *dios mio*, time to get ready for the meeting. It's the All Employees monthly meeting. Be there at 8:30 sharp. The area manager always starts on time. If you need anything at all, hon, you come see Momma Agnes." She gave Millie a quick hug and walked back down the hall.

Millie turned to look at what was not really an office, but a cubicle indistinguishable from all the others she just passed, except this one had no name attached. She took a step back, dumbfounded by the disarray she faced. The desk was barely visible under stacks of maps, manuals, and memos. Posters of wildflowers and pictures of flowering cactus, tacked up with pushpins, crowded the cubicle's cloth walls. Plant presses, field guides, more manuals, and a few dried-out plants, roots and all, were stacked willy-nilly on the waist-high metal shelves.

She felt a tap on her shoulder. Millie turned to see a short woman in jeans and a tan T-shirt. At nearly six feet tall, Millie perceived almost all other women as short.

"Hi. I'm Linda. I'm a range con. Come on, the meeting's in the warehouse."

Other resource specialists emerged from their cubicles. Millie kept pace with Linda, not wanting to get lost among these strangers. Linda said, "You'll get to know all these guys in no time. And get ready to be introduced at the meeting today." They left the main office building and entered the nearby warehouse. Metal folding chairs were already set up, enough to accommodate the hundred or so BLM Piñon Resource Area staff.

A man in his mid-forties stepped to the front. The crisp brown trousers and tan button-down shirt conveyed that this individual was in charge. His self-assured composure riveted the employees' attention.

"Morning, all. Before we get to the announcements, here's this month's safety video." The lights dimmed. A muffled groan went up as a sonorous voice on the video announced, "*Skin Cancer, Everybody's Enemy.*"

Linda leaned over and whispered, "That's the Area Manager, Wirt Hernshaw."

Half watching the video and half looking around, Millie felt out of place in twill slacks, a white, long-sleeve oxford blouse, and corduroy jacket. She thought dressing in what, back East, is considered Friday casual would be appropriate. Instead, her cleaning scrubs would have fit in better. Jeans appeared to be the norm for this crowd.

When the safety video ended, Wirt Hernshaw stepped back into view. Announcements included names of three new summer staffers. Millie slid out of her preppie-looking jacket seconds before Wirt called her name. "Miss Millicent Whitehall is here for the season filling in for Herb Thompson. She's from back East." Millie stood at her name, but was already collapsed back in her chair by the time he got to the back East part. *Why did I think wearing this bright white blouse today was a good idea.*

"Momma Agnes is next on the agenda. She has an

announcement." He motioned to Momma Agnes, who hustled to the front.

"We're having a potluck this Friday and I'm going to make tamales." This brought cheers and whistles from all parts of the cavernous room. "But, it's going to cost you—seven dollars. It's for Harrison Howdy's funeral expenses, so you'd better cough up." This last part brought dead silence.

Millie gave Linda a quizzical look. Linda signaled with finger to her lips that Wirt was about to speak. Millie settled back and turned her attention to the area manager. *Something happened here that disturbs everybody. Maybe this is who the news article was about in that Wellstown Chronicle I picked up in Cuba.*

Hernshaw took over. "You've all heard how Harrison died. Awful way to go, fell off that cliff, stone cold on the road when the field hand found him. He wasn't BLM, but most of you worked with him on BIA archeology consultations. He was like one of our own, and we'll miss him."

The area manager paused, then said, "So be careful out there." Millie rolled her eyes at the hackneyed expression but snapped back to attention when he continued. "The 'bagos are out, snowbirds from Phoenix going back north, retirees creeping along at five miles an hour. Be patient, don't pass 'em if you can't see around them. And keep an eye out for mares sneaking into sagebrush away from wild horse herds to drop their foals. Remember—rattlers will be starting to move around and you know how crabby they are this time of year." This last received quiet nods of agreement.

The area manager went on to cover several more items, most of which seemed to be a mix of names, terms, and acronyms that made little sense to Millie. Metal chairs scraping over the concrete floor signaled the end of the meeting. Momma Agnes motioned to Millie. "Hon, Wirt wants to meet with you after lunch. Come by my desk at 1:30. His office is just off the reception area."

* * *

By the appointed meeting time, Millie had the cubicle organized to her satisfaction. Only a computer, pens, and a yellow pad remained on the desk. Books on shelves were upright and arranged by category. The plant specimens were relegated to a bottom shelf.

Linda walked by and blurted out, "Holy cow. Hard to believe this was Herb's office. Bet you'll have it messed up in no time, just like the rest of us."

"Unh, unh. This is my first real office. I'm going to keep it this way. Besides, my folks have an office cleaning business. I know how to make a place look neat, even if it isn't."

On the way to her meeting, Millie skimmed an office directory to familiarize herself with names of people at the morning's meeting. She stopped at the unusual name, Agrippina Martinez, Front Office Supervisor. Millie smiled. *Her title ought to be mother hen and social coordinator.*

When Millie got to the visitor's area, Momma Agnes nodded in her direction and continued speaking into the phone. "Yes, sir, I understand your concern. I'm going to transfer you to Law Enforcement Officer Ramirez. Miss Ramirez will take down the location where the drip gas was stolen." Momma Agnes pushed a button on the phone, pushed another, and said into the line, "Robby, I've got another one for you."

Uninviting leatherette chairs lined one beige wall of the reception area. A brochure rack beside the front door displayed pamphlets on topics ranging from horseback trails to leave-no-trace hiking. Millie cocked her head at an arrangement of poster-size photographs showing a herd of galloping wild horses, a drilling rig, and a canyon sunset scene. A plaque on the wall indicated the photos were taken on the Piñon Resource Area. She couldn't resist. She stepped over and straightened the galloping wild horses, aligning it exactly level with the other photographs.

The office matriarch waved Millie over. "The area manager is on the phone right now. I'll let you know when you can go in. How's your first day on the job, Miss Millie?"

"It's not what I expected, Mrs. Martinez, but I didn't really know what to expect." She certainly never envisioned meetings in a warehouse, the prospect of rattlesnakes, or the casualness of her new office.

"One thing you need to learn right off the bat, you call me Momma Agnes, like everybody else does." She tapped a plaque on the counter. Glittering blue letters spelled out MOMMA AGNES. "Navajos make these sand paintings from colored sand or ground up rocks, like this turquoise here. Sand paintings used to be made only for ceremonial purposes. Now-a-days, you can get sand painted nametags, Christmas ornaments, most anything. Want a nameplate? I can put out an order for you."

Millie shook her head. "I'm only a temp. I don't want BLM to spend money on something I'd only need for the summer."

"Oh, hon, these aren't government issue. Each one is special made. See, this one has a corn plant and a stack of tamales by my name, that's because I make the best tamales of anybody in this office. Harrison Howdy gave it to me the first year I was here. He said Agrippina Maria Galleagos-Martinez was too much of a mouthful. So he started calling me Momma Agnes. God rest his soul."

"That's who Mr. Hernshaw talked about this morning? The Friday potluck is raising funds to cover his funeral expenses."

Momma Agnes touched fingertips to her forehead, heart, and each shoulder. "Harrison was the archaeologist for the Bureau of Indian Affairs. He was in here a lot, doing consultations on projects that cross over BLM and BIA land. That don't make sense to me, him falling off a cliff. He was strong as an ox and everybody said he knew the backcountry better than most." She leaned closer and whispered, "I still think there's something fishy about it, the way it happened."

Momma Agnes picked up the nameplate and turned it over, so Millie could read the maker's name written in pencil on the back. "Want one? I can put an order out."

Millie's eyes fixed on the turquoise blue letters, and the corn plant rendered in soft shades of sand. In her mind, the colors shouted, "I'm in New Mexico." She wanted one. "Sure, I'll pay for it," she said, without even asking the cost.

Momma Agnes ripped off a telephone message note and on the back side, printed a big M. "Millicent has two l's in it, right?"

"Oh, no, make it read Millie, that's M-i-l-l-i-e."

"I'll tell Ray Yazzie to make you one, next time he comes by."

"When's that?"

"No telling. I'll put word out on the moccasin telegraph that we want one, and it'll probably show up in a couple of weeks."

"But, when...?" Millie started to ask.

"I'll tell him to put plants on it. You like plants, right?"

"Okay, but no tamales." Millie hadn't ever tasted tamales, but considering the woman's girth, they certainly were not a diet food.

Momma Agnes glanced at the row of lights on her phone. "There, he just hung up." She called across the visitors' area toward an open office door, "Hey, Wirt, that new

15

botanist is here to see you."

∗ ∗ ∗

Wirt Hernshaw came around his desk, extending a hand. "Welcome, Miss Whitehall. We're glad to have someone with your qualifications with us for the field season." He motioned her to a chair and stepped back behind his desk. It was loaded with stacks of documents, framing the 5' 6" man in bureaucracy. Her new boss wasted no time in getting down to business.

"There's a half dozen federally listed threatened or endangered plants known to occur on the Piñon Resource Area. We got that pinned down in the early 1990s. You're going to be monitoring these for any significant changes.

"Also, be on the lookout for any of the sensitive species that occur in northwest New Mexico or could even be close by on our borders with Arizona, Utah, and Colorado. Sensitive plant species are those with limited distribution or special habitat requirements that could become endangered if impacted by development." He spread a large map across the paper mounds on his desk. "Here's what our GIS folks came up with for you. It overlays geologic formations, soil types, vegetation communities, roads, and well sites.

"We get a half-dozen or so APDs in here a month. Companies need to know which locations are excluded from drilling because of archeological sites, T and E species, wildlife habitat, and such. Having critical areas already identified saves headaches for everybody."

Millie shook her head. She had reviewed the BLM's official website that the agency oversees more public land than any other federal agency. But she did not understand the alphabet soup of acronyms that Wirt was rattling off.

"Wait a minute, can I borrow something to write on?

GIS, I know—Geographic Information System—it's great for looking at landscapes as a whole, but..."

Wirt stopped, seeing the baffled look on Millie's face. "Uh, APD, that's an Application for Permit to Drill, and we use T and E as shorthand for threatened and endangered."

He leaned back and ran tanned fingers through sandy hair. "APDs, wild horse round-ups, shoot—we're even getting movie studios wanting to film zombie scenes in some of our most remote areas. So, the idea is, we want to have a good handle ahead of time where sensitive species occur or might occur on this RA—this Resource Area.

"Did you know they used to call BLM the 'land nobody wanted'? When the West was settled and public lands divvied up, the National Forest Service got places that had timber of any value, the National Park Service got the most scenic areas, and BLM got the left-over land that nobody wanted. Well, that isn't so anymore." He gave a wry laugh "Now it's the land EVERYBODY wants."

He rolled up the map, handed it to Millie, and moved over to bookshelves along one wall. "This will help you get started." He handed her a massive, spiral-bound document. Millie read the title, *Piñon Resource Area Management Plan*.

"That's an *Astragalus* on the cover, right?"

"*Mancos milkvetch*. That's one of the endangered species on our Resource Area. Ugly little weed, don't you think?"

"All plants are beautiful to a botanist," Millie shot back.

He grinned at her, revealing sun-etched crinkles around his eyes.

He pulled out Volume II, another enormous document. "Say, this is a good one, too," and piled on a smaller, soft cover book, *New Mexico Vegetation, Past, Present, and Future*.

"This Wednesday, I'm going to the north unit, where there's a proposed drill site I want to check. I'm meeting with the company rep there. I'll show you some of the country you'll be working in. It's mostly P-J, uh, piñon-juniper, in that area, but I'll show you the few ponderosa stands still left on the RA."

He stood and held the door open for her. "One more thing, go see TJ in the Motor Pool tomorrow. He'll set you up with a vehicle to use."

Millie staggered out of the office, with the rolled-up map under one arm and hands clasped beneath the documents balanced against her chest.

* * *

That evening back in her rental house, Millie created two folders on her laptop computer. While taking a Plant Biology Methods course as a sophomore in college, Millie had adopted the habit of making field notes of two types, one couched in scientific language and a second set with personal reflections.

She labeled the first folder "Notes BLM T&E Inventory" and proceeded to list citations for the stack of references she'd brought home to look over. The second folder, she labeled "Notes A Season in the High Desert," and typed: *Good grief, what have I gotten myself into!*

Millie closed the laptop but sat staring at the pile of references. I can do this. Can I do this? I've got to. Anything beats carrying mop buckets.

3. TJ's Orientation

Three of every five on-site fatalities in the oil and gas extraction industry are the result of struck-by/caught-in/caught-between hazards. ... including moving vehicles or equipment, falling equipment, and high-pressure lines.
—U.S. Occupational Safety and Health Administration

Millie's first order of business the following day was to find the Motor Pool. "Wirt told you to go see TJ and it's only your second day here?" Momma Agnes grumbled, "Well, OK, pass by the warehouse and go through the green door next to the shop's double doors. You'll find TJ there." She winked and added, "Good luck, hon."

Millie wondered why Momma Agnes seemed so disapproving, but followed her directions and stepped through the green door. The odor of motor oil and rags soaked with solvent told her she was in the right building. Four doors on the left were marked Men, Women, Tool Room, and Viceroy of Vehicles.

She tapped on the partially open Viceroy of Vehicles door and stepped inside. "Hi. Wirt told me to see you about a vehicle I could use. I'm Millie."

TJ twisted a knob on the radio to mute loud country-western music. "You must be that girl from New JOYsey. Here to look at pretty flowers all summer."

19

Millie met his stare. "I'm here to survey endangered species, not pretty flowers."

"Whatever you say, girlie." TJ leaned back in his chair, clunking against a metal cabinet behind him. "I'll get your vehicle assignment authorization. You've got to go through the goddamned defensive driving class. You can do it on a computer. Try and stay awake while they tell you how to parallel park, which nobody ever does around here."

He tore the top sheet from a clipboard hanging on a nail next to the cabinet. "The government has enough paperwork to choke a horse. We never did any *defensive* driving when we worked on the drilling rigs. I was in the oil and gas patch, you know. Ten years, until I got part of my foot ripped off by a cable gone wild." He tapped the head of a cane hooked over the edge of the desk. "Take the test, fill out the form, and bring it back. And here, read this."

Millie reached for the instruction sheet and pamphlet, "Tips for Safe Four-wheel Driving." She wasn't about to admit to this creep that she had never driven off paved roads, but resolved to study every word.

"Voc-Rehab trained me for an office job and got me a job here." TJ seemed compelled to make her understand he could still pull his own weight. "A clerk job, jeez, that's women's work. I was lucky though, getting on with the government, steady paycheck and benefits. I got so I could do the paperwork just right and started helping these bozo college graduates do the simplest maintenance on vehicles. I always could fix anything, so here I am, in charge of a half-million-dollar fleet of vehicles. I make sure every single one is safe and fit for field work."

"What if I just used my SUV? Would the BLM reimburse me for gas?" Millie offered.

TJ dropped his chair to the floor. "Hells bells, that's a

good one. As if government wisdom would ever let that happen. Especially that junker you drive. Safety, liability, all that crap. The girl wants to use her vehicle. Wait till my buddies hear that one."

Still chuckling, TJ pushed himself up from the chair, took hold of the cane, and limped to a pegboard attached to the tool room door. He lifted a ring with two keys and a credit card holder. "The vehicle you'll be using is the tan Suburban. It's a little beat up, but it'll get you where you want to go. It's the last one under the shed at the back of the garage. Might need gas." He dangled the keys so that Millie had to reach for them. "Here you go, girlie. Take good care of them pretty flowers."

Millie's ire carried her to the end of the vehicle shed. *What a condescending attitude. 'Pretty flowers.' Does he have a clue he works for an agency required to protect endangered plants?*

There it was, a dented, dusty Suburban, with a tumbleweed wedged under the front tire. Millie scraped dirt off the key lock and opened the door.

"You've got to be kidding." A ragged piece of artificial grass carpet covered a split down the driver's seat. Millie wiggled in behind the steering wheel and adjusted the crooked mirrors.

With low expectation she turned the key. The motor puttered to life. Millie's sigh of relief was short-lived. The odometer read 108,058 miles while the gas gauge needle dropped to E. "Uh-huh, worse than the windowless cubicle."

Millie returned to the office and passed through the reception area. Something about Millie's body language caused Momma Agnes to wave her over. "Don't mind *him*. TJ hassles everybody. His name is Theodore Jackson. He hates to be called Teddy, thinks it's a sissy name. He hates getting called Theodore even worse." Momma Agnes whispered, "We all think TJ stands for Total Jerk."

4. Oil Field Parade

...consistent with the BLM's goal of good stewardship, "multiple use" does not mean every use on every acre.
—Bureau of Land Management Website

The next morning, shortly before 7:00 a.m., Momma Agnes waved Millie out the door with a *"Vaya con Dios."* Area Manager Wirt Hernshaw was already waiting in his Ford Expedition, a shining coach compared to the old junker assigned to Millie. She tossed her daypack on the back seat and slipped into the passenger's seat.

At the edge of town, Wirt pulled into a vast parking lot encircling a small grocery store. "Want a burrito for lunch?"

"No, thanks. I brought my lunch."

Dressed in jeans, short-sleeve tan shirt, and brown cap, Wirt blended in with the steady stream of customers revolving in and out of the store. He came out carrying lunch and a giant cup of coffee. A savory aroma emanated from the paper bag he placed behind his seat.

"This place must have the best food in town. It's busier than Grand Central Station," Millie commented.

"Naw, it's just one of the places that opens early for oil and gas field hands heading out for the day. You can count on getting a burrito or sandwich, a supply of junk food, and sturdy coffee that'll keep you going all day. You should see this place about five-thirty or six in the morning."

For the next hour they followed the paved highway, joining the parade of white pickup trucks, most of them sporting orange flags wobbling on poles above the cabs. As the distance from town increased, the trucks funneled off onto dirt roads, quickly obscured by dust and brush. Only the flags waving above sagebrush warned other drivers that another vehicle was nearby.

Wirt glanced at his watch. "We should get to the Lejos Canyon Road by nine-thirty, no problem." But less than five minutes later, he slammed a fist on top of the steering wheel. "Son-of-a-bitch," he growled. Seeing Millie's startled look, he mumbled, "Whoops, sorry ma'am, I meant to say, ah, this is going to slow us down. No telling how long we'll be stuck crawling along behind this bunch."

Directly in front of them was a pickup truck with lights flashing and a Wide Load sign attached to its back bumper. It was the last in a line of two dozen closely spaced trucks and trailers that occupied the highway.

"Big rigs are on the move," Wirt said in a singsong voice. "That's what we say when we get behind one of these companies moving equipment to a drill site. Sometimes we say a few stronger words if we get stuck behind one of these outfits for miles on end."

A half-dozen trucks had huge round tanks strapped to their beds. Other trucks were loaded with stacks of pipe. Three vans carrying men wearing hard hats were scattered among this industrial parade. All the vehicles were gray with red logos and lettering.

When the convoy slowed to inchworm pace, Wirt gave a sigh of relief. "Good, they're turning off here. Just a few more minutes and we can get by them.

"Say what you want about the oil and gas industry, but

you've got to hand it to these fellows that work the rigs. One day you pass an empty canyon, the next day there's a hundred-foot-high rig assembled and ready to drill. Once they start, they go twenty-four hours a day, maybe for weeks at a time, to reach the deeper formations. These guys *work*. You're probably looking at a couple million dollars' worth of equipment right there."

"Will they be using fracking?"

"Oh sure, there's hardly been a well drilled here for the last three decades that hasn't used some type of fracking. Now with directional drilling, it's a whole new ballgame. They go down a mile, maybe two, then sideways through likely formations."

"What about fracking chemicals getting into peoples' drinking water?"

"Here, they're drilling deep, through sandstone layers. Water wells in this area don't go anywhere near that deep. Back East, that's a different story—the oil-bearing formations are closer to the surface, so wells are drilled a lot shallower. What's a problem in one part of the country might not have the same impact where the geology is different. The saying, 'geology is destiny,' definitely dictates when it comes to mineral extraction."

Wirt slowed and turned at a mud-spattered sign— Lejos Canyon Road.

"It takes a lot of water when they do the frack job— maybe two to six million gallons."

"*Millions* of gallons? There's hardly any water around here. Where does it come from?"

"Uh huh, millions. That seems to be the big impact around here. Most of it is from the river. Some of it gets recycled over and over. Some is disposed of in deep injection wells."

Wirt shrugged. "It's all a balancing act. Under Flipma,

the BLM is charged with managing public land for multiple use. Nothing to it—we just need to accommodate recreation, range, timber, minerals, watersheds, and wildlife, and protect scenic, historical, and cultural areas. Easy right?"

"Flip... what?"

"That's F-L-P-M-A, short for Federal Land Policy and Management Act passed in 1976. Contrary to that, is the old Mineral Leasing Act from back in the 1920s, which mandates, *mandates* mind you, leasing oil and gas, coal, and other minerals on public land. Then there's the Endangered Species Act of 1973. That act says no disturbance of endangered species habitat. It came not long after the first Earth Day, which spurred a number of environmental protection regulations. Over time, this act and that act result in conflicting mandates. Makes you want to pull your hair out."

Millie tightened the rubber band holding her ponytail in place. "Is that kind of like one federal act giveth and the other taketh away?"

Wirt laughed and nodded. "It's kind of like walking a tightrope. The country needs oil and natural gas. Sometimes this basin is called a 'sacrifice area'."

"So, how did you choose to work for the BLM?"

Wirt laughed, "I was too smart to know better. My teachers in school kept telling me I had *potential*, should make something of myself. So I was dumb enough to start college. Ate it up—courses in range management, ecology, discussions on environment that covered things I never heard talked about at the feed store. I learned to see all sides of an issue. Best part of college was I met Pauline there. This June will make our twenty-third anniversary."

The area manager became more talkative and his shoulders relaxed the farther they traveled from the office.

He seemed glad to have a willing ear.

"I grew up on a small ranch in Oregon. Dad, he went on the rodeo circuit—he was away most of the time. I guess rodeoing had more appeal than putting up hay and fixing fence. Anyway, it fell to my brother and me to keep the place out of the creditors' hands. My brother was the oldest, so he was first in line to take over the ranch when Dad never made it home from a bad ride at the Cheyenne Frontier Days."

They rode in silence for a while, Millie reflecting on how different her path to New Mexico was from this man's. Her upbringing consisted of the small world of Milltown and the surrounding boroughs, mainly seeing her environment from the inside of the buildings where her family contracted the cleaning services. Unlike Wirt's older brother that inherited the ranch, her older brother, Bobby, was off in the army and she was expected to take over the family business.

"Doesn't working for BLM put you at odds with ranchers?"

"Not for me. I can talk to ranchers, get them to look at things from all angles. My first job with BLM was in Lander, Wyoming. The years went by, I moved up the ranks. They said I was good with the public, could settle a crowd at public meetings. So here I am, a ranch kid ending up as area manager in one of the heaviest oil and gas locations managed by BLM."

Wirt slammed on the brakes. A creature like none Millie had ever seen occupied the center of the road. Braced on all four legs, stretched up to its full three-inch height, it thrust an orange chin forward, claiming the road as territory.

Wirt shoved the gear into park and got out. Millie followed. He snatched up the creature and held it in cupped hands. "Horny toad—you handsome devil, you won't live long enough to reproduce this spring if you sit in the middle of the road."

Millie looked at the rumpled captive. "Handsome? Even a kiss from a princess couldn't help that toad."

"Aw, they're harmless. Not a toad at all, really. It's a short-horned lizard. I hate to kill a creature, even one that takes the prize for ugly." Wirt walked into the sagebrush and set the little desert dweller in a shaded spot.

He slid back in the driver's seat and sent a grin in Millie's direction. "My dog has a slightly different philosophy, he thinks of horny toads as chew toys."

5. Tailgate Meeting

There are some 21,000 active oil and gas wells in northwest New Mexico.
—New Mexico Energy, Minerals and Natural Resources Department

Millie tried to resist grabbing the armrest as the Expedition bumped along Lejos Canyon Road. The gravel surface made for a rough ride, especially where rain and vehicle traffic exposed baseball-size rocks. Wirt seemed not to notice the jolting that flung her ponytail from side to side.

The road followed Lejos wash, which funneled spring runoff from the surrounding canyons into the San Juan River. The stream bed sprawled nearly a quarter mile across, the rippled, sandy bottom outlined by banks no more than a foot high.

"This time of year you can see water in Lejos wash," Wirt said. "In another month, it'll look dried up, but don't try crossing it even then. It has spots of quicksand here and there."

"Yeah, sure," Millie tried to sound casual. She pictured herself driving along this road in the ancient BLM Suburban assigned to her for the season. *No wonder it looks so beat up.*

Wirt slowed at a small metal sign stating "Dagun," with a spouting oil well logo. He turned and followed a gravel road for a quarter mile. Millie let go of the armrest. This newly constructed road was wide enough to accommodate the big drilling equipment trucks she saw earlier on the highway, except that sagebrush along the roadside might tickle those huge, round tanks.

Wirt slowed when he reached the well pad. The raised, rectangular area was flat as a pancake, covering more than four acres, quadruple the area of a shopping mall parking lot back in Milltown. The pad's sides sloped down into the surrounding sagebrush and native grasses, but on the pad itself, not a leaf or stem of natural vegetation was left.

Wirt leaned forward over the steering wheel, peering at the ground. "Watch out for anchors on a well pad." He nodded toward a thick metal loop extending 12 inches above the dirt. "There'll be a half dozen anchors buried deep in the ground. When the drill rig is put up, steel cables tie into these shanks to stabilize it, similar to the way guy ropes hold down a tent."

"What happens if one comes out?" Millie asked.

"They don't. They stay put in the ground even after drilling is completed. Whenever the company needs to come back and do a work-over on the well, the anchors need to be there."

Wirt stopped next to a white pickup parked in the center of the pad. Two men leaned against the truck's shadowed side. Wirt got out of the SUV and extended his hand as he walked toward the men. He called out, "Buddy, you old vulture bait. You still getting to drive the bosses around?" Millie came around the front of the vehicle and noticed her footsteps barely made an impression in the hard-packed dirt.

The shorter man grinned and pulled off his cap. His

tan shirt had "Buddy" embroidered over one pocket in a flamboyant red script. The Dagun well logo was on the other pocket. Jeans and scuffed work boots completed his outfit.

Wirt turned to Millie, "Meet Buddy Maddox, the most experienced field hand working the oil and gas patch. This is Millie Whitehall, botanist for the BLM. She'll be survey-ing threatened and endangered plants. She's on for the season, carrying on for Herb Thompson who retired last winter."

"Pleased to meet you, ma'am." Buddy extended a cal-loused hand.

Millie returned the firm handshake. She felt like she had just crossed some kind of divide. Here she was Millie, the botanist. The invisible night cleaning woman, Millicent Whitehall, had faded away somewhere east of the Mississippi.

Buddy introduced the man with him as the petroleum engineer in charge of situating the well. He wore a similar tan shirt with logo, but his engraved name tag, "Clay White", and his pressed khakis signaled professional status within the company.

Niceties over, Wirt led off, "What are we looking at here?"

The engineer carried a roll of maps to the back of the pickup, dropped the tailgate down, and spread out charts and diagrams. The compendium of maps described their location, from a mile beneath the surface to a satellite view showing spacing of nearby wells.

Buddy motioned Millie toward the front of the three-quarter-ton Ford F-350 truck. He pulled two bottles of water out of a cooler on the back seat and handed her one. Millie leaned into the cab to look at the array of gauges and computer screen. Seeing her interest, Buddy began pointing out the tools of his place of work.

"Couldn't do without that GPS, but you can't trust it either. I know most all the roads to Dagun well sites, but sometimes there's a washout or something and you have to figure out another way to get where you're going."

He lifted a worn leather case off the front seat and unzipped it, revealing a stack of tattered maps. "I use both USGS topo quadrants and the BLM land-use maps, and maybe the compass in my head," he laughed, tapping a stubby finger on his temple. His knuckles bulged, showing signs of encroaching arthritis.

He flipped the visor down and unclipped an instrument the size of a hand-held GPS with a small, square screen. "I don't know if you BLM guys are issued one of these, but this is a hydrogen sulfide gas detector. Your petroleum techs probably all have one. A few gas wells have what's called sour gas. It can be deadly. They'll have a sign and a windsock hanging somewhere. Even if there's no sign, if I get a whiff of rotten-egg smell, I get my fanny out of there, pronto."

"Geez, you mean it's that poisonous? Why is that allowed?"

Buddy nodded. "Money, Miss Millie, these wells pump money." He gave each device a wipe with a microfiber cloth as he described it.

The cab's interior surprised Millie. "Your truck's cleaner than anything I've seen at the BLM."

"Yup, I take good care of my truck. I might drive two, three hundred miles in a day. Once we have 100,000 miles on a vehicle, some of the companies will just sign it over to us for a dollar. It makes a feller think twice about tearing around these roads just because it's a company truck and not their own personal vehicle. I'm going to retire in a couple of years and I will have one fine truck for a dollar when I do."

The tailgate meeting ended with the petroleum engineer rolling up his maps and the two men shaking hands. Buddy touched his cap and said, "Nice meeting you, Miss Millie. Be seeing you around the gas patch." His slight Texas drawl and disarming manner made Millie think Buddy was the kind of person who never met a stranger.

The Dagun truck circled the pad and headed toward Wellstown. Wirt turned in the opposite direction. "We'll eat lunch at the ponderosa pine stand, then drive around to a couple locations I want you to check out."

He seemed satisfied with the meeting. "I'm sending a message through this guy. Even though we've already approved their permit to drill, sometimes we need to emphasize the BLM is serious about the stipulations we put on it. We'll be watching to make sure they wait until roads are good and dry before bringing in loads of heavy drilling equipment."

A jackrabbit dashed onto the road. Wirt hit the brakes. The rabbit froze, then made a 180 degree turn in one prodigious leap, and ran back into the sagebrush. The area manager ignored the interruption. "Once they complete drilling and re-veg the well pad, we stipulated they have to fence it to keep out old man Attencio's cows. Not that Attencio would bat an eye about his cows getting a little extra forage, but he'd have my neck if one of them came up lame or anything else he could blame on BLM."

6. The Cliff

To live in hearts we leave behind / Is not to die.
—*Thomas Campbell, 1825*

They hadn't traveled far and were still at a low elevation when the road curved along the base of a massive sandstone cliff. It threw a shadow over the road, causing chill air to whirl into their open windows. "Well, will you look at that?" Wirt slowed to a stop.

"This is where they found Harrison Howdy's body. Somebody's made a marker for him." Wirt rested his hands on the steering wheel and studied the small pile of rocks on the roadside. "Good of whoever put up that marker. I'm not surprised. He didn't have any family close by, but everybody who worked with him liked him. They called me out that morning. Poor man died right at that spot."

Wirt got out and went to the memorial. He straightened what appeared to be the handle from a shovel with a stick wired across it, making the shape of a cross. Millie opened the door on her side, but hesitated, sensing he wanted a quiet moment. When he walked a few steps farther along the road, Millie got out and joined him.

"I need to tell the maintenance crew to get out here and rake over these vehicle ruts." Wirt shook his head as he walked along, looking at the ground. "You wouldn't believe all the trucks that were parked here by the time they finally put his body into the ambulance."

Millie moved closer to hear his quiet voice.

"It was Buddy who first reported it. He called 911 saying there was a dead man on the road. Then he called it in to his company. Dagun's office notified me since it was on BLM land. They told me their field hand was real shook up, that at first he thought it was somebody sleeping by the road. But when he turned Harrison over, Buddy said it made him vomit."

"Buddy? The man I met this morning?" Millie asked.

"Yeah. Don't know how he gets any work done. Stops to visit with everybody, so it's no surprise he'd stop to help out."

Wirt walked along the shoulder of the road, kicking off clods of dirt. "There were probably a couple dozen oil and gas company trucks backed up here, waiting to get by. Everybody had to take a look, but at least somebody got Harrison's face covered with a blue jacket.

"As soon as they got the 911, the sheriff's office sent out two deputies. It took them less than an hour to get here, pretty good time on these roads. I got here shortly after they did. Robby Ramirez had already arrived. She was checking on a report of illegal dumping not far from here. Robby had to shoulder her way in and let the sheriff's boys know that as a federal law enforcement officer, she has the authority to investigate a death on BLM land."

Wirt pulled a cell phone out of his shirt pocket and snapped a picture of the crushed sagebrush and tire ruts along the roadside. "This will remind me to send a crew out with rakes and shovels.

"It got like a crazy circus here that morning. The deputies called the sheriff out. It took the sheriff an hour to round up the medical investigator's field deputy assigned to this district. When the county's crime scene van pulled up, the MI stepped out in full investigative gear. She had on a yellow Tyvek suit and was pulling on latex gloves."

Wirt turned back toward the Expedition. "She looked over the site like a coyote scanning a hillside for a rabbit. The first words out of her mouth were, 'I can see this scene is thoroughly trampled.' She gave the sheriff a look and he pushed everybody back. Then she told any person who had touched the body to go stand by the van until they could be fingerprinted.

"The MI shot dozens of pictures from every angle before even getting near the body." Wirt circled the rocky marker. He seemed to be tracing the medical investigator's path.

"When the MI pulled that blue jacket away, you could of heard a pin drop. Harrison's eye, it was …had a yucca stuck in it. Buddy sounded like he was going to hurl again. I had to walk away myself."

"A yucca—stuck in his *eye*! That's horrible."

"Nobody said anything. Just watched. The MI took more pictures. Then making a show of checking the carotid artery for a pulse, she pulled out a tape recorder, looked at her watch, and pronounced him dead."

Millie was confused. "I thought you said Buddy already told them that?"

"Seemed obvious. Nobody could survive a fall like that. But you see, all that has to be done by the medical investigator's office. Whenever there's an unaccompanied death, not a clear cause, no doctor or anyone around, someone representing the MI's office has to investigate."

Millie listened as the scene played out—only words to her—but as a nightmarish memory for Wirt.

"Then the MI got his wallet out of a back pocket and

called out whether anybody could identify the body. I gave her Harrison Howdy's name and so did Buddy. Guess that was enough identification with what was in his wallet. She read his name into the tape recorder and put the wallet in an evidence bag. Next was the watch, which went into a different bag.

"That's another thing I don't want to think about, his stiff arm and the way the fingers stayed splayed out, rigor mortis having set in. And the gash on his head—looked about four inches long. The MI honed right in on that, measured, and took more pictures from every angle."

"Did the MI say how long he'd been... had lain there?" Millie asked.

"Once the MI was done with the preliminaries, she called Robby, the sheriff, and me over. Based on condition of the body, she estimated death might have occurred somewhere between twelve to twenty hours prior. The watch stopped at 10:36, the crystal was smashed, probably during the fall.

"She made a point of saying there was likely a skull fracture that would be x-rayed when the body arrived at the Medical Investigator's Office in Albuquerque. That was the peculiar thing. The gash on his head seemed to trouble her more than what happened to the eye.

"Finally, the ambulance got here. The driver had the siren blaring—ha, as if there might of been a stoplight or traffic for the last twenty miles of dirt road. It was noon by the time they loaded poor Harrison in the ambulance. The field hands had pretty well moved on by then. If they were feeling anything like me, they weren't too hungry for lunch that day."

The cliff top drew Wirt's attention. "It wasn't until the next day that Robby found Harrison Howdy's truck."

Millie's eyes followed up the steep rock face, with horizontal layers of gray rubble intermingled with sections of dense, red sandstone. The strata varied with some layers less than a yard to others more than 12 feet in height, altogether reaching 150 feet into the sky. Stepping off that sheer, steep precipice would result in no outcome other than death.

Head still stretched back, Wirt scanned the top of the cliff. "That was another peculiar thing. Robby said his truck was run up onto slick rock, not even parked so it was facing toward the way out, like most of us do. She wondered why he even stopped up there, that maybe something wasn't right."

Wirt turned and touched the makeshift cross on top of the marker. He lowered his head and stood a moment.

Millie slid into the passenger seat. She looked across low brush to where sunlight warmed the cottonwoods along the wash. Momma Agnes said that the archaeologist knew what he was doing. Yet he died in the field, doing his job. *This isn't going to be like a day hike back home at the nature center.*

7. Backcountry Lesson

More than any other plant, sagebrush evokes a sense of the wide open West. Its piquant scent, even dried within love letters, elicits memories of cloudless skies, endless space, and silhouettes of distant mountains...
—Thomas Lowe Fleischner, *Singing Stone*

The chill from the cliff's shadow over the roadside marker permeated the Expedition's interior for the next several miles. Finally, Wirt said, "Sorry for going on like that. I've never paid much mind to those *descansos*, until it became personal. That's what those markers are called, *descansos*—resting places in Spanish. Family or friends will put them next to a place where somebody died along the highway."

"I saw some of those on my way to Wellstown. They must mean a lot to whoever puts them there."

"Yeah, like I said, nice that somebody made one for Harrison. Kind of fitting they used a shovel, since he was an archaeologist and probably used a shovel on plenty of digs."

The road climbed and curved as Lejos Canyon gradually narrowed to two miles across. The canyon floor supported bunch grass scattered among sage and rabbitbrush. Rock-strewn slopes joined the canyon's floor to vertical, imposing, red rock walls. This transition zone between the canyon's floor and rim riveted Millie's attention. Massive boulders pried off by time and weather decorated the slopes in countless arrangements.

Oil field equipment dotted the landscape. After bumping along for twenty minutes, Millie had already counted six roads branching off into the sagebrush. "Do all these roads go to wells?"

Wirt nodded. "There have been about twenty thousand wells drilled in the San Juan Basin since the big boom in the nineteen-fifties. And hundreds more are possible if the companies decide to drill on all their lease holdings."

"So that's why you said it's important to know where rare species are, before development is planned?"

"Right. The more we know, the better job we can do to protect critical habitat. It's all part of the multiple use balancing act. Take the well site we're going to next, for example. It's one of the oldest on the Resource Area. Under current regulations, that particular location wouldn't be approved because of its scenic value. You'll see why after we take a little hike."

Wirt turned onto a side road. It looked like all the others to Millie, except for an inconspicuous wood sign, "BLM Scenic Overlook."

This rough road forced Wirt to slow, hunting for the least rutted spots. Millie watched his maneuvers, knowing she soon would be doing the same.

Wirt circled the well pad and parked pointing in the direction they had come. A chain link fence protected a massive tank and an octopus of pipes with tentacles emerging out of the ground, passing through a processor, and disappearing back underground.

Millie was out of the vehicle before Wirt had the engine switched off. A humming noise emanated from somewhere among the dull gray-green apparatus.

Wirt motioned Millie over to a closet-size shed outside of the fence. He used the edge of his hand to brush dust off a white placard bolted to the side of the shed. "If you ever get lost, just find a well site, and you can figure out where you are. Every well site displays the name of the company that operates it and the location's legal description. The first number is township, then range, then section number."

Wirt unfolded a BLM Piñon Resource Area map. Glancing back and forth between the map and the sign's string of letters and numbers, he drew a finger down the left edge of the map to find township, along the top to find range, then dropped toward the center of the map to find section number.

"We are in the northeast quarter. You can estimate even closer by reading the number of feet from the North and East section lines." His finger traced a dashed line on the map that indicated the road they came on; it ended in a small circle at the well pad where they stood. "See, we are right here."

Wirt handed her the map. "Here, you keep this."

Millie peered at the map, repeating Wirt's movements. When her index finger came to rest next to the small circle, she looked up, delighted. "Wow, I almost expected to see a little icon for your vehicle."

Wirt smiled. "Looks like we have a fast learner here."

Wind had blown the shed's door open. Millie poked her head inside and saw more pipes and gauges. "Watch it," Wirt called, "rattlesnakes like to hang out in those meter houses. They'll crawl in where it's cooler in the shade. Grab your lunch and we'll find some shade ourselves."

The AM retrieved the burrito from behind his seat. "By the way, it's always a good idea to park your vehicle heading toward the way out. If you ever need to get away fast, it can save you precious time. There's seldom anybody around here, but see that triangle there?" He tapped the BLM symbol on the door. "Some yahoos might think it's a target. If you ever see anything unusual, get the heck out of there and contact the office. We'll send Robby Ramirez or another law enforcement officer to check it out."

Millie looked at the emblem and shook her head. *Watch out for rattlesnakes, pregnant mares, geezers driving Winnebegos—'begos—he calls them, and now, yahoos. And then there's the poison gas Buddy talked about. I used to think that staying away from muggers, panhandlers, and flashers was what I had to worry about.*

Wirt led the way off the well pad and climbed up a slope, passing among widely spaced juniper trees and the occasional piñon pine. They took turns naming the sparse bushes—bitterbrush, serviceberry, big sagebrush, skunkbush.

He stopped by a knee-high bush with leafless branches sporting miniscule yellow cones. The bright green stems grew every which way, as if a deranged artist had glued handfuls of pick-up sticks into a bizarre sculpture.

Wirt snapped off a piece of stem, chewed briefly, and spat it on the ground. "Yup, I still hate that stuff. Mom used to make my brother and me drink it every spring. Mormon tea, *Ephedra viridis*. She said it was a tonic to flush out the winter doldrums. You just can't put enough sugar in it to make it even tolerable."

"Your *mother* gave you Ephedra! Isn't that the stuff the FDA banned a few years ago because of what it does to athletes—speeds up the heart or something?"

"Yeah, there was something about that in the news," Wirt shook his head, "I don't know why anybody would drink that stuff, but I guess the early pioneers didn't have a lot of choice. It makes a mild restorative tea. The tradition just carried on."

When they reached the stand of ponderosa pine, Millie stopped next to a big, gnarly yucca plant. She wrapped a hand around a fleshy, fat, round leaf and ran the area's plant list through her mind. Two species of yucca mainly occur here, banana and narrowleaf yucca. This was likely *Yucca baccata*—the high-elevation-loving banana yucca, named for its fleshy fruit. The narrowleaf yucca, *Y. angustissima*, was more common in lower elevations. She gave wide berth to the spines at the tips of its leaves; another name for *Y. baccata* is Spanish bayonet. Falling on one of those would cause horrendous injury, perhaps what drove Harrison Howdy over the cliff.

Despite its forbidding looks, Millie could see a fragile stalk about two inches long in its very center. This nascent stem would shoot up two, possibly three feet tall over the next couple of weeks, before unfurling rows of delicate bell-shaped blossoms.

Millie and Wirt continued calling out species, Gambel's oak and mountain mahogany, as they moved up the trail. "You're pretty good at this, Millie, never having been in this area before."

Millie mouthed a silent, "Yesss!" and swung a fist through the air. All that studying of high desert plants and habitats was paying off. Over preparation was the norm for Millie. School had been a get-away from doing the chores at home. She wanted to do well and studied every chance she had. College was even harder. She never knew when her mother might call to say Millie needed to fill in for a midnight shift because one of the cleaning staff called in sick. For fear of falling behind, Millie developed the habit of doing more than keep up, she read ahead in textbooks and did her best to complete assignments before deadlines. For Millie, as soon as the notice came that she got the BLM job, it was simply routine to study ecology and plant identification references about the high desert.

"I know what you meant about starting college planning one thing and ending up going in a different direction." Millie kept the conversation going, even though the climb was making her breathe faster. "I wouldn't be here if it wasn't for an intro to botany course. I started as a business major and it required a science course. Botany happened to fit my schedule. I loved it. It was all so organized. Family, genus, and species—every plant fits into a scheme. Who knew you could use a dichotomous key to identify every plant?"

"You're telling me you *liked* keying out plants?"

"Sure, it's like a puzzle or a video game. You find a plant and look at it. Are the leaves serrated or smooth? Do they grow opposite to each other or alternate their way along the stem? Choose right, and you get to move onto the next level. Keep looking. Do the veins run parallel or are they netting-like? Just eliminate alternatives until you find the right answer."

Wirt half turned and tossed a "you're kidding" look toward her.

"Yes sir, it was one thing in my life I was good at. The professor encouraged me to take more botany courses."

"I suppose you were the kind of nerdy student that could even key out composites."

"Well, yes. Sometimes I got kidded. I guess I overcompensated. You can't imagine the competition, the jockeying for attention by the smart set. I tried to wear the kind of classy clothes the other students had. Maybe that was silly. Sometimes I skipped lunch just to be able to buy gas to get to campus. Couldn't begin to afford to live in a dorm on campus. If my father hadn't worked for Rutgers and been able to get their employee tuition break for children, I'd have been lucky to even afford community college.

"I tried hard to fit in. I once forked over sixty dollars for a pair of designer jeans. Slipped on a rock and tore up my knee on the first botany class field trip. It bled like hell, but the rip in the jeans hurt worse. I eventually got on outdoor equipment websites, LL Bean, REI, Forestry Suppliers and accumulated the field clothes and gear I needed. That took doubling up on my hours on custodial jobs during Christmas and spring breaks.

"After a while, I gave up on trying to keep up with the rich kids, and just focused on botany." In no other aspect of her life could Millie find such certainty—be so confident she knew THE ANSWER. At the end of her sophomore year, she switched majors and added several more science courses to her transcript.

The trail was steep. Millie took deeper breaths, slowed, and looked up. Pine branches made filigree patterns against a brilliant blue sky. *I'm in the right place now.* She was glad to see Wirt had stopped farther up the trail and lengthened her stride to catch up.

"Take a look at this," Wirt called to her.

Millie reached his side, looked down, and took a step back. "Whoa, geez louise," she blurted out, startled by the vista before them. They stood at the edge of a steep canyon. A column of cottonwoods meandered along the valley below. From this distance, they gave off a soft green luminescence, assuring another season of survival.

Sweeping his arm along its length, Wirt said, "This is Split Lip Canyon. That's the largest riparian wetland tract we have on Piñon Resource Area. We've slowly cut back on the grazing allowance over the last decade and the native vegetation is coming back faster than we'd expected."

"Split Lip Canyon?" Millie giggled. "How did it get a

name like that?"

"Makes you wonder, doesn't it? It's a favorite hiking and picnic area. Let's eat."

Wirt motioned toward squared sandstone boulders shaded by a tall, straight-as-an-arrow ponderosa pine. He sat on one boulder, crossed his legs, and unwrapped the foil from his burrito, which still had enough warmth to give off a tempting aroma. Millie found a flat rock nearby. It was wedged next to another, slightly higher rock, making an acceptable table. She was glad she had stocked up on jars of jam and peanut butter; she would go through a good many PB&J sandwiches this summer.

* * *

In the afternoon, Wirt drove through the north unit, with Millie tracing their way on the map. They stopped at various sites to examine typical high desert grassland, desert scrub, and riparian plant communities.

They occasionally passed a white oil field truck, both drivers acknowledging each other with a nod and wave. At one point, they came head to head with a truck coming down an especially steep, scary-as-hell narrow road. Wirt maneuvered as close as possible to the hillside and stopped.

"When you meet another vehicle on a hill like this, the person coming down has the right-of-way, because they might not be able to stop on slick mud or loose cobble." The other vehicle passed with less than an inch of space between his side mirror and theirs.

Millie let out her breath. She appreciated the area manager's passing on lore of the field.

When they crested the hill, Millie leaned toward the windshield. Dead sagebrush and uprooted, splintered juniper trees extended back from both sides of the road.

"What happened here? Looks like a tornado went through."

"It's been chained over, did it a couple of years ago, really opened it up."

"Chained? Like, chained up? Were the trees trying to get away?"

Wirt gave her a quizzical look, apparently not sure if she was joking or not. "Two big tractors drag a heavy chain stretched between them over the ground. Helps to open it up."

"Jeez, it looks devastated. Why?"

"Taking out competing vegetation promotes more forage grasses. It allows increasing Animal Unit Months on a grazing allotment. We added five more AUMs on this allotment. Five more cows with calves, or some equivalent of sheep, can summer here. You'll see several chained areas like this."

"You mean hundred-year-old junipers get wrecked just so a calf can get a little fatter to go get butchered?"

Wirt winced. "You've got to remember where the BLM came from. Way back, in the 1800s, there was a General Land Office created as the nation expanded west, later there came the U.S. Grazing Service. These two parents, I guess you could call them, were combined in 1946 to form the Bureau of Land Management. Those early ranchers had a lot of influence, still do." Wirt's voice took on a low growling sound, "Wish I had a nickel for every time somebody's told me, 'I'm, by god, going to call the governor's office about this.'"

Millie realized she had overstepped. She turned to the window, focusing on memorizing the turns and landmarks of the north unit.

A green Subaru Outback came hurtling along a side road. It looked certain to collide with them if neither vehicle slowed down. Wirt slammed on the breaks. The

Expedition skidded to a halt.

The small car popped onto the road just in front of them. The driver's door flew open and a burly figure came stomping toward them.

"Uh oh, Millie. You're in for a treat," Wirt whispered.

An Amazon-sized woman presented herself squarely in front of their vehicle, waiting for them to come out. The woman greeted Wirt with, "Who's this?"

"Belva, meet Millicent Whitehall. She's on for the season, monitoring sensitive plants. Millie, meet Belva Banks. Belva is a member of the Old Broads for Public Lands Protection. She keeps us on the straight and narrow."

"Damn right I keep watch of you guys. 'Bout time you get somebody on that does more than just sign off on drilling permits all day," Belva bellowed out and pumped Millie's hand.

Belva was a bit taller than Millie; this was one woman she could look up to. From the faded sun hat to her flip-flops with a cactus spine lodged in the edge of one sole, Belva looked like one tough cookie. Wrinkles piled above her knees told of thousands of hours in the sun, the muscles of her legs attested to years of traversing desert and mountain trails. Her canvas shorts were shiny with wear. The cotton blouse with rolled up sleeves gaped over her ample bosom. Gray streaks fought with black strands in the hair plastered with sweat to her neck, the gray streaks winning.

Wirt deflected a few more of Belva's barbs, giving Millie the impression that they were long-time sparring partners. He lifted his wrist making a show of reading his watch and started easing toward the Expedition.

Belva turned to Millie. "I'll be watching for you at the next Old Broads' meeting." She clomped back to her car and plopped behind the steering wheel.

"Well, Millie, you got to meet Belva the Bulldozer on your very first day in the field." Wirt gave a sigh, apparently relieved to be back in the protection of the vehicle. "She's something else. Gives BLM, Forest Service, National Park Service, everybody and anybody hell any time an acre of public land gets scheduled for development. In this seesaw of using versus preserving public lands, she puts a lot of weight on the preserving end." He grinned, appearing pleased with his own pun.

The Subaru charged off ahead of them. Once the dust cleared, Wirt rolled down his window, steered close to the left edge of the road, and grabbed a sprig of sagebrush. He rolled its gray-green leaves between his fingers, sniffed them, and pushed the stem into his shirt pocket. Looking a bit self-conscious, he said, "I don't get in the field much anymore, so I like to take a bit of it back with me, just as a reminder of the old days when I did my work on horseback."

8. Lunch Company

Nothing can bring you peace but yourself.
—Ralph Waldo Emerson, 1841

Two weeks into the job, Millie was loving her days in the field. Her schedule was routine now, up at dawn, long drives to locate rare plant sites marked on maps from previous surveys. These were cursory field checks to find the locations and make quick observations of conditions. Millie was targeting the earlier-blooming plants, especially those species that were almost indistinguishable after their flowering period. She would return later and conduct systematic transects of these sites, to compare current plant density with the earlier records.

She planned today's route to put her near Split Lip Canyon Overlook at lunchtime. She left the Suburban on the well pad where Wirt had parked and climbed the trail leading to the overlook. Millie had more in mind than a beautiful place to have lunch, she sought out the banana yucca she encountered that day Wirt took her to the field.

"Yeees! You did it."

The venerable old yucca displayed the miracle that it had performed for many seasons. Its center stalk was now three feet tall, as big around as a broom handle. A glorious drape of ivory-white flowers tinged with a hint of rose spiraled around the apex. Millie moved closer, careful to keep clear of the yucca's sharp points. She gently lifted a bell-shaped blossom by one finger and inspected its interior decorated with amber pollen.

"Such beautiful blooms you have, big yucca! No wonder yucca is New Mexico's state flower."

Millie sat her backpack on the ground and pulled out a camera. She photographed the blossoms, and then took several steps back to frame the whole plant from the pockmarked, insect-chewed whorl of leaves at its base to its newest buds ready to open at the tip.

The view from the edge of Split Lip Canyon was just as breathtaking as two weeks earlier. Leaves on the cottonwoods along the canyon floor had progressed from an early shade of chartreuse to mint green. By summer, they would take on a deeper, glossy shade.

Millie settled onto the same sandstone boulder she'd used that day with the area manager and arranged lunch on the adjacent flat-topped rock. She folded a paper napkin into thirds, put it left of the sandwich and aligned a plastic spoon on top of it. She sat a yogurt cup to the right where a water glass would normally be placed, replicating a proper table setting. Even in this remote location, she could not shake the influence of orderliness that her mother had impressed upon her.

Hungry as she was, Millie could not resist checking photos from her morning's triumphant accomplishment—finding the endangered San Juan cactus. She got the camera out and flicked through the pictures. She wanted to make sure she had acceptable documentary images. The rare *Sclerocactus sanjuanensis*, averaging a mere two and a half inches high, would be almost impossible to find once its blossoms dried up in another month.

She had spent the morning taking GPS readings along

the perimeter of the cactus plot. She avoided treading across the few acres where the plants grew. The small cactus plants were barely detectable among pebbles and the ground's rumpled cryptobiotic crust that stabilized and nourished the soil. Even footsteps could disturb these hidden, living organisms. Before leaving the plot, Millie dropped to her knees next to an especially large specimen to photograph its cluster of eight, vivid fuchsia flowers, each blossom half the diameter of a dime.

The San Juan cactus was a fairly recent discovery in botanical terms, being first described in the 1990s. Subsequent plant inventories found only two locations where San Juan cactus grew, both populations occurring within the north unit of the Piñon Resource Area.

Sclerocactus sanjuanensis was notorious for being loved almost to extinction. When word of a newly discovered species spread, it was almost decimated by cactus collectors, driven to possess a specimen other cactus aficionados would envy. With efforts to keep locations vague and stricter protections, the collecting activity tapered off over time.

Millie breathed a sigh of contentment that this engaging cactus continued to survive. She put the camera back in her pack, fished out a tube of sunscreen, and slathered it on for the umpteenth time. She spread the BLM area map across the red rock to plan her route for the afternoon, peeled off the yogurt's cover, and probed for fruit at the bottom of the cup. The ponderosa pine's shade cut the noonday sun and provided soft background music when a breeze rustled its branches. The view stretched for miles across Split Lip Canyon and the gray-green landscape beyond. "This job has perks I never even considered."

A blood-curdling screech fractured the silence. Millie clamped both hands over her ears. She looked skyward, then ducked. A shadow slid across her left shoulder. A great, black bird glided to a nearby branch, almost at eye level.

"Raven! Did you have to scare me like that?" Millie scolded and returned the raven's probing stare. The raven gave another ear-splitting scream. Millie called back with a line of Poe's memorable poem. *"Once upon a midnight dreary, while I pondered, weak and weary..."*

Tilting its head, listening, the raven called again, this time more softly.

"I didn't bring enough lunch for you, Raven, but I'm glad to have your company."

Chuckling, balancing forward and back, the raven tipped its head sideways, focused on the foil yogurt cover. Their vocal exchanges continued. The bird hopped closer.

At the sound of crashing branches, the raven swooped, snatched the shiny foil, and dropped from sight over the canyon's edge.

Millie stood, not knowing what could make that much noise in the bushes. A human form stepped into the clearing. She could see, and smell, a sweaty young man. He gave a wave in her direction, and bent down, swinging long black hair over his face. He brushed the top of his head, scattering bits of juniper bark and needles.

Between deep breaths, he puffed out, "My grandmother talks to ravens all the time."

9. Deer Don't Read Maps

Wild plants, fruits, and nuts were gathered in the spring, summer, and early fall. Gathering parties made encampments in the regions where pinion nuts, broad leaf yucca fruits, sumac berries, and Indian rice grass were harvested.
—Woods Canyon Archeological Consultants, *Moving Across the Landscape*

"Hi, I'm Ben Benallee." The stranger walked toward her, clutching a ragged map under one arm, and extending his hand in greeting.

With her back against the rock, Millie had no choice but to accept the handshake. She guessed he was a couple years younger than herself and about four inches shorter.

He stepped back and lowered a well-used leather shoulder bag onto a nearby rock. The tooled leather case showed figures of bear, mountain lion, and other wildlife. Even the shoulder strap was etched with a parade of smaller creatures—rabbit, ground squirrel, and ringtail cat.

He unbuckled one strap to open the bag enough to fish out a granola bar. "Man, I'm hungry. Been following a radio-collared mule deer all morning."

Millie eased back onto her seat. Ben took her place

leaning against the rock, taking in the view across the canyon. He looked rock-hard himself. From sun-bronzed face to well-muscled calves below frayed cut-off shorts, he was a picture of health and fitness. Millie would have taken him as a hiker or rock climber except for the official-looking short-sleeve shirt, with button-down collar and pens, small notebook, and mobile phone in the pockets.

He turned an arm toward Millie. "Yeah, I'm a wildlife biologist for the Jicarilla Apache Game and Fish Department. They're big on deer and elk hunting. Make a fortune off rich big-game trophy hunters." The yellow and red patch on his shirt sleeve backed up his words, showing the tribal insignia and a trophy-sized mule deer. Still winded from trailing after the deer, he stopped to take a deep breath.

"Hi, I'm Millie," she was able to get in before Ben continued.

"Never thought the Jicarilla would hire a Navajo, considering how much they fought with each other in the past. But 'let bygones be bygones,' my Auntie Louise would say. They liked it that I had a bachelor's degree in wildlife biology from Northern Arizona University and I'm already in a master's program. Yup, I'm getting paid to do deer research and get a thesis out of it at the same time."

"I'm with the BLM doing T and E plant surveys," Millie slipped in.

"BLM, huh?" Ben upended the granola bar packet, funneling remaining crumbs into his mouth. He pulled out the Forest Service map tucked under his arm. Millie pulled her map closer. She was sure, but double-checked, that she was inside BLM-administered land, indicated in yellow on her land status map. She figured that he must have crossed the Carson National Forest colored in green on the map and was well beyond the orange-shaded sections of tribal territory.

Ben balanced his map with one hand and traced a zig-zag path with the other.

He slumped against the rock. "Damn it! We got a dozen does fitted with radio collars. Satellite signals off their collars have been making neat little clusters just where you'd expect them to be. All of a sudden, this doe, THIS ONE, decides to go sightseeing. Maybe a mountain lion chased her, something caused her to bolt. Now she'll probably drop her fawn on BLM, for cripes sake."

"Guess deer don't read maps," Millie offered.

Ben swiped at the sweat on his forehead, looked back at his map, and began laughing. "Okay, okay, Wildlife Management 101—animals do not respect boundary lines on a map. They go where they can best survive." He ran an index finger along a winding course, pointing out a slice of private land shown in white on the map. "That doe led me clean across state, federal, and tribal land, even this rancher's place."

Millie laughed too. The raven, and now this Navajo biologist, were noisy intruders on her quiet lunch spot. Ben's shoulder-length hair was as black and shiny as the raven's feathers.

"Well, that doe's long gone by now. I'll pick her up later with the next satellite reading off the radio collar. This is the damnedest country to work in. Not like the desert around Phoenix where I grew up. This is even meaner than Beautiful Mountain where Auntie Louise made me go visit relatives every summer." Ben pushed himself up on the far end of Millie's lunch table rock, fannying back into the shade.

"No wonder that guy walked off a cliff. Did you hear about that guy? A fellow called Buddy told me about it. He's the one who found the dude dead on the road."

"I heard about it at the BLM office. He was an archaeologist. His name was Harrison Howdy. They held a potluck lunch to collect donations for funeral expenses, even though he worked for the Bureau of Indian Affairs."

Ben barely stopped long enough to take a breath. "First they thought he'd been run over. When they turned him over, his eye was hanging out of its socket. Like by his *nose*." Ben shivered at the thought. "Seems there was the end of a yucca spear stuck right in his eye. Something like that would drive ya' crazy. They figure it blinded him and he stepped off the cliff. All scraped up he was. His truck was up on the mesa top. Just think of that. Skewered by a yucca spike."

No wonder Wirt looked so shaken when he stopped at that marker. This grisly detail attached itself to Millie's image of the steep cliff and humble roadside marker. How could yuccas put forth such delicate blossoms and be armed with such deadly spikes? *This land is beautiful and cruel all at the same time.*

Millie folded her map and gathered up empty lunch containers, hoping he'd take the hint that it was time to leave. When Ben didn't move, she stood up, pulled her backpack closer, and stuffed the lunch remains in it.

With one quick jump, Ben was by her side. "Say, can you give me a lift back to my truck?"

"No problem. I can spare a few minutes to drop you off. Let's go."

Had Millie known it would take two hours to deliver Ben to where he'd first started tracking the deer that morning, she would have left him at the edge of Split Lip Canyon.

Between bumps and jolts, they compared the programs required for their biology majors. Despite having hiked many miles, Ben practically bounced in his seat with energy, apparently eager to impress this pretty girl from an East Coast college. "The research I'm doing now is going to make a great thesis. Hardly anybody's done research on how deer interact with oil and gas development. In other places, maybe, but not in northwest New Mexico."

Ben motioned to the steering column. "You might want to put it in four-wheel drive."

Millie sighed, not wanting to take her eyes off the road. With a quick glance down, she shifted into 4-low. The drive for the last several miles had taken them snaking up a Forest Service not-quite-a-road, used for logging long ago. Then it got worse. They crossed onto the Jicarilla Apache Reservation, following barely visible two-track grooves.

Ben recounted how competing in high school science fairs led to scholarships at Arizona State. "I always knew I'd go to college. Auntie Louise and Uncle David made sure of that. I lived with them all the time I was growing up.

"Auntie Louise works at the Phoenix Area Indian Health Center. She's a physical therapist, which makes her a commissioned officer in the Indian Health Service. She has to wear a snazzy uniform, kind of like being in the military.

"Uncle David, he's different. He hates to dress up. He's part of a big law office, so he has to put on a suit and tie when he goes to court. Even so, he'll bush his hair out, so it hangs over his collar. He tells his lawyer colleagues that when he is defending Native American rights, he wants everybody to know whose side he's on."

Ben's voice softened when he talked about his mother. She had left him at her sister's house when he was two years old. "All I remember about my mom is standing at their front door. She was hugging me so tight. When Uncle David opened the door, she pushed me inside. She told him Louise was the good sister and would take care of me better. Then she ran down the street. No one in the family has seen her since."

Millie saw her own mother's tired face again. She couldn't remember ever seeing her mother look anything but worried. Yet, her mother was always there. Maybe some mornings when her mother had left early for work, it was just a bagged lunch left on the kitchen counter for Millie to take to school. Maybe it was a light touch on Millie's cheek from a calloused finger that transferred a mother's kiss to her sleeping daughter, but Millie had known only security and protection all her life.

Ben shrugged and ran a hand under his shirt collar to loosen trapped strands of hair.

"But don't think I'm a city boy. Every summer, my Auntie Louise took me to her folks' sheep camp. I could have been going to Wet 'n' Wild Water Park like the other kids. But, unh-unh, not with my Auntie Louise. She wanted me to learn traditional Navajo ways. She said being in clean mountain air among her own people kept her sane. Easy for her to say. After two weeks, she'd go back to Phoenix. Left me all summer with Grandfather and Grandmother Sageman at sheep camp. It's way up on Beautiful Mountain.

"Bored, bored, bored. Can't tell you how bored I was there," Ben grumbled, choking on the second "bored" when the Suburban lurched across a deep rut.

Ben regaled Millie about all he learned from his herbalist grandfather, Harvey Sageman, and his grandmother, Emma Sageman. Ben accompanied grandfather Sageman on his trips to collect plants from as far away as the San Francisco Peaks in Arizona and Mount Blanca in Colorado, always staying within the four sacred mountains that delineate the Navajo traditional homeland. Ceremonies handed down from nomadic ancestors prescribed certain herbs to be used, which must be gathered from the proper location at the proper time of year.

"People still come to Grandfather at all times of the day or night. They ask for certain herbs to prepare traditional teas or ointments to use for healing. He showed me all kinds of things—where to find quail, how to tell a coyote track from a bobcat's, how to know when plants are ready for gathering, depending on their intended use."

Ben described Grandmother Emma as smarter than any of the professors he had for ecology courses. "She told me over and over again, 'respect all creatures, even the small and homely ones.' She'd say, 'never step on a horned toad, it represents your Cheii, who protects you. Cheii— that's my maternal grandfather. Ants clean our surroundings; do not disturb such hard workers. Every creature matters,' she'd say."

Millie saw her chance to add something to the conversation. "Did you know horned toads are actually in the lizard family? I was with the BLM area manager when he stopped for one. It was right in the middle of the road."

"Of course. *Phrynosoma douglasii* is the species around here. Had that in zoology. Most people call them horny toads."

Ben flung out his arm, almost blocking her view of the road, and pointed toward a rounded rock formation taller than any others around it. "See, way over there? That's Gobernador Knob. That's where First Man found the baby, White Shell, and brought her to First Woman, who placed her in a cradleboard. When the baby grew up, she became Changing Woman and gave birth to twin brothers, Monster Slayer and Born for Water. In our creation story, the brothers got rid of the monsters and made the world safe and beautiful for us Diné, Navajo people."

Millie sent a questioning glance toward Ben.

"Yeah, Grandfather told me that when I was just a little kid. There're lots of teachings like that. Elders make sure we all learn them."

Contemplating this for a rare quiet moment, Millie replied, "I suppose that's about the same as Adam and Eve starting the human race. Do you think Changing Woman looked anything like Eve in the Garden of Eden?"

"Who knows, maybe they knew each other." Ben countered, with a grin.

"Hold up, stop by that big Engelmann spruce. I want to show you something. This is one of the places Grandfather Sageman came each summer. Seemed like it took him forever digging, clipping leaves, or brushing seed heads into a bag. He'd say a prayer by every plant before gathering it. He said he was explaining to the plant why it was needed and that it would be put to good use. 'If you do not honor the plant,' he said, 'Mother Earth's balance and harmony are broken. If you are respectful, Mother Earth will continue to provide for her people.' Almost killed me, all that waiting around for him.

"I'll be right back." Ben dodged around the big conifer and trotted toward a clearing, leaving the passenger's side door hanging open.

Filtered sun through nascent aspen leaves and the trickle of water from late snow run-off pulled Millie's senses back to days of tramping through the woods with Aunt Nina.

It was her aunt who gave Millie a glimpse of another life. Aunt Nina operated her own vegetable stand in the next town over. She was the proud owner of 70 fertile acres and claimed she was the one that kept Garden in New Jersey's state nickname. Other family members whispered about Aunt Nina—why didn't she ever get married, why doesn't she move into town where it would be easier, why is she so—odd. Millie didn't care. Millie loved to visit Aunt Nina's farm, especially when the rows of multi-colored gladiolas were blooming and the strawberries came ripe.

Sometimes Aunt Nina invited Millie to go adventuring. Anytime she could evade another cleaning job was a good day in Millie's book. Sometimes they went to the seashore, but usually it was to a state forest. In the spring, they watched for lady slippers to unroll their delicate pink flowers, later they'd follow the rotting scent of skunk cabbage right into swamps, and in the fall, marvel at golden and scarlet leaves floating into their outstretched hands.

Ben landed on the passenger seat and held an open hand in front of Millie. "Yup, I was right. Grandfather scraped this kind of lichen off the rocks over there."

Millie took a pinch of the oatmeal-sized orange flakes from his palm. They crumbled to powder between her thumb and index finger. "That little stuff? What's it for?"

"Grandfather sells it to the rug weavers who spin their own wool and use natural dyes for different colors in their designs. I think this is the one that makes a kind of burnt-orange color."

By the time Millie pulled the Suburban next to the Jicarilla Game and Fish truck parked in a clearing surrounded by ponderosa pine, Ben was rambling on about how everything he learned summers with his grandparents put him way ahead of other students in his classes. Grabbing his leather shoulder bag, he nodded and said, "Yeah, I aced every test and lab exam they could throw at me. Hey, I'll take you up to our sheep camp. You've got to meet my folks. Thanks for the ride."

The door slammed. Millie savored the silence before turning the Suburban around and heading down the mountain. So much for the stoic Indian stereotype.

10. Nobody – Everybody

That which is not good for the bee-hive cannot be good for the bees.
—*Marcus Aurelius, 2ⁿᵈ Century Roman Emperor*

Millie hoisted a can of Bud Light in celebration of surviving her first two weeks as BLM botanist. "Here's to me, and to gloomy cubicles, horrible roads, exquisite cactus flowers, superlative scenery, a gazillion gas wells, ravens, and toads that aren't toads. Rather than the Land of Enchantment, New Mexico could be the Land of Contradiction."

Perched on the top step of the rental's front porch with her laptop computer nearby, Millie watched a teenager clunking a skateboard along the sidewalk, a couple strolling hand-in-hand, and cars and SUVs passing on the street. Activity in the neighborhood and her tired body told her it was Friday night and time to relax.

Millie returned a wave from an elderly woman walking by, who was being pulled along by a Jack Russell Terrier bent on sniffing and peeing on each yard they passed. When the dog strained its way toward Millie's foot, an orange flash zoomed into Millie's open front door. It was the scruffy cat that slipped off the porch the last few nights when she drove in after work.

"Come on out of there," Millie called to the intruder, but made no effort to move. She was too tired to get up and the spring air was delightful. She didn't mind the cat, really. In fact, she looked forward to its presence every night. It made the dreary rental less lonely. She maneuvered sideways to lean against the porch post, so she could see into the house, watch activity on the street, and gaze up at fluttering leaves of the cottonwood that made her decide to rent here.

The bold cat showed no indication that it heard Millie's command. It padded around the living room, rubbing its face along the couch and armchair, claiming territory. Millie sipped her drink, ignoring the prowler.

The cat, the raven, and Ben Benallee made three visitors for the day. The animals were welcome company, Mr. Benallee, however, had been a real pain. *What a wasted day.*

No, not totally wasted, an uber-good morning. She had located the San Juan cactus, a plant so rare that the US Fish and Wildlife Service officially designated it as endangered. *Just a wasted afternoon, well, sort of, that Ben was kind of cute. And wouldn't it be interesting to meet his grandfather who knows about native herbs.*

Millie picked up the laptop, balanced it against bent knees, and tapped it awake. She reviewed notes from the prior week's field visits. She corrected punctuation and deleted extra spaces. No one else would ever read the notes, but capitulating to her methodical mind, she made the edits anyway.

What a privilege to observe San Juan cactus in bloom. Getting to photograph an endangered species didn't happen every day. Its limited distribution in only two locations was a key factor for being listed in the most stringent category designated by the 1973 Endangered

Species Act. Should wildfire or some calamity devastate this small plot, the cactus would be on the edge of extinction. If something happened to its counterpart a couple of miles distant, a unique gift of beauty would be gone forever.

Of the half-dozen species of special interest plants occurring on the Piñon Resource Area, three were in the most critical category of endangered. The others were classified as threatened or rare, meaning their fate was less precarious but merited special protection to avoid decline into the endangered category. Once extinct, a plant's ecological role, its potential for use as medicine or other benefit yet to be discovered, and simply its special-ness as a unique life form, could never be recreated.

Millie gazed up into the cottonwood's convoluted branches. With all the oil and gas development on the Piñon Resource Area, will there be enough room left for San Juan cactus?

This thought triggered snatches of words in Millie's mind from an advanced seminar in "Species Loss and Restoration in a Changing World—Issues and Opportunities." It was the professor's voice that kept the information reoccurring to Millie. The young professor spoke rapidly with the urgency of a general preparing for war. "The Endangered Species Act put teeth into protecting rare species, making it a federal crime to take, malicious-ly damage, or sell plants and animals classified as either threatened or endangered. The ESA offered protection in national parks, national forests, national wildlife refuges, military bases, and other federal lands." Millie was in awe of this young professor and was pretty sure no student passed through her classes without forever after feeling a twinge of guilt about tossing plastic bottles into the trash.

Millie's own research before leaving for New Mexico

tagged along in her thoughts. New Mexico passed its own Endangered Plant Species Act in 1985 to safeguard flora occurring in its many habitats from Chihuahuan Desert Scrub in the southern region of the state to Alpine Tundra in the north.

Millie shifted her attention back on her notes. She organized the week's data into columns for plant community type, elevation, GPS coordinates, weather, and general observations. She checked and re-checked the GPS coordinates she took that morning around the perimeter of the San Juan cactus plot. Something didn't fit.

Millie hunched toward the laptop screen, oblivious to the returning skateboarder rocketing along the sidewalk. The site map that emerged did not match the area outlined from previous surveys. The old maps showed a larger perimeter. Perhaps she had made an error taking GPS readings, or maybe the earlier surveyors were a bit sloppy with their mapping. She needed to return to that cactus plot next week.

The orange cat leaped onto the table Millie used as a desk, landing neatly in the space where the laptop usually would be, and looked back at Millie. "Gutsy creature, aren't you?" The cat lowered into a meatloaf shape and continued watching Millie, perhaps curious what was so interesting about the square box on her lap. "Make yourself at home, Ragged Ear, why don't you?" His left ear had a notch in it and the right ear hung down. This fellow had been in a few fights in his time.

Millie leaned back against the post, hooked her hair behind her ears, and let her eye lids slide shut. Every day, bumping along the back roads, she had seen activity that validated the area manager's words during that first meeting in Wirt's office—"the land nobody wanted, but now everybody wants."

Something soft touched her hand. She opened one eye to see Ragged Ear sitting with his back to her, lolling his tail side-to-side, as if touching her was by shear accident. The cat stood, sauntered to the edge of the porch, and resumed a meatloaf position.

Millie swirled a finger over the trackpad to bring the screen back to life and closed out the field notes folder. With a slight grin, she opened a new spreadsheet and labeled it "Nobody – Everybody". She started with the current day and typed in "Ben Benallee—wildlife research." Then she jumped back to the day Wirt first showed her the unit and typed, "Buddy Maddox—oil & gas field hand. She added Clay White, petroleum engineer planning drilling locations, and Belva Banks—Old Broad for Public Lands Protection hiking the back country." She remembered the lunch spot and typed, "scenery to die for."

Oops, 'die for' is not the best phrase to use. That poor man who fell off the cliff. Horrible the way Ben described it. Everybody seems to know about it. No wonder, I guess, with the number of times I pulled up behind a couple of trucks, the drivers just stopped in the middle of the road to talk. Seems like these guys know each other and keep up on happenings all around the gas patch.

Filling in the Nobody—Everybody column for other days, Millie added road graders and cattle trucks, and chopping firewood for the men she saw at the chained area. Gathering traditional plants also went on the list, based on Ben's description of his herbalist Grandfather Sageman.

Millie switched to the folder where she kept her personal musings, "Notes: A Season in the High Desert," and added:

"No need to worry about getting lost in the wilderness. Roads are everywhere, people driving all over, well sites in every nook and cranny. This land is beautiful and harsh all at the same time.

"I'll do my part to watch over the rare plants. We need many habitats for many species to maintain biodiversity. The first rule of intelligent tinkering is to save all the parts.

"Got to get back to that San Juan cactus plot. Something's not quite right there."

Millie drained the last drops of beer from the can. At the snap of the laptop's lid, Ragged Ear disappeared over the edge of the porch.

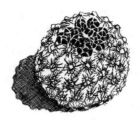

11. Buddy – Everybody's Friend

Although not a large employer, the mining sector, especially the oil and gas industry, contributes significantly to the state's gross domestic product... and workers in the sector earn among the highest average weekly pay in the state.

—US Energy Information Administration, New Mexico Profile

The mid-morning sun behind a tall water tank cast a shadow over Millie's map. She stood a few inches from the location plaque wired to the fence surrounding the well equipment.

The crunching of gravel caused her to look up. A white truck stopped next to a padlocked gate on the opposite side of the fenced area. Millie recognized the Dagun logo and the driver sending a friendly wave in her direction.

"Hi there. Miss Millie, isn't it?" Buddy Maddox called over. He fingered a key ring on his belt, found the one he was looking for, and let the gate swing open. He walked around to see Millie, a slight hitch in his gait. "I could tell that was your vehicle, they always give the beaters to the summer temps. How's the surveying going?"

Millie let go of one side of the map just long enough to shake his outstretched hand. "Hi, Mr. Maddox. I'm remembering what you said about not being able to rely on a GPS out here. Sometimes I think I'm going right to a place and I end up going back and forth, back and forth on roads that all look the same, until I could just about throw the darn thing out the window."

"It's not about the destination, it's about the journey, so they say. And everybody calls me Buddy."

"OK, Buddy. It's just that I'm sick of bumping along on these roads all day. I've got to get to four more locations, and it's already late April. A lot of species will be done flowering soon."

"I've been working this gas field for twenty-eight years. Been over every road. Then a company puts in a new well some place, another company shuts one in and rehabs the road that used to be there. I'm back to doing just what you said, driving back and forth, until I can spot where I need to get to."

"I'm not interested in the journey, Buddy, I just want to get to this destination." Millie jabbed a finger at the map. She thought about the traffic on these back roads. Maybe they were lost half the time, too.

"Let me see, maybe I can help." Buddy ran a stubby finger along the map, zigzagging to the spot Millie indicated. "Hold on while I tinker with this well and you can follow me to this turn-off here. Then go another half mile and you'll be pretty near it."

Millie studied the map a few minutes more, while Buddy whistled his way back to his truck. He pulled out a canvas tool bag and walked through the open gate to the pump house. It was painted the same dull, sage green as the tank and pipes inside the fence. The door made of sheet metal gave a bong-like noise when Buddy pulled it open.

"Christ almighty!"

Buddy backed away from the shed and trotted to his truck. He grabbed a shovel and motioned Millie over. "Want to see a rattler?".

Standing next to Buddy, Millie swept the floor of the shed with her eyes, not seeing anything. Then following Buddy's stare, she saw the shiny loops of a snake twined along the pipes, resting its head on a round pressure gauge.

"That's a big one for these parts, nearly three feet long," Buddy commented. "The western prairie rattlers we get around here aren't near so big as your spaghetti western snake-in-the-bedroll diamondbacks."

"Yikes, Buddy, what are you going to do?" The triangular head and unblinking eyes gave her the willies.

"Stand back, I'm going to toss it out toward those weeds. You know what Aldo Leopold would say, well maybe not about rattlesnakes, but he wrote it somewhere. The last word in ignorance is the man who says of an animal or plant, 'What good is it?'"

Millie didn't have to be told twice. In fact, she was already inside the Suburban by the time Buddy, using the shovel, gently herded the creature beyond the fence.

"Now I can get these gauges regulated right and we can get going," he called to her.

Millie pulled the Suburban behind Buddy's truck and rolled up the window to keep out dust. Twenty minutes later, Buddy stopped by a nondescript two-track road. Millie pulled up beside him, putting the BLM shield next to the Dagun logo. Buddy got out of his truck and motioned to Millie to roll down her window. "We're right here," he said, pointing to her map with an assurance Millie wished she had regarding these crisscrossing roads.

At that moment, a screeching sound reached them, along with a rumbling through the ground. "There they go," Buddy declared, pointing into the distance. "They've started drilling. I saw them putting up the rig a couple days ago. It's a beautiful sight."

The drill rig looked to be nearly a half-mile away, only the upper third visible beyond the intervening mesas. Millie shook her head. The high-pitched noise made her blood run cold. *Maybe to Buddy it was a beautiful sight, a technological marvel.*

"Don't be alarmed, Miss Millie. When the drill bit first hits hard rock, it screeches like that." With a wave, Buddy returned to his truck, soon disappearing down the road in a plume of dust.

Millie stared after him in bewilderment. This man quotes Aldo Leopold, doesn't hurt a snake, and calls a drill rig beautiful. Environmentalists and oil and gas industry are supposed to be adversaries. Maybe that's multiple-use. It's not always us against them. Here—it's everything.

Millie thought back to the parade of equipment she'd seen that first day out with Wirt. Amazing how all those parts could be assembled in a couple of days, tall enough and sturdy enough to reach the deep formations where gas and oil deposits lay undisturbed for eons.

For several minutes the screaming sound continued as the diamond-hard drill bit plunged into the ground. *It sounds like Mother Earth crying out.*

12. Cowboy

I've got spurs that jingle jangle jingle, as I go riden' merrily along...
—*The Old Chisholm Trail*

Millie stretched and massaged her neck. She was tired from walking transects back and forth in the hot sun. She scanned the ever-changing landscape, fascinated by how the passing sun gave light to hills and boulders, then later would camouflage them in shadows. Piñon and juniper trees growing midway up the mesas cradled an expanse of sagebrush, edged by brighter green rabbit-brush along the wash.

She gathered gear to carry back to the Suburban and shuffled the backpack until it accepted clipboard, plant guide, map, GPS, and flannel shirt she had shed in the warm afternoon sun. She folded the one-inch magnifying loupe into its hard shell that hung on a lanyard around her neck. If the loupe ever got lost it would be disaster—maybe not quite disaster, but it was a fond token of good times keying out plants in botany classes.

The magnifier was essential for identifying San Juan cactus. Other small, ball-shaped cactus, *Echinocereus* or maybe *Pediocactus*, occurred on the Piñon Resource Area, but the loupe verified the San Juan had curved fishhook spines, putting it in the *Sclerocactus* genus. The sharp hooks looked vicious when magnified, even though the spines were only the length of an eyelash. The colony of San Juan cactus showed healthy reproduction for this time of year.

Her eyes followed the road that sometimes teetered on the edge of steep banks of the stream bed at the bottom of Lejos Canyon. In other places, in order to keep to a more direct route, the road pulled away where the wash almost curled back on itself. She lost sight of the road where it disappeared through the gap at the top of the canyon. This narrow gap warranted one of the few signs Millie encountered after leaving the paved highway, "Caution One Lane Road." She smiled, thinking of the times she had stopped right there, risky to pause in the narrow pass, but worth it to enjoy the view that extended for miles.

The fatigue she felt was due to more than a long day in the sun. She could not shake the niggling in her mind for why the boundaries she outlined for this San Juan cactus population did not coincide with the old surveys.

She had followed protocol to survey the plot. She walked a wide area, circling inward until spotting the first specimens. She shoved one spindly, knee-high wire with its white flag into the sandy soil to mark the edge of the plot. She continued this process until white flags outlined the egg-shaped plot, encompassing approximately two and a half acres. Next, she walked the plot's perimeter, punching the GPS unit's *Mark* button at each white flag. Walking transects at 20-foot intervals within the marked area had filled the rest of the day. Back at the office, she would use the GPS readings to produce a precise location map, then compare her count of individual plants with earlier survey data to determine any change in density.

One more walk around to pick up the flag markers

and she'd be done for the day. Still, she spent a few more minutes scrutinizing the area. She wanted to embed every aspect of the location into memory.

Two quail whooshed into flight across the plot, causing Millie to wheel around and peer in their direction. A horse stopped short and snorted. The tawny buckskin and its rider's black hat blended with the shadows.

The cowboy's head shot up. "What are you doing here? Easy, Dunnie, easy."

"Stop. Don't let that horse step on these cactus. Stay away," Millie shouted.

"What da' ya' mean. Those little cactus won't hurt Dunnie any," he called back.

"Yeah, but it won't do the cactus any good to get trampled. Breaking up this cryptobiotic soil won't help either."

"Lordy, lady. You must be one of those BLM scientist types." The man wore leather chaps, and had a coiled rope and rifle case slung from his saddle.

With an almost imperceptible move of the man's wrist and shift of weight, the buckskin took a few steps backwards, then circled in her direction, staying outside of the flagging. Again, with no noticeable signal, the horse stopped just far enough from Millie to allow for conversation without the need to shout.

"Dunnie, here, he won't cause any trouble." The cowboy made no move to dismount, just rolled his slim hips backward as if he were relaxing in an easy chair.

"You just go riding your horse wherever you want to?"

"Yes, ma'am. This is public land and I'm a public," he said, with a smart-alecky grin.

When he pulled off his hat and hooked it over the saddle horn, he appeared to be in his 40s, although he had one of those craggy, movie star-type faces that made it impossible to tell age. He wore the usual demarcation across his forehead of those who work in the outdoors. Tan creases climbed above penetrating blue-gray eyes until they met an inch of bleached skin reaching into his dark hair.

"I'd heard there was supposed to be some kind of special cactus around here. So, this must be it. They're kind of cute little things. I'll be sure to watch out for 'em. I get through this way every once in a while. In fact, I do some work for the BLM myself."

"Sure you do," Millie rolled her eyes.

"Well, it's not like office work. Sometimes, when they get ready to do a round-up on the Waterhole Mustang Herd, they pay me to keep track of them for a couple weeks ahead of time. That's if I'm available. You see, a wild horse herd travels around some, but not so much that you can't predict where they will go to water. That's where the trap will be set up. Catches a few mustangs and gets them off the range.

"Dunnie, here, he was caught in a round-up. When I can get away, I do some work for my uncle Eladio Gomez. He has a big allotment and runs a couple hundred head of cattle all summer. He's so dirt poor, he can't really afford a hired hand. So he lets me bunk at his ranch, keep my horse there, and ride herd on his cattle."

The visitor seemed to mean no harm, nor be in any hurry to move on. Millie let her backpack drop to the ground and walked toward the horse, extending her hand, palm upwards. She had seen big Thoroughbreds on occasional trips with her father to Belmont Park racetrack and couldn't resist reaching out to this compact mustang. Millie rubbed the mustang's nose and slid her hand along his neck, the tangled black mane dropped below her elbow. She was standing almost at the cowboy's knee. She pulled her hand back, noticing a row of white hairs beneath the mane.

"What's that on his neck? Looks like a scar."

"It's a freeze mark, ma'am." The cowboy reached forward and gathered up the horse's mane to reveal a row of what looked like hieroglyphics defined by white hairs along the buckskin's neck. "Mustangs rounded up on Forest Service or BLM land are given a freeze brand and put up for adoption. The mark has a code for the state where the horse was caught, its year of birth, and an individual registration number. I help with all that. It's pretty good pay for some off-and-on work. So, see, I work for BLM, too."

Dunnie nuzzled Millie, starting at her hand, working up her arm, and sniffed her breath. Apparently satisfied with this proper introduction, the horse lowered his head and closed his eyes.

Millie shifted to a comfortable stance at an angle from Dunnie's shoulder. This cowboy might make an interesting addition to her field notes.

"Dunnie, I could see he came from good stock. Some people think mustangs are these noble beasts directly descended from Spanish horses brought over by conquistadors." The cowboy patted his pride and joy.

"You should hear Fritz go on and on about 'the noble mustang, symbol of freedom in the great American West.' Have you met the German? You'll see his camper around. He takes photographs of the Waterhole Herd and scenery, sunsets, things like that. Says the European magazines can't get enough of pictures of the West. He leads tours, too. Charges people good money. 'Land of Enchantment Wild Horse Tours,' he calls them. Tells the dudes he has a special way with wild horses. So if they're real, real lucky, they might get a chance to see a genuine mustang. Ha, his special way of knowing is that there are only so many water holes where horses are bound to be."

The cowboy's laugh caused Dunnie to open one eye. "Your average mustang is a runty little cuss. But others are domestic horses that have just been turned loose. I could see Dunnie here had a lot of Quarter Horse breeding somewhere in his ancestry and enough mustang in him to carry a man all day and never miss a step."

Millie stepped back, taking in the horse's full length. "He's no runt. That's a nice-looking horse." Millie was glad to pay back the cowboy for enlightening her about wild horses.

"Hear that, Dunnie, the lady thinks you are a fine specimen of the equine world."

Millie started toward the nearest white flag.

The cowboy shifted and the horse turned toward the outlined cactus plot. "So ma'am, you say there's something special about that dirt?"

"See that dark layer in between plants? It's cryptobiotic crust—actually thousands of tiny, living organisms that hold water and nitrogen and keeps the soil from blowing away. Crushing it might take years for it to build back up. It may be part of the answer as to why these San Juan cactus exist here."

"You know, I've seen these little-bitty cactus over there, too." The horse and cowboy turned as one, to face toward the road. "The soil looks about the same. Same kind of hillside, faces south like this one."

"Where? Show me."

"You see that clearing over there below the P-J?"

Millie's eyes followed his outstretched arm, looked across the road, beyond the wash, and spotted the opening nearly a mile away.

"Now see that big boulder just above it? It's got petroglyphs carved on it. I camped by that boulder once. That little cactus was a little south of it."

"I'll check it out. Thanks."

Millie looked at the cowboy just as he ducked his head, either because he was lifting his hat from the saddle horn to settle it back in place, or because he was muttering, "I should have known better when I got a closer look at those little cactus the next morning. That's where I hobbled Dunnie one night."

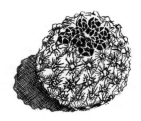

13. Interruptions

The curation of silence is nearly a lost art.
—Erica Olsen, *Recapture*

Millie arrived early at the BLM office. Momma Agnes was already behind her counter and had coffee brewing in the break room. "You owe me twenty-five dollars." Momma Agnes was grinning, holding out a sand-painting nameplate. "I told Ray Yazzie to put plants on it, told him you like plants."

Millie maneuvered her backpack so she could accept the nameplate. Cradling the artwork with both hands, she nodded and read **M-i-l-l-i-e** in bold letters rendered in fine, black sand.

"I love it, Momma Agnes. I'll be right back with the money." Millie walked toward her cubicle, scrutinizing the soft green streaks of colored sand that formed sagebrush and an image of a piñon tree branching over the M. The tree was drawn with many shades of fine lines from tan to brown to charcoal.

"Hey, plant person, watch where you're going," Robby Ramirez called out, deliberately stepping into Millie's path. She had a BLM badge on her tan shirt and wore the law enforcement officer's tool belt on her slim hips like she was born with it. The wide leather belt held a holstered gun, along with baton, radio, and items Millie didn't even recognize.

Robby's laugh and good-natured fist bump to her shoulder almost made Millie drop the nameplate. "Look at this. Look at the shading, all made with just sand."

"Can't now. Our favorite citizen is up front. Wants to tell me how to do my job." Robby quickened her pace toward the admin area.

Millie dropped the backpack on her desk, unzipped the front pocket where she carried money, and strolled back to the lobby. She was about to hand the bills to Momma Agnes, but pulled her hand back.

If looks could destroy, Momma Agnes's stare would have splintered the area manager's closed door. "How dare she! Do you know what she said to me? She said, 'I don't need no stinkin' badge.' Said it to my face. Well, it happens to be *my job* to sign in visitors and give them a visitor ID tag. Just because Belva Banks has bothered every person here at one time or another doesn't mean she can just barge into Wirt's office, demanding to talk to a ranger!"

Even through the closed door, Millie could detect Wirt's voice getting in a few words, but she could easily hear Belva sounding off about bozos running ATVs off trail and chasing wild horses. The door opened and Wirt guided Belva out, followed by Robby.

"Robby, take Miss Banks to the map room so she can show you exactly where she saw those ATV'ers." Wirt winked at Robby.

Taking the lead down the hall toward the map room, the Old Broad for Public Lands Protection glanced back at Robby. "What're you doing in the office anyway? Why don't you get off your skinny ass and get out there where they're tearing up *MY PUBLIC LAND.*"

"But, ma'am, ma'am, there's a million acres in the Piñon Resource Area to cover and there's only two of us... That's more ground to patrol than the whole state of Rhode Island. Can't be everywhere all the time."

Their voices trailed off down the hallway. Wirt locked eyes with Momma Agnes. His face was as red as Entrada sandstone. "It's all right, Momma Agnes. Nobody could stop Belva. I've got a lot of respect for the Old Broads organization, for what those grandmothers do for public lands. But that woman, *THAT* woman. Well, she can swear worse than I can, and I was in the Navy!"

This made Momma Agnes laugh. Millie felt it was safe to approach the counter. She handed over the money and pointed at the nameplate. "I can't figure out what the little crisscross design is on here."

"It's a cradle board, hon. Navajos wrap babies tight in a cradleboard. Keeps 'em quiet, just like going back into the womb. Can hang it on a tree or lay it on the couch. Baby goes to sleep. Everybody gets some rest."

"But what's that got to do with me?"

"Well, Miss Millie, you gotta' be pushing thirty. It's high time you be thinking about such things."

Millie drew a breath, turned on her heels, and headed back to her cubicle.

A man sat in her office chair, running his hand along the neatly arranged bookshelves. *Now what? Am I ever going to get back out to check that plot today?*

He popped out of the chair, took a couple steps, and positioned his fanny on a corner of the desk, acting like he owned the place. "Hi Millie. Thought I'd gone down the wrong hallway—hardly recognized my old office. I'm Herb Thompson."

"So you're the former denizen of the 'herbarium.' Hope you're not back to reclaim your old territory. I wouldn't be surprised though. Everybody has nothing but good things to say about your work here."

"Maybe that's what they say now that I've retired. I've had some pretty good rounds in my days. Almost got run over by a bulldozer once. I told the driver to quit right where he was. He thought it would be just a grand idea to straighten out a little road to his company's well pad. Couldn't see a thing wrong with plowing over three-hundred-year-old junipers."

Millie could picture this wiry old man standing his ground no matter what. About two-thirds Millie's height and well past usual retirement age, Herb looked as tough as a three-hundred-year-old juniper. Suspenders held up sagging jeans that folded over his shoes.

"Never thought I'd say it, but I miss working here, going out in the field. I miss seeing the wildflowers come into bloom after a hard winter. Purple locoweed, orange globe mallow, pure white sego lily. And the cactus—prickly pear's peach blossoms and claret cup with those killer-red flowers. Nobody can tell me that there's nothing to see in the desert."

Millie wished she could peek into the visions that were floating behind his eyes—eyes that had witnessed many seasons come and go in the high desert.

"Know what I miss most of all? I miss the silence. Turn off the engine, and if you're not anywhere near a compressor station, just listen. Listen to nothing. Most people don't even know what it's like to be in real quiet." He paused for a moment, enfolding them both in the recollection of silence.

"I kind of miss seeing the folks I worked with, too. I don't mean just the guys and gals who work here, but the characters I'd run into out there. I'd see Buddy almost every week. He'd fill me in on what wells were going in where. Real nice guy."

"Buddy Maddox? Works for Dagun?" Millie chimed in, "Wirt introduced us the very first day we went in the field. We ran into Belva Banks that day, too. Do you know Belva?"

"There's nobody in this office that doesn't know Belva. Seems she's *always* out there hiking around. Belva probably knows the Piñon Resource Area as well as any of the specialists here.

"Yeah, she's a regular out there. Have you met Fritz yet? He comes all the way from Germany about this time of year. Camps out and takes pictures of wild horses. Not one of your back-packer tent types. Not Fritz. He's got a rig tricked out with all the comforts of home and a ton of photography gear."

Herb was an office legend. He had the reputation of being able to spot a rare plant from a vehicle going 40 miles an hour. He led the team of resource specialists who did the original T and E survey in the '90s. Whenever Millie heard another staff member talk about Herb, the tale inevitably included the time he reamed out a visiting senator who was considering weakening the Endangered Species Act. Millie was torn between getting back to work and prompting him for more stories.

Maybe she could do both. Reaching into her backpack, she pulled out the worn and crumpled field map of the earlier survey. Herb's face lit up. "How are you doing checking on my T and E plots?"

"I was here just yesterday," Millie said, pointing to the San Juan cactus plot. "They're still there," she assured him, not ready to discuss her observation that the population may be decreasing in size.

"Are they still in blossom? Don't they have the prettiest little flowers you ever did see?" Herb sounded like a grandfather gushing over a new grandbaby.

"Yes, sir, awesome. Delicate." An invisible spark leaped between their kindred souls.

"And you know what? Yesterday, a fellow riding a mustang came along and said he knew where there are more San Juans—'those little-bitty cactus' he called them."

Quick as a flash, Herb pushed himself off the desk and was leaning over the map. "Where? Show me." The old botanist's unkempt eyebrows almost touched each other in concentration.

"Did the fellow say he worked for Eladio Gomez?"

"That's him. I didn't get his name. Right there, on the other side of the road from where we were. He said by a big boulder that stood out about halfway up the mesa, a boulder that has petroglyphs on it."

"I know that boulder," Herb mumbled, studying the map. "Could be. Could be. Right elevation, right habitat, right soil. Maybe could be. Cowboy's a pretty good hand."

"What's this cowboy's name?"

"Um, don't know. Never thought about it. Everybody just calls him Cowboy. He almost got a range science degree at New Mexico State University, but went and signed up to fight in the Gulf War. Wasn't the same when he got back. Goes off for months at a time. Some say he goes on drinking binges, but I don't believe it. Old Man Gomez lets him stay at the ranch. Cowboy keeps an eye on the cattle that the old cuss gladly lets run anywhere on BLM land. Guess the situation works for both of them. One thing though, Cowboy knows his blue-stem from muhly grass, that's for sure."

Herb's eyes gleamed with anticipation. "You going to go check it out?"

"I'll get there this afternoon or next week for sure," Millie assured Herb. "I've got to have TJ look at my vehicle."

"My old work horse truck needs a little TLC, too. Got it at a government surplus sale. Used to be a Forest Service vehicle. Since I got back from the Oregon coast, it's been a little fussy about running at high altitude. Once I get that taken care of, I'll go check out what Cowboy said, too."

Millie could hear Herb making his way along the hallway, stopping to chat at almost every cubicle.

Punching her computer on, Millie switched gears to focus on her purpose for coming in early. She was eager to download the GPS data gathered the day before.

No question about it, outlines on the computer screen of the San Juan cactus plot she recorded did not match the boundary shown on the earlier survey map. Her field map was worn and crumpled. She needed to look at the original maps for accurate comparison.

Millie veered off from entering the map room when she heard Belva's loud voice and Robby's overly courteous replies. There was another chore to take care of this morning. She took a deep breath and stepped into the Motor Pool shop. TJ was bent over a wire cage sitting just outside his office door.

"TJ, the Suburban's *check engine* light is flickering on and off. Can you take a look at it?"

TJ stood upright, giving the cage a nudge with his cane. Millie saw a quick movement in the cage and heard a thump. A snake, bigger than Millie had ever seen except for in zoos, lay in two and a half loops in the three-foot cage.

"Ain't he a beauty?" TJ bragged. "About the biggest bullsnake I ever caught."

Millie's wide-eyed stare shifted from the cage to TJ. The self-proclaimed viceroy of vehicles launched into the whole capture story. He and another scouting volunteer make a trek into the mesas south of town to acquire a special treat, the Bully Surprise, for the annual Wellstown Boy Scout rally.

"Yesiree, we get one of the newbies out on the ball field to play catch. Once the kid gets warmed up, we wave him back farther and farther until he can just barely catch the ball. Then one of us, real sneaky like, pulls out the snake and tosses it to the kid. You can hear a pin drop 'cause all the older kids know what's comin.'"

TJ nudged the cage again. Another thump from inside. "Last year, this kid..." TJ was laughing so hard he could hardly get the words out. "This kid, he peed his pants right there. Kid pushed the Bully off himself and ran like the devil was after him. God, I love doing the Bully Surprise."

"Does the Scout Master know you're doing this, scaring a kid like that?"

"Well, it usually happens when the official guys have gone to town for groceries or something, if you know what I mean."

Millie leaned over to see into the cage. She winced at the big snake's bloody nose. "How does the snake fare with all this," Millie said, more of a statement than a question.

"Ah, don't hurt it none. Might get a little scraped up. Just crawls off when we're done messing with it."

Millie scowled, but got back to business. "So, when can you work on the Suburban? I've got to get back to a place where some cowboy said he might have seen San Juan cactus growing. If he's right, it would be a new location."

Still chuckling, TJ nodded. "I'll have it ready by noon, if there's nothing major. That's the endangered one, right? I'd be real interested to know if you find some more of them cactus."

14. Discovery

The immense expanse of country lying within the water-shed of the San Juan River encompasses an equally immense variety of soils and local climatic conditions. ... Within this remarkably diverse landscape is a similarly diverse flora and vegetation, including numerous endemic species and plant communities found nowhere else on earth.

—Heil, O'Kane, Reeves, & Clifford, *Flora of the Four Corners Region*

True to his word, TJ had the Suburban ready by noon. Millie didn't waste time getting to the field, just munched granola bars for lunch and sipped from a water bottle along the way. An hour and a half later, taking one dirt road then a still smaller, bumpier one, Millie reached her target.

Standing in the same spot where she met Cowboy the day before, Millie traced her finger along the San Juan cactus plot outlined on the old survey map. "I was right. There's a real difference. The perimeter of my survey covers about two-thirds of the original area," Millie muttered out loud. "What is going on here?"

She worked though explanations for the discrepancy. Climate change—warmer winters affecting plant distribution? Grazing?—no indication of hoof marks or cow patties. Too rocky, too nondescript to attract ATV riders.

Yet, there were more individual plants filling in the center of the plot than indicated in the old survey. Higher density per square meter, good reproduction, but shrinking area. Weird.

Though hardly visible above the soil, the tiny, young cactus balls with first, second, and third year growth were evidence of a healthy population. That explains why none of the field checks made by BLM staff in the past reported any problems. Without meticulous comparison to original survey maps, the difference would not be noticeable.

Millie pulled off the band holding her hair in a ponytail and shook her head, making a breeze across her neck. "How could this cactus plot have good seed reproduction while shrinking in size?" Normally, her thoughts would settle into some semblance of order. But they remained muddled in a stew of questions; this site seemed to be going against nature's tendency to expand.

She looked at her watch and glanced toward the mid-afternoon sun. Still enough time to hike to the area that Cowboy had pointed out. It wouldn't take long to figure out what kind of cactus he saw.

Millie rolled up the map and scanned the lay of the land. From her location at the edge of the P-J, the sagebrush-covered ground sloped to where the tan Suburban blended with the dusty side road. This spur ran a half mile through the sage to connect with the road that skirted the wide Lejos wash.

The Lejos Canyon Road, named because of the great distance it ran north-south, probably originated centuries ago as a footpath followed by Native Americans. It was later used by Spanish conquistadores in dusty armor, riding tired horses, bent on civilizing this *Tierra Adentro.*

pack, only joy. She broke through brush where the hillside flattened out and she saw a white truck with the familiar spouting well logo. Buddy was hobnobbing with Cowboy, who was leaning toward the truck's open window and resting crossed arms on the saddle horn.

Buddy waved her over. "Knew that was your truck, Miss Millie. Just wanted to make sure you were okay."

The buckskin horse shuffled his back legs, swinging its rump aside to make room for Millie to join the conversation. Cowboy glanced toward the petroglyph boulder. "Did you see 'em? Those little-bitty cactus?"

"Sure did. You were right. I believe that's an unrecorded population of San Juan cactus! I need to check the taxonomy references back at the office and get expert consultation, but I believe you are right."

Millie found herself spilling every detail, starting with seeing the fuchsia blossoms, her estimation of acreage involved, even the number of photographs she took.

"Well, that's something I've got to put on my map. Tell the office about it," Buddy said. "Nobody had that location marked for an endangered species."

An approaching vehicle broke up the afternoon chat. Buddy started his truck, gave a goodbye wave and headed toward Wellstown.

"I thought you'd be mighty interested in that spot, Miss Millie." Cowboy nodded and gathered up the reins.

Millie watched as he angled Dunnie across the road and into the sagebrush. *Wonder what Cowboy meant by that?*

15. Tea in the Sagebrush

Go West, Young Man, Go West.
—*Attributed to Horace Greeley*

Wait until Wirt hears about this! I'll get to the office first thing Monday morning. Momma Agnes will want to hear all about it, too. A good day's work, if I say so myself, and a beautiful Friday afternoon, to boot. Why not give myself a little reward with a visit to Split Lip Canyon Overlook before heading back to Wellstown.

She was surprised to see a dark green vehicle occupying the spot where she usually parked on the well pad next to the overlook trail. She circled the equipment enclosure and passed the medium-size, self-contained camper.

An awning was spread out along the camper's side facing the trail. It shaded a small table covered with a red and yellow tablecloth, supporting a silver tray with a china teapot and sugar and cream containers. Millie stopped and sniffed. The unmistakable fragrance of pipe smoke hung in the air. *This must be the German photographer Herb Thompson talked about back at the office. Herb said he had a decked-out camper.*

A man relaxing in a lawn chair under the awning lifted his pipe in a gesture of greeting. Millie, overcome with curiosity, approached the rig. When the man stood, he had to scrunch down a little to avoid brushing his head on the awning.

"Welcome, madam, you are just in time for tea. Will you join me?"

The man's wavy amber hair showed a touch of gray at the temples. His white, button-down shirt with rolled up sleeves revealed well-tanned arms. A wide leather belt tooled with figures of mustangs and cactus could not overcome the conspicuous creases in his pressed jeans. The carefully draped soft gray neckerchief was the crowning touch. The man presented the classic image of a foreign tourist visiting the American West.

Too taken aback at finding this dash of elegance miles from nowhere, Millie could only mutter an uncertain, "Thank you. I mean, *Danke*."

Smiling at her response, the German disappeared into the camper's side door, pulling it closed behind him. Millie stared after him. The man's accent transported her back to the summer she spent in Europe.

Balancing a cup and saucer in one hand and maneuvering a second folding chair in the other, her host eased out the camper door, closing it with a slight backward kick. He settled the chair on the uneven ground and motioned Millie to sit. *"Guten Tag.* I am Fritz Müller, here to photograph this beautiful country. And you, madam? Are you here to watch the sun set over Split Lip Canyon?"

"I have a long drive back to Wellstown, so I can't spend much time here," Millie waffled, unsure just what his invitation to watch the sunset might entail.

"I see you drive a BLM vehicle. Might you be acquainted with that fine gentleman named Herb?"

"Yes, yes. He told me about you. I'm following up on his T and E plant surveys now that he's retired. I'm Millicent Whitehall." She didn't know why she gave her full first name, but somehow his urbane speech triggered a sense of formality.

"Ah, your botanist colleague retired. So that is why he has not come to join me for tea. And you follow in his footsteps seeking out rare plants. It would be enlightening to know where those footsteps lead."

"You might see him out here. I told him about another location for San Juan cactus. He was the first to survey the Piñon Resource Area for it. He said he'd check it out. I can't wait to hear what he says. All indications look to me like it is a new, unrecorded site."

He stopped, holding the teapot in mid-air. "San Juan cactus, you say. That is a rare one, no? I would be pleased to know if my friend agrees with you."

With great formality, Fritz resumed pouring the steaming tea. Without checking her preference, he used tongs to add chunks of crystallized sugar and added a dollop of cream into one side of the liquid.

Catching scent of the tea's aroma, Millie closed her eyes and took a deep breath. Again she was back in Germany, biking across the countryside, succumbing to a carefree companion. "Is this East Frisian tea?"

Fritz responded to the delight in her voice. "Ah, you must have been to *Deutschland,* my country."

"I had a one-month internship at Ruhr University. It even paid for the flight over. It was part of an exchange program to expose first generation college students to international work. I worked at the university's amazing botanical garden. After I completed the internship, I toured around on my own—sort of. It took almost all my savings, but I figured I'd never get to travel like that again."

Millie described her travels, leaving out what was behind the "sort of on my own" part. One morning, while she was savoring buttery croissants at a sidewalk café, a chance meeting began her greatest adventure that summer. A very good-looking American about her age was wending his way among the tables, looking for a spot not already occupied. On impulse, Millie motioned him to the empty chair at her table. In no time, they discovered they both were attending Rutgers.

The fit young man was a business major, which explained why they had never encountered each other on campus. He convinced Millie the only way to fully experience Europe was by bicycling. The next week, Millie found herself pedaling side-by-side with him across the countryside. At the end of each day, they sought a secluded spot and set up camp. Millie had never felt such freedom, nor such desire when they lay together in the tent at night.

Their affair didn't last long back on campus that fall. She didn't have time to linger over coffee at the Student Center, nor watch his crew team practice. And she was concerned that if he parked his BMW in the neighborhood where she lived, the hubcaps might vanish.

"I remember camping along the Rhine River."

Fritz's nostalgic sigh matched her own. "A beautiful river is the Rhine. I must admit, and pardon me if I offend you as an American, but I was a little disappointed when I first saw your Rio Grande River." He pronounced it Rio Grandee.

Millie laughed, and said she felt the same just a couple of months ago, this being her first experience in the Southwest.

Fritz nodded. "I always wanted to experience the American West. Like many boys in my country, I was fascinated by the legendary Karl May's books. He published adventure stories of the American West, even though he wrote them well before your Theodore Roosevelt became president. I wanted to *be* Old Shatterhand and ride with my Indian blood brother Winnetou, the noble Apache chief. I would have no qualms about punching a bad guy or shooting the town's villain. *Ja, Ja.* I would be the upright, stalwart protector of the wild and woolly West.

"I would escape my reality of being in a bleak classroom with forty students sitting in straight rows by imagining myself as being one of the big boys in a one-room schoolhouse. I would fetch firewood for the pretty school marm. Oh, how I envied their freedom and independence, all the characters Karl May wrote about, even the villains."

Fritz's bent head wagged side-to-side. "But I'm too late, I fear. I find here pickup trucks, beer cans strewn along roadsides…"

"It's not what I expected, either. There are roads everywhere. I imagined myself camping on a hillside, mountains looming in the background. The only sign of human intrusion being a lantern light shining through the sides of my lone tent. That's how I thought it would be—like the cover of an REI catalog."

They sipped tea in companionable rapport and gazed toward the trail leading to the canyon overlook, tuning out the low hum of the gas well equipment behind them. The narrow path through sagebrush became lost from sight as it reached the scrubby piñon and juniper trees and continued up the slope into tall ponderosa pines.

"You know, in my country, there are still Karl May festivals. People dress up like cowboys and Indians. I have yet to see a Native American here wearing a breech cloth," Fritz chuckled and filled Millie's cup from the still warm teapot, then refreshed his own.

"Perhaps it was never real." His voice took on an ironic tone. "Karl May wrote all those western books before he even stepped onto this continent. He never got farther west than Buffalo, New York.

"But I do not want to mislead my guest." He spread his arms wide. "I love this high desert. Sunsets are better than either Karl May or Zane Gray could evoke with mere words on a page. Stories of your wide-open spaces, they still draw us Europeans with great fascination."

Fritz drained his cup and continued, "One can still run into the rugged soul. Let me show you." He ducked out of the awning, opened the camper's passenger-side door, and eased out a rectangular box. Before setting the box down, he snatched up the napkin by his cup and saucer, and whooshed it across the tablecloth to chase away any dust.

The box was the kind used by museums and libraries to contain specimens or important documents. Fritz folded back the lid attached to the box like a clamshell. He lifted a photograph and, supporting it with both hands, held it toward her.

Millie gasped. Her eyes dazzled with an explosion of gold, vermilion, cerulean, and purple colors. Slowly the landscape underpinning the sunset slid into her consciousness. "That's Split Lip Canyon from the overlook, isn't it," she breathed, not taking her eyes off the masterpiece, first created by nature, then framed by a photographer's eye and rendered by the camera's lens.

He placed the image in the box's lid and lifted out the next photograph. Millie jerked back with surprise. There stood horse and rider, a silhouette against a setting sun, angled and cloaked in shadow giving the viewer an impression of seeing a centaur. Cowboy would have been unrecognizable, except that he was in the same rolled back, relaxed position as when he told her about wild horse round-ups. Dunnie's long mustang mane, dangling below his neck, filtered the sun's rays.

"This will be the portfolio I exhibit. I will sell prints,

signed and numbered by myself. Other photos I sell to magazines. Magazines that tell people how wonderful it is to visit the American West. Some tell their readers that they, too, can make pictures like this if they go on Fritz Müller's Wild Horse Tours. Thus, I have money to come back next spring. I bring here people from my country. I show them where to stand when the sun goes down. It is a wonderful cycle, no?"

"They're beautiful," Millie cooed. One after another, Fritz amazed her with ten more images, each one portraying iconic Southwest scenes.

"I camp and explore for a few days, then go to Wellstown for a nice motel and spicy Mexican food. Mr. Herb, he tells me many times, I may not camp for more than fourteen days on BLM land. How could I? I cannot exist on beans and trail dust like the cowboys did."

Fritz returned the portfolio to the camper and came back with a business card for Millie. Superimposed on a colorful sunset image, an elaborate script announced:

Land of Enchantment Wild Horse Tours
Capture the Spirit of the West
Fantastic Images of Wild Mustangs Guaranteed
Frederik (Fritz) Müller—
Photographer, Exporter, Adventurer

The sun edged toward the horizon. She'd be lucky to get back to pavement before dark and still had a half-hour drive after that. "Fritz, you can have the sunset to yourself tonight. It was a pleasure meeting you. Your photographs are awesome."

Millie ducked out of the awning but stopped next to a photographer's tripod set up by the camper. Each leg was composed of three sections designed to slide into each other, so it could be collapsed or extended to its current five-foot height. Millie ran a hand along one rounded, wooden leg, feeling a slight dent from much use and noticing how clean and well-polished it was. "I've never seen a tripod like this."

"It is a German tripod, madam. It is made of ash wood, from something once alive. It absorbs vibration when the camera operates. It is a very fine piece of equipment, no?"

"It is beautiful. Thank you for the Frisian tea, it is a real treat."

"My pleasure, madam. When you see my camper again, do come for tea," Fritz called after her. She heard the clink of china being gathered on a tray as she closed the door of the Suburban.

* * *

Millie did not see another vehicle for the last few miles before hitting pavement. Oil field trucks were long gone by sunset and anyone from the scattered ranches would be back from town by now.

Millie breathed a sigh of relief when she reached the BLM office before the night security guard locked the vehicle yard. She backed the Suburban into its stall at the end of the row and grabbed her backpack and roll of maps. She fished in the glove compartment for a flashlight. "Damn it, batteries are dead." She muttered a "double damn it" when she tapped the flashlight icon on her mobile phone and found it was out of juice as well.

On her way through the dark to her own vehicle parked in front of the office building, a rustling sound made Millie jerk to a stop. On alert, her senses honed in on a box in the shadow of the Motor Pool shop. *Thump, thump.* She heard the pathetic protests of TJ's captive.

Knowing she'd be sorry, Millie veered toward the cage and peeked over the edge. *Thump, thump.* The bullsnake seemed caught in a trance of repetitive movement. Millie stepped back, just wanting to get home. *Thump, thump.* She could not do it. She couldn't walk away.

She inspected the front of the cage, took a deep breath, and wiggled a peg out of the hasp. *Thump.* The door flew open. Millie let out a "yikes" and jumped back.

It's not like she minded snakes. After all, they are a part of the natural world. She didn't even mind handling them. She remembered the field trip back in a botany class where the professor picked up an eastern garter snake and told students to form a circle. Standing in the center, the instructor coached them how to let the creature glide from one hand to another. Millie was amazed at its dry, light feel as it glided from her right hand over her left palm and onto the next student's outstretched hand.

But this dude was *BIG*. Not like the slender, ribbon-sized garter snake. And it was crawling toward the vehicle shed.

"Oh, no. You can't go there. He'll find you." Millie spotted a push broom left against the building. She plunked the broom down squarely in front of the bullsnake. It stopped. She winced at the sight of its bleeding nose. "That direction," she whispered, "go toward the fence."

Angling the push boom alongside the snake, stepping left and right, Millie herded the brown and amber shape toward the chain link fence. As it got closer to freedom, the creature moved faster and faster. Easily slipping under the fence, it disappeared into the sagebrush and darkness.

"Good luck to you, big fellow. And no bully surprise for some young boy scout, either. More of a surprise for the two-legged bully, I'd say." Millie returned the push broom to the exact same position against the wall. She stood still a moment to let her heart stop racing. Before picking up the backpack where she had dropped it, she looked around by the cage, found the peg that had held the door closed and broke it in two. Maybe it would look like the snake had banged the door hard enough to break it.

Millie continued walking quietly to the Explorer, alert for any other sounds. In the dark, the SUV's sangria red paint looked like the dried blood inside the snake's cage. Millie was relieved to climb inside, glad the day was over. Before starting the engine, Millie leaned her head back against the seat. *What a day. I find an unrecorded population of an endangered cactus. I have tea in the sagebrush. I dance with a bullsnake. I never expected this job would be anything like this.*

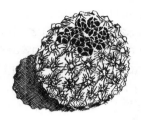

16. Devil's Claw Café

Red or Green?
—New Mexico's Official State Question

Millie trudged back to her cubicle, not seeing anything but the worn carpet in front of her feet. It wasn't because of Monday morning doldrums. The area manager's reaction to her announcement of a new San Juan cactus population was not what she anticipated. It was, in fact, disheartening.

His first words were, "You haven't told anybody about this, have you?" He was standing, leaning toward her, both hands on his desk, or they would have been except for the inches of paper between his palms and the wood.

Her mind flickered through the way Cowboy's horse kept trying to nibble the orange flag on Buddy's truck and the aromas of pipe tobacco blending with Fritz's East Frisian tea. Millie took a deep breath, and recounted what she did and everyone she talked to after discovering the cactus.

Wirt dropped back into his chair and lifted a hand to rub his eyes as if trying to blot out the words she was saying. "Are you sure? Don't you know enough not to go blabbing to everyone about *finding* an unrecorded location for an endangered species on the Piñon Resource Area. You told Buddy? He's got the biggest mouth in the gas patch. And you *think* it's a San Juan cactus? Show me where it is."

She pushed the contour map toward him, pointing out the new plot. "It's not all that far from the one Herb found in the early nineteen-nineties. It's by a big boulder that has petroglyphs on it."

"Let's get that fellow from the community college to look at it. He's supposed to be the cactus expert around here."

Wirt hit the intercom. "Momma Agnes, get Officer Ramirez in here. Then get me the number for the college."

Momma Agnes' voice came over the speaker, "Sorry Wirt, Robby signed out this morning to go check on a cattle trespass."

"Call her back in here, now," Wirt ordered.

Millie rolled up the map and started toward the door. "Don't mention this to anybody else. You understand?"

"Yes, sir."

* * *

Millie positioned the oversized taxonomy book on the copy machine. She wanted to have the official San Juan cactus classification along when Wirt, the cactus expert, and the law enforcement officer went to check out her discovery. The two pages of description would be easier to carry in the field. Voices and the sound of a shuffling cane caused her to look up.

With his free hand, TJ was flipping open a Piñon Resource Area map. A smiling Fritz was right behind him, now wearing a flamboyant turquoise neckerchief and corduroy jacket complete with leather elbow patches.

TJ's cane struck the corner of the copy machine. He stepped next to her as if in line to use the copier, but a little too close. "Girlie, the Boy Scout Jamboree was a big bust. There wasn't any Bully Surprise. Maybe you already knew that."

Millie turned a shoulder to block TJ's view of the copier. Wirt's angry words still stinging—don't tell anybody about the cactus. "Gee, that's too bad, TJ."

"Ah, the botanist lady hard at work. Good morning, Madam Whitehall." The tone of Fritz's greeting was considerably more cordial than TJ's.

Millie lifted the tome off the platen and slid the two warm pages inside the book. She nodded to Fritz and turned toward the hallway. TJ directed Fritz to steady the map that he flopped on the copier. In a louder than normal voice, clearly for Millie's benefit, TJ said, "Yeah, Fritz, whenever you need to know anything about this BLM area, you just come to me. Me and my hunting buddies have been over every inch of this land."

The phone was ringing when Millie reached her cubicle. It was Wirt's voice. "Robby is here. Get your gear and meet me in the lobby in five minutes. We'll pick up Dr. Arnold at the college."

Millie kicked off her sneakers, pulled on field shoes, and grabbed maps and backpack. She got to the reception area at the same time as Robby padded in, carrying her shoes. They sat next to each other outside of Wirt's office. Millie leaned down to finish lacing up her field shoes. Peeking through the curtain of hair draping her face, she saw Robby was pulling boots on over Hello Kitty socks. *That can't be regulation uniform*, Millie thought, but wasn't going to challenge anybody wearing a gun.

Sitting next to this fit female, both bending over their feet, Millie thought back to her middle school gym class, where they were supposed to sample various types of dance. The two weeks devoted to ballet were Millie's favorite. She could almost feel the slippers with their smooth ribbons, wrapping them around one ankle, then the other. That was another world. Instead she continued crisscrossing leather laces into eyelets on clunky field shoes.

* * *

Dr. Arnold was waiting in front of the community college. He waved them to the curb and had to nearly fold himself double to fit into the Expedition, dominating three-quarters of the backseat. Robby had to edge closer to her door.

Wirt half turned to the backseat, and said, "Dr. Arnold, this is Millie Whitehall, and you already know Officer Ramirez. Sorry to pull you away on such short notice."

"Hi Robby. No problem, glad to get out on a nice day like this. So, this is the summer temp who thinks she's found a new location for San Juan cactus? Well, I've got to tell you, ever since I did my Ph. D. research on cactus genetics, I get about a half dozen reports a year that somebody's found a new species. Not one of them have panned out yet."

Wirt nodded and said, "Yeah, if this turned out like that, it would simplify my life, that's for sure. We'll stop at the Devil's Claw Café for lunch."

Millie slumped lower in her seat. *Great, just great, lunch will take another hour. I just want to get this over with.*

Devil's Claw Café was at the intersection of the paved highway and the turn off to Lejos Canyon. The parking lot was crowded with white pickup trucks, rickety flatbed ranch trucks, two pickups with horse trailers, and a couple of passenger vehicles, their relative cleanliness and out-of-state licenses marking them as tourists passing through.

The sign on the cafe's door welcomed all customers—

Open, Abierto, Yah-ta-hey. Millie followed as Wirt and the others bee-lined to a booth, weaving around shelves and display cases offering everything from toothpaste to salt licks to cans of motor oil.

Without asking, the waitress poured coffee for all and nodded as Wirt, Robby, and Dr. Arnold identified whether they wanted beef or chicken burritos, with red or green chile sauce. Millie hesitated, not sure if she could keep anything down until she knew whether she her cactus identification was right or whether she was going to get fired.

Robby whispered, "Try Christmas, that means partly covered with red chile and partly with green chile."

The waitress saw her blank look and said, "How about a bean burrito, hon, with Christmas sauce?" Millie nodded.

As Wirt and Dr. Arnold caught up on news about people they both knew in common, Millie took in the Devil's Claw Café's eclectic wall decorations—an oversized, blue velvet Mexican sombrero with sequined trim was flanked by a charcoal drawing of an Indian child holding a lamb and a poster of a grizzled, toothless cowboy.

A question from Robbie got Millie's attention. "Did you know that New Mexico has an official state question?"

"State question? Like a state bird or state flower?"

"Yup, the question is short, and the answer is even shorter. Red or Green? As in chile. If you live here, you've got to be ready with the answer."

The order arrived and Millie sampled both ends of the burrito. She decided the half with puddles of green chile sauce was tastier than the red half. She'd be better prepared next time to respond to New Mexico's official question. Green!

Millie felt a twinge inside her stomach. It wasn't a burn from eating the burrito. *Oh no, not now.* She excused herself and went to the shelves of supplies. She breathed a sigh of relief and picked up a package of tampons. Millie laid her purchase and dollar bills on the counter where the same waitress was at the cash register. Inside the glass counter, an elegant turquoise and silver necklace caught Millie's eye. It lay alongside bracelets made from juniper seeds interspersed with tiny red beads. Next to these, for no apparent rhyme or reason, was an assortment of breath mints, Tums, a hairbrush, can openers, and bungee cords.

The waitress glanced at Millie, swooped up the dollar bills, and poked at the cash register. She met Millie's eye and whispered a sympathetic, "Sorry, hon." *Sisterhood happens.*

Millie returned from the restroom in time to pay her share of the bill and toss a couple dollars into the tip pile. She was the first one out the door and into the Expedition's front seat.

Dr. Arnold was the last one to settle himself in the backseat. He tapped Wirt on the shoulder, and said, "Drive on, Jeeves, let's continue this wild goose chase."

Millie squared her shoulders and looked straight ahead. *Maybe I am from New JOYsey, but I can read a taxonomic guide just as well as a Ph.D. dude.* She was 99% sure she was going to show Dr. Arnold, Wirt and Robby a new location for San Juan cactus.

17. Note on the Wind

Women are like tea bags. You never know how strong they are until you put them in hot water.
—*Attributed to Eleanor Roosevelt*

"**W**ell, that's one for the record books," Dr. Arnold declared, tucking his magnifying loupe into a shirt pocket. The big man pushed himself up from a kneeling position after studying several specimens. "I've got to apologize to you, Millie. This whole BLM Resource Area was surveyed for San Juan cactus. Then here comes a seasonal temp and she finds a new location for one of the most endangered cacti in the Southwest. You know your plants."

Relief flowed through her whole body. If she had been wrong, if this were just another common cactus, well, she might as well pack up, go home to Milltown, and start filling mop buckets. Instead, she let out an exultant, "Yeeesss!"

"This makes three locations for *Sclerocactus sanjuan-ensis* that we know about." Dr. Arnold's voice held relief and delight.

He pointed across the wash. "The hillside way over there that we can just see—where you met that cowboy, Millie—was the first location where this species was discovered. Herb Thompson came across that plot, back in the nineties when he was doing the ecosystem health inventory. He thought it looked different from any of the other fishhook cactus around here."

Turning toward the south where the road curved over a rise, he said, "Not long after, archaeologists discovered a second population near an old homesteader's cabin they were stabilizing. Herb and I collected some specimens for verification by renowned cactus specialists. It took two years for the official taxonomy to be published. It took another year and a half for the Fish and Wildlife Service to approve adding it to the federal endangered species list. Herb was pretty excited about it. We got to calling those two plots T-one and T-two, after Herb Thompson."

Dr. Arnold's broad hand clasped Millie's shoulder, giving a good-natured shake. "Maybe we'll call this one the 'Millie plot.'" His wide grin matched Millie's. "Now with this new plot, we have three separate locations, at least two miles apart. That's kind of like having insurance—if something should wipe out one or the another, at least the species would survive."

Hmmm, Millie plot. She liked the sound of that. A little bit of recognition of her botany work felt darn good.

Millie continued guiding Wirt and Dr. Arnold around the perimeter of the plot. For several steps, the men tiptoed at a snail's pace, being careful to steer clear of the small cactus. Millie assured them that if they followed in her wide circle, there was no danger of intruding on the distinctive, cobbled patch of ground where San Juan cactus found its niche.

They rejoined Robby, who had waited in the shade of the petroglyph boulder. Wirt said, "Let's not put this location in any reports just yet." He paused, making sure he had their full attention. "I need to check an Application for Permit to Drill that's on my desk for signature. I'm thinking the plan showed the drill rig to be placed somewhere in this locality."

Despite this caution, by the time they reached the vehicle, Wirt and Robby were caught up in the botanists' exuberance. As they drove to the T-one San Juan cactus plot that Dr. Arnold wanted to look at, Robby revealed her Texas roots by launching into song at the top of her voice.

"Come a ti yi yippee, come a ti yi yea."

Dr. Arnold burst out laughing and joined in. "Come a ti yi yippee, come a ti yi yea."

Robby began waving her hands, pretending to conduct the refrain. "Come along boys and listen to my tale, I'll tell you of my troubles on the old Chisholm trail."

Millie and Wirt joined in, "Come a ti yi yippee, come a ti yi yea, Come a ti yi yippee, yippee yea."

Caught in mid-yippee, Robby called out, "Stop! That looks like Herb Thompson's old truck. You can tell from that faded out Forest Service yuck green." They all saw the flash of afternoon sunlight reflected from a windshield. "What's that old fart doing off the road like that?"

Ruts led to a vehicle that appeared to have run off the road, plowing 20 yards through the sagebrush.

Wirt pulled over to the roadside and stopped. Millie and Dr. Arnold came around the front of the Expedition just as Wirt and Robby stepped into the sagebrush. Suddenly Robby raised her arm, stopping them with a whispered, "Stay here."

The command in her voice halted their forward momentum as if they hit a sandstone wall. Wirt met Dr. Arnold's quizzical expression. "I don't know. Robby's got that cop's sixth sense when something's wrong. We'll just stay here until she finds out."

Like a stalking cat, Robby moved soundlessly toward the pickup, hand hovering over the pistol on her hip. They watched her run the last few steps to the driver's side door that was hanging open. Reaching in with one arm, Robby frantically waved for them to come.

Robby's back obstructed their view, but they could see a blue-jeans-clad leg hanging out the door. Robby stepped aside but still held two fingers against the man's neck, checking for the pulse that should have been surging through the carotid artery.

An open pill bottle was tipped sideways in a rigid hand, a few pills caught in the creases of the jeans and spilled on the floor. The other arm pressed against the chest, hand clamped around the opposite arm just below the shoulder.

Robby straightened up. "He's passed." For a moment, it seemed like the wind stood still, the sagebrush stopped growing.

Wirt's face was pale. "Goddammit. That's Herb. It can't be Herb. He was just in the office a couple of days ago."

Millie's voice shook. "I told him about the new plot. He said he might go look at it. I should never have mentioned it." She could not reconcile the contorted, ashen face before her as belonging to the vigorous man she met.

Wirt seemed to be in a daze at the sight of his longtime colleague. Robby took charge. She stepped directly in front of Wirt, forcing his attention.

"Wirt, you and Dr. Arnold go back to our vehicle. Call the county sheriff's office and tell them to send an ambulance, and the medical investigator. Take Dr. Arnold back to the main road so he can direct emergency personnel."

She turned to the professor. "You remember how to get here, to this side road?"

"Sure, no problem. I'll help in any way I can."

"Wirt, you get back here as soon as you can, but stay in the vehicle to keep in communication with emergency services."

Robby put a firm hand on Millie's arm, led her a few yards away from the body, and faced her in the direction the men had gone. "Millie, you stay right here. Don't let anybody get closer to Herb's truck than you are right now. Don't let anybody touch anything. I'm going to take a jog around a wide perimeter and see if I can spot something that might have caused him to run off the road."

The sun was high and direct. Even so, Millie shivered. She stood still and closed her eyes. The dangling leg persisted in her vision. Deep breaths, one after another. Gradually she opened her eyes and saw that her foot was resting on a prickly pear cactus. She stepped aside and shook off a pad stuck to her boot. She brushed against a knee-high bitterbrush. Its pale-yellow flowers, just coming into bloom at this time of year emitted a sweet odor. A breeze jiggled a scrap of paper caught on one of its branches.

Millie reached for the scrap before the breeze sent it further. Millie hated littering. About to tuck it into a pocket to toss in the trash later, she noticed scribbled black letters that coalesced into words. The letters fell down the page, but Millie recognized her name in the scribbled marks.

CACTUS

MILLIE

GONE

Every detail on the paper seared itself into Millie's mind, trauma making her senses more acute. The 3-by-5-inch note had perforated holes across the top. Bits of chad clung to a few openings as if it had been torn off a small notebook. A pen made the scratchy marks. The letters showed a shaky hand, like on the letters Millie had received from her beloved Aunt Nina just before she died.

Not wanting to, but trying to make sense of the message, Millie looked toward the pickup wedged in the brush. Lying in the dirt beneath the open door, directly under the dangling boot, was a black pen with silver top, the kind guaranteed to write in the rain used by people who work outdoors.

My name. Why did Herb write my name?

Millie shifted to watch Robby circling at a distance. Robby walked head down, scrutinizing the ground for tracks of any kind. Finally, Robby's path brought her back to their BLM vehicle. Wirt got out to join her, but Robby motioned him back into the Expedition. They talked for a few minutes.

"County's got two deputies on their way. Ambulance is just starting to roll," Robby reported as she approached Millie. "We're going to be here a while. I didn't see anything that would make him run off the road like that."

"I found this," Millie said, handing Robby the slip of paper.

As soon as Robby deciphered the scribbled letters, she pulled a plastic bag out of her pocket and dropped the note inside, being careful not to touch it any further. "Where'd you find this? You didn't go over there, did you?" Robby snapped.

Millie touched the small bush that caught the note in the breeze. "I have no idea what these words mean, or why my name is on it."

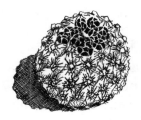

18. Word Spreads

District Managers and Field Managers are responsible for implementing the BLM special status species policies and program within their area of jurisdiction by: ...Ensuring that all actions undertaken comply with the ESA*, its implementing regulations, and other directives associated with ESA-listed and proposed species. (*Endangered Species Act)
—BLM Manual 6840

It was long after sundown by the time Robby asked a sheriff's deputy to give Millie and Dr. Arnold a ride back to town. Herb's body was on its way to Albuquerque accompanied by the medical investigator. Oil field hands that had stopped to see what was happening had all moved on. Robby and Wirt stayed at the scene until the other deputies finished stringing crime scene tape and cleared out.

When Millie got to her driveway, Ragged Ear appeared out of the dark and leaped onto the hood. The cat looked peeved. He swirled in circles by the front door until she got it unlocked and flipped on the living room lights. "You want your munchies, don't you?" He ran directly to the bowl of cat food that Millie now kept by the kitchen sink.

Millie leaned against the refrigerator and watched

Ragged Ear devour the dry nuggets. His contented purr filled the kitchen. When the last crumb was gone, the cat walked over, leaped onto the counter next to Millie and nuzzled her shoulder. She reached around and collected the little warm body in her arms. Ragged Ear nestled against her chest; the first time he had let her touch him. He purred louder, rhythmically, until her heart beat slowed and her eyelids drooped. "I thought I'd never sleep tonight. I was right about the cactus, but what a hellish ending to the day. Now I'm feeling exhausted. I guess this is what they call fuzz therapy."

* * *

By mid-week, word of finding Herb Thompson's body had spread throughout every department. The office atmosphere was one of somber bewilderment.

Momma Agnes herself made the trip down the hallway to Millie's cubicle to deliver the message that the area manager wanted to meet with her. The office mother hen looked like she had been crying. She patted Millie's arm when they reached Wirt's office.

Wirt motioned Millie to the chair in front of his desk. "Sorry you had to go through that, Millie, seeing Herb like that. Two men found dead on the Piñon Resource Area within two months of each other. In all my career, nothing that crazy has ever happened. Herb worked here for years, and almost all of us met up with Harrison Howdy at one time or another." Wirt's voice trailed off. He was probably reliving the death scene just as she had, over and over. "That's just not something a seasonal should have to deal with. You doing okay?"

Millie put on a good front and told Wirt she was staying busy with the plant inventories.

Wirt scanned her face and nodded. "There's something

else that I called you in here for." He tapped a thick report in front of him. "There may be a problem about that new plot of San Juan cactus you found. This is an Application for Permit to Drill a natural gas well in the same location. Just preparing the site prior to drilling would pretty much take out that whole plot."

"What do you mean, 'take out'?" Millie demanded.

"According to the site diagram, the access road goes across the lower end of where the cactus are, and the well pad itself is thirty yards farther up the slope."

Hoping the thumping of her heart wasn't as loud as it sounded to her, Millie gulped and said, "That can't happen. A road there could destroy the whole colony. Disturbance anywhere around there could impact soil moisture. We don't know enough about San Juan cactus ecology to know what a change in drainage might do. That can't happen!" Millie knew her voice was rising.

"Hold on, hold on. It's a federally listed endangered species, Millie. We can't let this APD go through the way it is. The Fish and Wildlife Service will need to be consulted. There may be avenues for mitigation, re-routing the access road, moving the whole drill site if necessary."

Millie sat motionless, glaring at the area manager.

Wirt shuffled his chair back a few inches. "I'll need some time. This APD sits on my desk until I've talked to the company myself. They aren't going to like the idea of delaying drilling for a little cactus you can hardly see. They're going to raise holy hell."

Millie shook her head, wanting this to all go away. This couldn't happen to HER cactus. Wirt was rubbing a hand over his eyes again.

"I'm walking a tightrope here. There's likely to be some political push-back on this. I need to alert the BLM State Office to expect a call from a legislator or two.

"Look, I admire your passion for protecting the resource. You're the right person for this job." He paused, seeming to be working out strategies in his mind. "Meanwhile, keep the location to yourself. Gather any information available on habitat requirements for San Juan cactus. Walk the area at least a half mile out from where you saw the plants, look to see if there might be more of them growing anywhere around there. Analyze the site for overall vegetation cover and soil type. Based on what information you put together, we can put a No Surface Occupancy stipulation on that area. An NSO prevents disturbance on the lease surface to protect special values. Doesn't mean a company couldn't still use directional drilling to tap gas or oil beneath the surface."

Millie wasn't convinced. Development plans tended to only gain momentum, regardless of words on paper. She shuddered at the thought of that quiet patch of ground supporting these unique cactus turned into a bald, lifeless well pad. That can not happen.

* * *

Most staff were leaving for the weekend by Friday afternoon when Millie returned to her cubicle from poring over BLM manuals in the resource room. She now had three pages of notes on what was required to designate an area for No Surface Occupancy. She found Robby Ramirez pretending to look at the wildflower poster on the wall. "Let's go talk in the conference room, Millie. Nobody's using it right now," her tone was more commanding than inviting.

Robby took a chair across from Millie and laid a notebook on the oblong table. "I want to go over anything that you and Herb talked about the day he was in the office. Maybe it'll shed some light on what happened out there."

Millie's baffled expression caused Robby to elaborate. "The sheriff's office recommended I pull together the BLM side of what happened. When we finished up that night, after you and Dr. Arnold left, we were waiting around for the sheriff's office guys to clear the scene. The medical investigator came over and talked to Wirt and me, kind of off the record. She said it was probably cardiac arrest. Happens when the heartbeat becomes irregular."

Robby picked up the notebook and flipped through a few pages. "Arrhythmia is what the MI called it. Those were nitroglycerin tablets that Herb was holding. She said they are prescribed to people with angina. The tablets dissolve under the tongue and go into the system pretty fast. Looked like he was experiencing chest pain and trying to get one in his mouth, but didn't do it in time. The fact that he had a prescription meant he was under a doctor's care for coronary artery disease. But what triggered it just then, well, I'm trying to figure that out.

"That note he left, with your name on it. Why would he take the time to write that if he knew he should be getting that pill into his system? Maybe I've just got a cop's suspicious mind, but something doesn't feel right about this."

Millie shook her head, seeing the note again in her mind.

CACTUS

MILLIE

GONE

She tried to reconstruct her conversation with Herb as much as possible for Robby. "At first, I was a little perturbed about the way he seemed to make himself at home in my office. But then we talked a lot. He told me all about San Juan cactus. I'm sure that's why he was driving around there. I never mentioned that there aren't so many mature specimens as what he recorded back when he first surveyed. I don't know why I didn't say anything, but I guess I just didn't want to see him disappointed. Maybe that really bothered him, seeing some cactus gone."

"Gone! He wrote *gone* on that note," Robby almost shouted. "We've been focusing on your name on that note. That's not what it was about. Herb was telling us those cactus are GONE.

"Let's get back out there. Meet me Monday at 7:00 a.m. and we'll go take a look around. See if that was what Herb was trying to tell us. You know, it's not just cattle rustlers us law enforcement officers get alerts on. Anymore, it's just as likely to be cactus rustlers."

19. Invitation to Sheep Camp

Ask any veteran fry bread maker what's the best flour to use, invariably they will answer, "Blue Bird."
—*Navajo Times, 2010*

The next morning, Millie was in her usual Saturday position leaning against the porch post, balancing the computer against her knees. Ragged Ear was being his stand-offish self, abandoning Millie to sit in a sunny spot on the farthest corner of the porch.

"Lighten up, cat. I didn't plan to get home late. Robby had a lot to tell me. How about a head rub, old boy?" Ragged Ear merely twitched his good ear and rolled belly-up into a sunbeam.

Determined to keep up on recording details of the week's fieldwork, Millie had made good progress translating most of her scribbled notes into readable daily reports. But she could no longer put off covering last Monday's encounter with death. The blank page blurred before her eyes, and the dangling blue-jeans-clad leg took its place. She heard her own voice telling Robby, "I have no idea what these words mean or why my name is on it."

She forced her fingers to recount Dr. Arnold's qualifications. Then she listed the characteristics he had called out as he inspected several specimens, leading to his pronouncement that she had correctly identified San Juan cactus. She rendered the thrill of locating "the Millie plot" into bland scientific terminology, ingrained in her mind from reading botanical journals.

The words came tortuously slow, interrupted with flashes of the horror that had replaced their earlier excitement. A stretcher carried by four men, being lifted over sagebrush. Wirt's saying, "*It can't be Herb.*" Hushed voices passing bits of information among the line of white pickup trucks parked along the road.

gone…Millie…cactus. *My name. Why did Herb write my name?*

She felt a bump on her elbow and Ragged Ear's raspy purr pushed away yesterday's sights and sounds. A furry paw hit the spacebar and the cursor flew off the page. "You're right, that's enough for now, you old skank."

Millie hit the save button and closed the "BLM T&E Inventory" document. She opened the "Nobody–Everybody" spreadsheet to catch up on her observations about the multiple uses of BLM land. Remembering running her hand under Dunnie's mane, she typed in mustang round-ups and cattle grazing. This jumped her mind to photography and guiding tourists. Her fingers wouldn't type any further, resisting putting *place to die* on this list.

Why did Herb write my name?

A flashy red Miata jerked to a stop in the driveway, pinging bits of gravel onto Rust Bucket's back bumper. Ragged Ear zoomed inside the house.

"Hi, Millie. You working on a Saturday? You're just too dedicated." Ben Benallee's voice reached Millie even before he got to the porch steps.

"How did you find out where I live?" Millie demanded.

"Momma Agnes told me. Nice day isn't it. How about a soda pop? Got any Dr. Pepper?" Ben settled himself on the porch steps, peering upward through the cottonwood's fluttering leaves.

Millie sighed. *I need to have a discussion with Momma Agnes. She can't be sending men that I barely know to my house. Might as well see what he wants now that he's here. Beats writing up field notes.*

"Ben, I don't have any Dr. Pepper. You'll have to do with whatever is in the fridge. Wait here." She hadn't planned on company and wished she'd pulled on a sports bra that morning along with the T-shirt and shorts.

Millie shouldered back out the screen door, holding a tall glass in each hand, and letting her freshly combed hair sway around her face. Ben accepted the iced tea, with not quite a scowl but not with a thank you either. Millie eased down on one step below Ben, putting their heads nearly at the same level.

"Heard there was more trouble on the Piñon Resource Area. I was wondering how you were doing. Momma Agnes said you were one of the people who found that man in his pickup. Must have been awful."

"It was horrible. I—I can't talk about it." Millie drew her legs in against her chest and rocked back and forth for a moment. "And Momma Agnes talks too much."

Ben said, "Yeah, it's just that Momma Agnes worries about everybody, you know? I thought you might want to go for a ride this weekend. My relatives are up at sheep camp. It's kind of an annual gathering of family. My Auntie Louise is coming from Phoenix."

Millie took a slow drink of iced tea. *What's he up to? Maybe it's OK if his relatives are there. For sure, it's something I've never done before.*

"Where is this sheep camp?"

"The Sageman sheep camp is south of Shiprock, halfway up on the side of Beautiful Mountain. You turn off before you get to Buffalo Pass, or else you'd be in Arizona. Lots of us relatives go and help fix up the camp. The shade house always needs fresh branches piled on, firewood gathered for cooking, that kind of thing. Grandfather Sageman has a neighbor truck the sheep in each spring. He and grandmother used to take turns moving the flock around to graze, but grandfather does most of it now, since grandmother can't get around much anymore."

"Why sheep?"

"Sheep? Well, sheep is what Navajos do."

Ben caught sight of Ragged Ear peering out the front door. "Navajos don't let cats and dogs come into the house, but I kind of miss that one my roommate keeps back in Phoenix. Cats are pretty smart creatures, you know?"

Millie wondered if the roommate was male or female.

"One thing, though, up at sheep camp you can't get Internet. I told you they were traditional. No electricity. Cook over hot coals. Know what my Auntie Louise said when I was trying to check my email? She said, 'Sure we're wireless. Most all hogans on the rez are wireless. Have been for centuries.' Very funny. That's a Navajo's idea of a joke."

Ben's grin flashed in the bright morning sunlight. "Know what my grandfather said when I told him I just might stay in school all the way through a Ph.D.? Know what he said to me! He said, 'I got me a P-H-D.' He took me over to the back of his truck and picked up an old post-hole digger. 'This is my p-h-d, couldn't do without it,' he said. That old man—I know I'm supposed to respect the elders, but sometimes…

"Anyway, you've got to meet Grandfather. He can tell you anything about plants."

Millie shot him a surprised look, "You asking me for a date?"

"Naw. If it was a date, I'd be picking you up."

Ben stood up and stretched to touch fingertips to the lintel. Bronze muscles in his arms competed with glistening black hair swinging side to side for Millie's attention.

"Meet me at City Market tomorrow morning."

"Meet you *where*?" Millie called out, as Ben neared the Miata.

"The grocery store. In Shiprock. Everybody knows where it is."

"Wait—what time?"

"Whenever you get up. Takes maybe forty minutes from here. Call me when you pass the Hogback, I'll find you in the parking lot."

"What time?" she called after him, but the car was already out on the street.

Hands on hips, Millie scowled. "I don't even have his phone number. What is a sheep camp? What do people wear to a sheep camp, anyway? I need details, give me some details." No one heard except Ragged Ear.

* * *

Millie made her way through Shiprock's smörgåsbord of fast-food restaurants—KFC, McDonalds, Little Caesar's Pizza, and Burger King—and turned by the City Market sign at precisely 9:30 a.m. She circled the wide parking lot, watching for a parking space. She had to stop once for a stray dog looking for handouts and was distracted by the giant Navajo rug designs painted on the grocery store's exterior walls. At least 20 feet high, each painted rectangle showed a different geometric and color pattern.

On her second trip around, Millie pulled in next to a truck with hay bales stacked high in its bed. She had barely turned off the engine when the red Miata zoomed up behind her Explorer. Ben leaned across and pushed the passenger's side door open. "Knew you'd come. Get in."

Millie was still fumbling for a seat belt as Ben turned onto the highway that stretched straight south. She breathed a drawn-out "Oooh... Ship Rock—I've wanted to see this from the day I knew I was coming to New Mexico." Ragged peaks of dark stone, remnants of an ancient volcano, towered above the desert floor. The distinctive geologic formation shared its name with the second-largest town on the Navajo Reservation.

"It's called '*Tsé Bit'a'í*' in Navajo. It means 'rock with wings.' You can see what looks like wings going out from two sides. That makes more sense than what the early *bilagáanas* called it—'ship rock.' They thought it looked like a big sailing ship. Whoever came up with that one here in the middle of the desert had *some* imagination."

Before the grand, ragged monolith passed from view, Ben turned off the highway and pulled into a dirt parking area occupied by three pickup trucks. Vendors stood by open tailgates that served as improvised display shelves. One offered 25-pound sacks of dried beans, another offered crates of oranges and burlap bags of potatoes. Ben stopped next to the pickup with a sign, "Kneel Down Bread."

He popped out and greeted a middle-aged woman wearing jeans, checkered cotton shirt, and a straw hat with a crumbling brim. She greeted Ben with a big smile and gentle handshake. "You that Benallee boy, went off to college? I went to school with your mother."

They fell silent for a moment, avoiding any more mention of Ben's mother, until Millie joined them. Ben introduced Mrs. Roanhorse and nodded toward the insulated chest on the ground, under the shade of the pick-up's open tailgate.

"How many you want?" Mrs. Roanhorse asked.

"One plain and one green chile. We're going to Grandmother's sheep camp for lunch."

She opened the chest, picked out two bundles about the size of hot dog buns, and quickly closed the lid.

"I love these things," Ben said, holding them toward Millie. "Which one do you want?"

Millie took the plain one and removed the paper towel wrapping. "Corn husk?"

"It's inside. Unfold one end."

Millie loosened a slim band of corn husk knotted around one end of the broad, slightly flattened bundle. Watching Ben do the same, she worked open the pliable corn husk cover, and sniffed a savory aroma. She pinched off one end of the bread-like dough, eased the warm morsel into her mouth, and felt an overwhelming sense of comfort.

"Yumm, this is wonderful. How do you make it?"

Mrs. Roanhorse seemed glad to hear of Millie's interest. "It's from the sweet corn my family grows. You take the husks off, set them down and flatten the leaves for later. Maybe sprinkle a little water on them so they don't dry out. Then you have to cut the corn kernels off the cobs, and smush them all together with a little salt, until it looks kind of like cooked oatmeal. Shape a handful in your palm, so it's about the length of your hand. Put just the right amount on the corn husks, fold them over lengthwise, then fold up the ends, and tie each end with a little strip of corn husk. Takes a lot of time."

Ben nodded, "Used to be, women ground the kernels off by rubbing them against a rock. They had to kneel down to do it."

Millie savored another bite, noticing its slightly sweet flavor and texture due to the bits of yellow kernels she could see. "This is warm, and looks roasted."

"It is," Mrs. Roanhorse nodded and gave a big smile, "That's why you put it back in the corn husk, so it cooks just right and tastes good. That's how come it takes a lot of time. You have to make a fire in the outside oven and let it burn most of the night so the oven is evenly heated, then put the bundles in for two or three hours to cook."

"No wonder it's so hard to make. That kneeling down must hurt your knees."

"I have a special shortcut," Mrs. Roanhorse winked at Ben, who almost choked to keep from laughing. "I use a food processor. We got electricity now, you know."

"Can't believe you fell for that one, Millie." Ben handed a few dollar bills to Mrs. Roanhorse. "Come on, we better get going."

"Just for that," a red-faced Millie said, "you can buy me another one. I like kneel down bread."

Ben pulled out of the parking area and continued on a road that led away from the highway. They passed through a low ridge of loosely piled black lava that formed the south wing of Ship Rock.

"'*Tsé'* is rock in Navajo. Wish I knew more words in Navajo so I could talk better with Grandmother Sageman. You'll meet her at sheep camp. Sometimes the elders say if I'm smart enough to go to college, how come I can't tell stories in Navajo." Ben shook his head. "I learned some Navajo when I spent summers in the mountains with my grandparents, but there weren't many others around to hang out with. Kids my age, well, they called me an Apple Indian."

"An apple?" Millie said, peeling the corn husk back from the second kneel down bread, and deliberately holding it out of Ben's reach.

"You know, apple—red on the outside, white on the inside. Not my fault I grew up in Phoenix. Always wished

I could be in a drum circle, be part of a pow wow. That would be so cool."

Soon the road became steeper and curvier. Oakbrush closed in on both sides of the road replacing the sparse desert vegetation. She pressed her head against the window to look up at statuesque ponderosa pines that filtered a startling blue sky. "I had no idea that New Mexico had mountains like this."

Ben nodded and focused on negotiating the hairpin curves.

Millie envied Ben's summers of freedom. "At least you had a beautiful place to roam around and grandparents to teach you about nature. Once I was in high school, I had to spend summers helping Mom clean buildings whenever she needed me. In between times, I got to go to the town's swimming pool, if my brother was going. He was older than me, so we could go on our own. We'd hang out there all day. Get a Coney hot dog for lunch. But the best days, the best days, were when Aunt Nina took me adventuring into the woods. Or even better, over to the coast to walk along the seashore."

Ben laughed, "Seriously, Coney Island hot dogs? What are those?" Before Millie could answer, he slowed, turned onto a dirt road, and announced, "All right, we're here in plenty of time for lunch."

He pulled into a clearing, where a dozen cars and pickups were parked willy-nilly. He maneuvered two folding lawn chairs and a giant bag of potato chips out of his trunk. His smile grew wider and wider as they walked toward the cluster of men, women, and children gathered around and under a brush-covered shade house.

Ben shook hands with each man as he introduced Millie, explaining, "I found her up at Split Lip Overlook. She's working for BLM, surveying plants." Along the way, he managed to greet the youngsters, tousling their hair, sometimes pulling a pigtail, or tipping a cowboy hat over a little boy's face. The women were grouped around the fireplace.

Millie picked out Aunt Louise even before Ben gave her a bear hug. The stately woman wore perfectly fitting jeans, a sleeveless cotton blouse, and silver bracelets on both wrists. Thick black hair, even longer than Ben's, framed her handsome, oval-shaped face, which was set off by earrings with dangling dream catchers.

Extending a manicured hand, she said in a warm voice, "Welcome to the Sageman sheep camp. I hope you like lamb, Millie."

Without dropping Millie's hand, Louise led her toward a woman sitting in a wheelchair. "This is my mother, Emma Sageman."

With a grunt, the woman stood up and balanced herself with a cane. Millie looked down on a faded blue kerchief wrapped over hair as white as the freeze brand mark on Dunnie's neck.

Millie dropped to one knee to be at the same height as the diminutive woman. The elder's face reminded her of the deep fissures in an ancient cottonwood tree's bark. Millie took a frail hand, saying, "Hello, Mrs. Sageman. Thank you for letting me share your beautiful camp."

A smile touched the woman's lips and shone through onyx-like eyes.

"Mom pretends she only speaks Navajo," Louise winked, helped her elder back into the wheelchair and arranged a Pendleton wool blanket back over her lap. "Come over here, Millie, help us make fry bread. The meat is almost cooked."

Millie took her place between Louise and a woman introduced as Louise's little sister. Flames crackled beneath an iron grill set over cinder blocks stacked waist high in a U-shape, which left an opening for inserting firewood. Little sister leaned over the grill, turning over pieces of mutton, which made sizzling explosions as grease dropped into the fire. Millie maneuvered to the other side of Louise, trying to escape the smoke and unfamiliar odor of roasting mutton.

"Take about a handful of dough, make it flat and round like this, and slide it into the frying oil." Louise eased her dinner-plate-size round of dough into hot oil bubbling in the biggest cast iron frying pan Millie could ever imagine. Louise scooped up another handful of dough from a huge mixing bowl on a nearby table and handed it to Millie. A can of baking powder, a round box of salt, and a pitcher of water surrounded the mixing bowl. A half-empty, toddler-size cloth bag of flour lay on its side, draped over the table's edge. It had a blue bird design stamped on it.

Millie concentrated on working her hands in the flip-flopping motion that Louise used. Plop—the dough hit the ground. Bending down, Millie heard the communal intake of breath, then laughter.

"Don't let that girl waste food," came from the direction of the wheelchair.

"It takes practice," Louise said, handing her own almost-shaped dough to Millie. "Remember to make a little hole in it before putting it in the oil, so it cooks evenly."

Millie pulled and stretched the outer edges a little more. Making a small hole in the center was not a problem. It was minimizing splits to just one that took her full concentration. She slid the glob into the pan, all the while willing the meal to be ready soon.

After a few more agonizing minutes, Millie's third misshapen fry bread lay draining on paper towels next to dozens of perfectly round ones. Someone banged the bottom of a washtub. Children came running from every direction.

Ben appeared and handed Millie a paper plate. "That one yours?" He picked up the mushroom-shaped fry bread and dropped it on his plate, along with a piece of mutton. They joined the line moving around two six-foot tables loaded with potluck dishes—a dozen macaroni salads of different shapes and colors, boiled potatoes, Jell-O offerings of many flavors and sheet cakes, round cakes, and cupcakes.

Ben set his two folding chairs at the edge of the shade house, leaving the cooler center area for elderly relatives. Grandfather Sageman made his way to a rickety vinyl recliner, permanently planted next to the brush arbor's center pole. Ben looked up to see his Auntie Louise pushing her mother's wheelchair, handed his plate to Millie, and ran to help. They settled the wheelchair next to her husband's recliner, and someone brought Grandmother Sageman a plate of food.

Millie listened to snatches of conversation, some in English, some in Navajo. From the elders, Millie could only distinguish syllables that sounded like the shushing of moccasins along a sand wash.

Ben is lucky. He's not an outsider here like me. He has an instant family simply by being born into a clan.

Even back home, I felt out of place at family picnics. The fried chicken would beat roasted mutton any day, but what a chore to fend off my aunts' questions about how many kids I planned to have, fake it with cousins that I had been to the new store at the mall. All of us crammed into somebody's back yard. Huh, one thing that's no different, men are plunked into lawn chairs while women are bustling around doing the cooking.

As the plates emptied, the visiting increased. Ben was

Millie spotted a well pad squeezed in between the road and Lejos wash. She could park there. The wash would be easy to cross, having only a small rivulet of water at this time of year. By following a gully that angled up the mesa, then cutting left a short distance, she could get to the lone boulder where Cowboy said he camped.

She wove her way through P-J and sage, keeping the big boulder in sight, her mind churning. Cowboy probably saw nothing more than a patch of Fendler's hedgehog cactus or Simpson's pincushion cactus. But how cool would it be to find a rare San Juan cactus population never previously recorded! Not likely. Nevertheless, it was charming the way he described that "little-bitty cactus" and worth checking out.

Catching her breath in the shade of the boulder, Millie scanned the ground. No more than ten steps beyond the boulder's shadow, she glimpsed a spot of color. Creeping closer, easing to one knee, Millie gasped. *Could it be? No other fishhook cactus has flowers of such deep fuchsia.* She exhaled, visualized the description of *Sclerocactus sanjuanensis*, and switched into the botanist's systematic process of keying out a species.

Yes, mature plants had clusters of three to four stems, slightly spiraled ribs. She opened the magnifying loupe on the cord around her neck, fished in a pocket for a metric ruler, and scuttled closer to the specimen that first caught her eye. This one still had bright blooms, but most of the others already sported crinkled brown tops transitioning from pollinator-attracting, bright flowers to dried seed capsules.

Yes, its cluster of stems was less than six and a half centimeters above the soil, each rounded, globose stem no more than three centimeters wide. The tubercle bumps protruding from stems, about the size of a grain of rice, had the distinctive three central spines. The tips of the spines were faintly hooked, placing it in the genus *Sclerocactus* within the Cactaceae family. *Sclera*—coming from a Greek term meaning hard, sometimes interpreted as cruel.

Leaning even closer, Millie focused on the radial spines skirting the three central spines. These spines, lighter in color and softer looking, were no more than a millimeter and a half long. Yes, that fit. *S. sanjuanensis* taxonomy dictated eighteen to twenty-four radial spines, always an even number.

Lastly, Millie inspected the red-violet flowers. Okay, four diminutive flowers crowded the apex of each of the mature stems. Their petals described as a dark pink, the usual botanists' understatement. These bits of beauty were a flamboyant, vibrant fuchsia color.

Millie stood up and realized her lower left leg had gone to sleep. She shook it out and limped to the backpack. *I've got to get good photos of this. I think it is. I'm sure it is! I've got to document to the nth degree. This makes a third location for an endangered species! That's monumental. It could make the difference, if something happened to the other two plots, between survival or extinction.*

Every hundred steps or so, Millie dropped to both knees and photographed a sampling of specimens in various stages of growth. She estimated the widely spaced cactus occupied approximately three acres.

Circling back to her original find, she again knelt down, this time to savor its specialness, its beauty. "Thank you, small flower, for holding on this long, for letting me find you and your community."

* * *

Millie worked her way to the wash and trotted toward the road, not feeling the hot sun or the weight of the back-the center of attention among the relatives sitting closest to him and Millie. He was describing how he tracked radio-collared deer with satellite signals. Millie felt a tug at her back. Looking around, she found a little girl with a shy grin separating her hair into strands.

"That's Spring Benallee," someone said, "she's Ben's grand-niece." The little girl giggled at being singled out. Millie felt tugs and twisting of her hair, but pretended not to care, until a tickle in her ear told her it was time to notice. Spring draped one braid over Millie's right shoulder and another over the left, each pigtail tied with a bit of red yarn. Ben reached back and lifted the squealing youngster up over Millie's head and tickled her so hard she plopped on her bottom at their feet.

"There's that grandson of mine," Grandfather pointed a walking stick in Ben's direction. "He's always up to something." Some folks shifted to watch the entertainment. Grandfather Sageman was ready to hold forth.

"So, grandson, when are you going to come back to where you belong. You know no Navajo should go beyond the four sacred mountains. It's bad luck."

"Grandfather, I've told you, I'm working now. I'm almost done at the university." Ben tried to sound exasperated. Millie had the impression this conversation had occurred before.

"This young one, he thinks he can learn everything from those professors over at the university. Why, he hardly knows the difference between a goat and a sheep."

Grandmother Sageman handed her plate to her husband and came to the young man's rescue. Speaking in careful English, she said, "Watch it old man, 'cause just maybe I'll trade you in, just like that lady said."

Aunt Louise, along with the others surrounding their beloved hosts, stopped talking in order for the elderly woman's voice to carry throughout the gathering.

"What lady?" somebody called out.

"That lady that was hitchhiking up the Bisti Highway. It was July, too hot for an old grandma to be out like that." Millie smiled at the idea of this wizened woman in a wheelchair calling someone else old.

"So I gave her a ride, of course. I had to move the groceries off the front seat. She climbed in but kept looking at the back seat. 'What's that?' she says. 'It's a bottle of whiskey,' I told her. 'I got it for my husband.' We got past Twin Rocks before she said another word. Then she says, 'Good trade.'"

Everybody laughed. Confusion clouded Millie's face. Then it came to her. She started laughing. She laughed hard, harder than she had in years. The storyteller poked her husband's arm with a crooked finger and reached for the cup cake left on her plate.

Ben winked at Millie, she grinned back. They now had something in common, being the brunt of Navajo humor.

"Come with me," Grandfather Sageman waved an arm to the children, long finished with second and third helpings, and getting restless. "You too, Ben, and bring your girlfriend."

Ben held out his hand to help Millie up from the lawn chair. She sniffed and slapped it away. "What have you been telling him?"

Leaning a bit on his walking stick, but still ramrod straight, Ben's surrogate father led the way along a dry streambed. At first, the children gathered around him like a flock of sheep, but soon fanned out, working off energy by chasing after lizards, dueling with pretend swords made out of sticks, or turning over rocks hoping to find some hidden treasure.

A warmth swept through Millie's being. The warmth

of summer's sun, of a meal she helped prepare, and the warmth of family. *Maybe this is the Land of Enchantment.*

Grandfather pointed his stick at various shrubs and grasses, nodding when Ben, and often Millie, called out their correct name.

"We Navajos used to move across this land according to the seasons, following the migration of game animals and finding different places where useful plants grow. Now many Navajos live in big cities like Albuquerque, Phoenix, and Los Angeles. Some of them still want to follow the old ways. They come to me for bee plant to dye wool and piñon nuts for sweets."

The elder placed a hand on Ben's shoulder. "My grandson, he helps them buy the gifts that Mother Earth makes available to us. He walks in two worlds—the White Man's and the Navajo."

Ben laughed. "I operate a website for him. He has a whole garage in Shiprock full of shelves stocked with every kind of herbal medicine, teas, and bundles of sweetgrass to burn for incense. Big demand for Mormon tea, too. It's not just Navajos that order from him."

Millie saw what looked like a handful of black hair move on the sand. It scurried toward the shadow of a stone, but stopped and rose up on its hind legs.

"Cool, a tarantula," Ben said and asked for his grandfather's cowboy hat. He held the hat in front of the creature and nudged it with his toe. Ben lifted the hat slowly and turned it as the tarantula fingered its way along the rim. "Look at all those eyes, Millie. There are eight of them, but they mostly sense things by those hairs on their legs."

Millie gazed at her image reflected in the eight black eyes. Realizing she was inches from the tarantula, she jumped back. "These things are dangerous, they have venom in their bite."

Sageman's expression did not change. "No creature is good or bad. You always have a choice. Ben threatened it with his finger, so it stood up on its hind legs and said, 'I'm giving you this warning.' If Ben lets it go into the shade under the rock where it wanted to go, then it is harmless."

Ben did just that, stepping near the rock and shaking the tarantula off the hat. "Go find a girlfriend, big spider."

"There is always a reason if something good happens. There is always a reason if something bad happens. We have the choice, to live in harmony or to cause disruption. I fear for our future, for what will be left of the earth for the children of Ben's children."

Ben rolled his eyes. It seemed that he had heard this lecture before. "Let's head back. There's got to be some desserts left over."

Most of the pickups were gone and only a tall, blue-enamel coffee pot sat on the fireplace grill. Louise and the remaining few relatives were moving lawn chairs next to the fire.

Louise looked into the pot and called out, "Tea is ready." Then seeing the returning threesome, she said to Millie, "Did Grandfather fill you full of when to pick this plant and how to use that plant? Help yourself to some Navajo Tea."

Millie followed her actions by using a folded dish cloth to lift the big pot by its hot handle and poured the steaming liquid into a Styrofoam cup. The earthy scent of freshly-mowed grass prompted Millie to remove the lid and looked inside. Millie swirled the pot around a little to stir the contents, and a bundle of dried stems, tightly wrapped with white string, bobbled to the surface.

Tapping one of the chairs, Louise said, "Ben, come sit next to your Auntie and tell me all about what you've been doing lately."

Pointing to the adjoining chair, Louise said, "Millie,

you sit there, where the basket is. Grandmother Sageman wanted me to give it to you. She made it herself, a few years ago. It's woven from coyote willow stems. When she was younger, her baskets won prizes at the Window Rock fair. She cut the thinnest branches in spring when they are most limber. She'd strip the bark off with her teeth, back when she used to have teeth."

Millie raised the gift, slowly turning it around, tracing out the over and under patterns which locked its twigs together. "Please thank Mrs. Sageman for me. This is beautiful."

She settled back in the chair, clutching the basket to her chest. "Just for now, just for a little while," Millie whispered to herself, "stop seeing scribbles on that note blown by the wind. Stop counting and counting cactus plants. Be in the moment." She breathed in the calming fragrance wafting from the brownish tea, becoming mesmerized by the fragments of leaves and stems floating in it, and let the day's joy and the native drink warm her body and soul.

20. One Of The Best

Older women have the experience and maturity to offer the greatest service and skills to society of any segment of our population. They are at the peak of their promise. ...Since we are the natural care-takers in this world, I feel the greatest good that women can do is help the environmental movement.
—Anne LaBastille, *Woodswoman III*

Millie leaned her backpack against her desk. She remembered to put in an extra water bottle at dawn this morning when she grabbed the last hard-boiled egg and a packet of cheese and crackers for lunch. It had been so late the night before by the time Ben dropped her off from the sheep camp adventure and she drove home from Shiprock, that she just dumped more kibbles in Ragged Ear's dish and went to bed.

"You ready?" Robby appeared at Millie's cubicle promptly at 7:00 a.m., as agreed the previous Friday. "Millie, I'll meet you in the vehicle yard and follow you out to the T-one cactus plot. Then I've got to be back in Wellsville by 1:30 to testify at a hearing. You can go do whatever you do with plants."

An hour and half later, Millie came to the yellow crime scene tape still looped across the sagebrush where they had found Herb Thompson's body. She slowed to glance back at Robby in her BLM ranger's Chevy Tahoe. Robby waved her forward.

They continued on to the T-one cactus site. Remembering Robby's caution that morning to stop well back from where anyone would likely park to reach the plot, she pulled the Suburban to the roadside and reached for her backpack. Robby was soon by her side, carrying a notebook and camera. Eyes glued to the ground, Robby motioned to Millie to walk behind her.

"OK, there they are. The impressions in the sand here match the tires on Herb's truck. He was here all right." Robby said, and crouched to photograph the tracks. "Let's see if there are any other tracks near those cactus."

They walked to the spot that Millie used as a base for setting out flag markers earlier. Robby stopped short. "Somebody else was here. These hoof marks are from a shod horse."

Millie described her encounter with Cowboy and Dunnie, which led to her discovery of the new San Juan cactus population.

Holding the copy of Herb's original 1990s plot survey so Robby could see, Millie laid her newly mapped perimeter over it.

"Herb saw some were gone, all right," Robby said, "there's a real difference here. Let's take a walk around."

Concluding their circuit of the plot's perimeter, neither Robby nor Millie spotted anything amiss other than Dunnie's tracks and faint indentations that Robby said matched the type of shoes Herb was wearing.

"If this place was any cleaner, I'd think somebody had taken a broom and swept it," Robby said.

Millie hadn't noticed it before, but the area did appear tidier than other openings she had traversed in and around P-J habitat. Except for the native clumps of grass, few shrubs or forbs were evident that would shade the small San Juan cactus. Millie scanned more carefully. There were almost no dried up or decayed cactus specimens.

Robby started back toward the vehicles, "Let's stop and pick up that yellow tape. I'll take another look around, then I have to get back to Wellstown and testify at a hearing about illegal sewage dumping. But tomorrow, I want you to show me the other San Juan cactus site, the one Dr. Arnold calls T-two. Bring your maps. Maybe plants are missing over there, too."

Robby led the way back to the death scene, unmistakable because of crushed sagebrush strung with yellow tape and the rutted road where emergency vehicles had parked. As soon as Millie pulled in behind the ranger's SUV, a dusty Subaru skidded to a stop next to them.

Belva Banks scrambled out and growled, "What's going on here?"

Belva's face clouded as Robby pointed along the path of crushed sagebrush. Her eyes watered as Robby described what happened in terse, officialise sentences.

"Goddammit! I hate to hear that," Belva spoke in an angry voice. "Herb Thompson was one of the best. He loved this land."

Robby's head drooped.

Belva softened her tone, "I know I give you BLM guys a ration of shit a lot of times. But you know, I admire the work you do. You hold the line the best as law and politics will allow. If it wasn't for you BLM and Forest Service folks, no telling what these public lands would look like by now."

Robby's head shot up, a dumbfounded look on her face.

"I just make a lot of noise to counteract all the shenanigans the developers and land grabbers try to get away with. In these days, organizations like Old Broads for Public Lands Protection have to shout loud and long to even begin to balance the seesaw of federal land use and misuse."

Belva paused, then threw her shoulders back. She pointed to the furrows torn up along the road. "Now what are you going to do about this crypto-muerto soil here?"

Millie and Robby simultaneously said, "What?"

"You botanists call it cryptobiotic crust, meaning hidden life. Once it's stomped down like this, I call it crypto-muerto—dead-as-hell soil." Millie couldn't help herself, she giggled, then laughed out loud. Robby began to laugh. Belva joined in with a raspy chuckle.

21. Storm

Then the storm burst with a succession of ropes and streaks and shafts of lightning, playing continuously, filling the valley with a broken radiance; and the cracking shots followed each other swiftly till the echoes blended in one fearful, deafening crash.
—Zane Gray, *Riders of the Purple Sage*

Robby headed for town and Belva stomped back to the Subaru saying she was off to find Fritz Müller for a cup of tea. Millie had several hours of daylight left to get started on Wirt's assignment. She arrived at the petroglyph boulder by noon, settled in its cool shade, and unwrapped her lunch. She surveyed the patch of San Juan cactus spread in front of her and began planning how she would map out a buffer zone of protection.

By mid-afternoon, Millie had more than half the perimeter of the San Juan cactus area flagged. She stood erect with hands on hips and leaned backward to stretch her tall frame. If she worked late, she estimated she could get the entire plot marked by the end of the day.

She pushed a wayward strand of hair back behind her ear and watched feathery clouds drifting across the blue sky. She applied another coat of lip balm and continued searching for specimens.

A *tick-tick-tick* sound reached her ears. A brown-checkered stick swiveled where she was about to put her boot.

"That... that is a rattlesnake," she gasped, bent over trying to catch her breath. Looking around, she realized she had just sprinted clear to the opposite side of the plot. "Oh my god, how did I get here? That thing rattled at me. Oh no, I probably stepped on the cactus!"

After more gasps and a concerted effort to still her racing heart, Millie started analyzing the situation. "Okay, I go find a juniper branch, make a walking stick, and poke ahead of myself as I walk. Just like Mr. Sageman said, no creatures are inherently bad. They give you a warning when you are intruding. Okay, we can coexist here. I'll warn you where I am and you leave me alone."

Even more focused now on scrutinizing the ground while moving around the plot, Millie did not notice the dimming daylight until a rumble in the distance caused her to look up. Black clouds low in the sky were turning the late afternoon into twilight. The T-one San Juan cactus plot on the distant hillside lay in deep shadow and a dark curtain of rain was steadily advancing toward the Suburban.

Making sure she had clipboard, GPS, and all equipment accounted for, Millie turned and hiked toward the Suburban. She abandoned poking the improvised walking stick ahead of every step and began taking long strides, hoping to reach the vehicle before the storm hit.

Glancing up every few steps, Millie watched a wave of rain obscure the narrow sandstone pass on the road that led back to Wellstown. Fat raindrops plopped on her hat and arms just as she tossed gear onto the back seat and slipped behind the steering wheel. She needed to turn the windshield wipers on full-speed by the time the engine caught and she got the seatbelt buckled. Hail, like rice tossed at newlyweds, pelted the windshield.

Millie turned on the headlights but only rested her hand on the gear handle. She could not see 10 feet ahead. Good judgment told her to stay put and wait for the storm to let up. She was astonished at how rapidly the sky had transformed from fluffy clouds to menacing. A day-long cloudy sky would precede such a rainstorm back East.

Experienced field hands had already joined the parade of vehicles, large and small, skedaddling out of the back-country like ants racing from an anthill attacked by a badger. Oil field hands stayed vigilant when clouds started billowing up on a distant horizon. If the clouds turned black and strong winds pushed a storm in their direction, they knew it was time to get off soon-to-be slick muddy roads.

Lightning cracked like a whip, followed immediately by a horrendous thunderclap. "Yikes, that was right over my head. I'm not going anywhere until this lets up." Knowing she was safe in the vehicle insulated by four rubber tires provided only a modicum of comfort as the storm raged overhead.

Finally, Millie could count to four seconds between a lightning flash and its accompanying thunder. The storm was moving away. She took a deep breath, slowing her breathing that had been coming in short puffs since that first explosion of lightning.

Then a rumbling, unlike the now-sporadic thunder, caused Millie to look toward the pass. Between sweeps of the wipers, she could see a cloud of dust where the pass opening should be. In a few more minutes, the rain quelled the dust. One side of the pass was transformed from what had been a nearly vertical sandstone to something that now looked like an uneven flight of stairs.

With a sinking feeling, Millie put the Suburban in

gear and drove toward the pass. The rain diminished to a sprinkle and then was gone. She was going so slow that she barely touched the brake to stop a good distance from what had been the pass. A car-size boulder leaned over the road, and rubble was scattered in all directions.

Millie's cell phone chimed. She pressed the button and recognized Wirt's voice. "Thank heaven you're in cell tower range. We just got a call in from one of the oil and gas companies. There's been a landslide about where you are working. Millie, what's your situation?"

"I'm sitting here looking at it, Wirt. And I'm on the wrong side of it. There's a humongous boulder nearly blocking the road. I'm not sure if I can get around it."

"You stay right where you are. A landslide is unstable. Don't even think about driving anywhere near it." Wirt's voice held both command and concern. "You'll need to stay out there tonight. Road crews will get after it in the morning. What have you got for supplies?"

Millie assured him that she had a container of survival items stashed in the back of the Suburban. Wirt was about to sign off when Millie heard Momma Agnes commandeer the phone. "You all right, hon? I won't be able to sleep a wink tonight, until I see your vehicle back here in the parking lot."

Her reassurances to Wirt and Momma Agnes that she would be fine spending a night by herself helped lift Millie's own spirits. Their concern warmed her heart. Just as this fierce rain forced seeds into soil crevices to take root, her connections to this land and its people were taking root and growing.

She turned around in the road and nosed along until spotting a level place close to where she usually parked to hike to the petroglyph boulder. She backed the Suburban in, satisfied that the surrounding sagebrush and juniper provided a private place to settle for the night.

Adhering to women's ancient nesting instinct, she opened the back hatch, dug into the emergency box, and set about arranging items. Remembering the afternoon's rattled warning, Millie mumbled, "Okay for cowboys to sleep out under the stars, but I'm sleeping with steel around me." She spread the space blanket along the back seat and rolled up a shirt for a pillow.

She slipped a small flashlight into a pocket and pulled the five-gallon water jug closer for easy access. She tossed the multi-tool Leatherman knife onto the space blanket to be within easy reach. She popped open the plastic shoebox crammed with packaged food items, a few paper plates, and hand wipes. She picked out a bag of trail mix and a protein bar and set aside a packet of vanilla cookies as a bedtime snack.

Millie perched on the back of the Suburban, opened the protein bar, and dumped the trail mix onto a paper plate. With plenty of time to kill, she arranged the pieces into categories. She nudged green M&Ms together for a salad, red M&Ms for tomato bisque, peanuts for a protein main course, and clustered the rest of the M&Ms as a mixed-vegetable side dish. The raisins went into another pile for dessert. "I won't be hungry at all after this five-course meal. Why am I talking to myself?" She laughed, remembering there was no one within miles to hear.

A pink glow in the sky caught her eye. It spread, shimmering from pink to rose to gold. The sun had already slipped below the western horizon, but its rays bounced back from the dense clouds remaining after the storm. The colors progressed to the sky over her head, creating a breathtaking kaleidoscope. Fascinated, Millie watched as minute by minute the array of colors painted the sky horizon to horizon.

Enthralled, Millie fumbled in the backpack for her camera. The moment she raised the viewfinder to her eye, the eastern sky dimmed. With surprising speed, Mother Nature put away her glorious painting on this rare night, never to be repeated in just the same way. Snapping photos toward the western sky, Millie was disappointed at the lackluster images in the playback mode. But then, no human could capture such a scene in any media. "I must lock this marvel in my memory and keep it for as long as I live."

Twilight vanished from the entire sky. Millie tried to convince herself that she would get a good night's sleep wedged into the backseat and the space blanket would be perfectly cozy. Twirling to take in the darkening scene from horizon to horizon, Millie stopped, almost stepping on her own foot.

Lights bounced in the far distance. Peering hard, she discerned that she was looking at a vehicle's low running lights. Somebody else was on this side of the landslide. Somebody was driving rain-slicked roads, without headlights. Why would anyone be out now, not using headlights?

She stood motionless, eyes fixed in the direction where they found Herb's body. The lights disappeared—either the driver had stopped or a hill blocked her view. She waited and watched. Minute after minute passed, but neither lights nor sound penetrated the dark.

Millie relaxed a little. The Suburban was secluded from the road and its doors locked from the inside.

Just before climbing into the back seat, she pinched off a few sage leaves, crushed them between thumb and forefinger, and rubbed them on her left wrist. She hoped the scent would be calming. She learned this technique on a shopping trip to a JCPenney's department store for her eighth birthday. Her mother had ushered Millie to the cosmetics counter and they tried "tester" bottles of perfume until both wrists and a spot between still non-existent breasts exuded exotic scents. What would her mother think of exchanging White Shoulders for *Artemisia tridentata*?

Millie slept fitfully. Visions of tilting boulders, sticks that moved, and unnerving lights in the night competed with knees and elbows that disputed every position she tried for fitting into the back seat. When the call of nature superseded all of these, Millie gave into full consciousness, found the flashlight, and eased the door open.

Storm clouds were long gone, replaced by a half-moon and a rain-scrubbed sky more pristine than any nighttime spectacle Millie had ever experienced.

The light-colored sand offset the night's efforts to dim a pathway. Eyes adjusting, Millie realized her own sight would cover a wider distance than the flashlight's circle. She put the flashlight into a pocket and walked a short distance from the van.

"Starrrrs. I have never seen stars so many stars." The longer she looked, more stars revealed themselves, deeper and deeper into the night sky. "This must be what a state of nirvana feels like." The nighttime chill eventually intruded. She shivered and climbed back under the space blanket.

The sun was halfway above the eastern horizon when Millie maneuvered her stiff limbs out of the backseat. Catching the clean, after-rain fragrance of juniper and sage, Millie contemplated the bizarre events of the last twenty-four hours. The morning's trip to the T-one cactus site where she watched Robby's keen observation skills at work, detecting old hoof prints and faint tire tracks. Then the somberness hanging over the death scene, and the Old

Broad grumbling about "crypto-muerto" soil. This contrasted with the afternoon's satisfaction working around her cactus plot, assuming she hadn't squashed any while retreating from the rattlesnake. Storm, landslide, lights in the night, and a stunning sunset. So much for an uncomplicated season in the high desert.

Turning her back to the warming sun, she was presented with the kind of light that attracts artists to the Land of Enchantment. Millie noticed a juniper tree she had walked by several times without giving it a second thought. Lightning from a storm many years ago had peeled away half its trunk, but it still clung to life, supporting a few live branches. The sun's low aspect touched this desert survivor's heartwood. At this moment, it glowed— bronze, copper and cinnamon.

In the space of a few breaths, she watched the sun's upward climb leave the half-dead, half-alive trunk to fade back to silver-gray. *Old juniper, how many countless sunrises have put you in the spotlight? I'm probably the only human to witness your heart's grandeur.*

22. Watched

The desert will take care of you. At first it's all big and beautiful, but you are afraid of it. Then you begin to see its dangers, and you hate it. Then you learn how to overcome its dangers. And then the desert is home.
—Hosteen John, quoted in *Gillmor and Wetherill, Traders to the Navajos*

Millie jumped when the chime of her cell phone broke the morning silence. She swallowed the last of the second granola bar she was having for breakfast and answered.

"You sound in good spirits, Millie." She smiled at Wirt's voice. She didn't mind that he was checking on her and was glad to hear his update. "Here's what's going on. Dagun has a maintenance crew in that area and they said they'd go ahead and clean out the landslide for everybody. They thought it wouldn't take more than half the morning."

"That's good news. Thanks. And tell Momma Agnes I'm okay." In fact, she was more than okay. She was pleased with herself. She had prepared emergency supplies, got to use them, spent a cold night out by herself, and witnessed a spectacular sunset and an awesome sunrise.

"For once, I beat Momma Agnes in, but I'll tell her when she gets here. I'm sending a couple of our engineering techs out to help with the clean-up and assess whether any more grading will be needed for erosion control. They'll ride out with Robby Ramirez. They'll bring your vehicle back when they get done."

Before she could protest having her only means of transportation appropriated, Wirt continued, "Robby says she wants you to show her the second colony of San Juan cactus, that T-two site that Dr. Arnold talked about. When the road gets cleared, meet her at the landslide. Robby will bring you back into town. There's something that keeps eating at her about finding Herb's vehicle plowed into the sagebrush like it was."

Millie glanced into the back seat. She'd better get her scattered gear rounded up and ready to transfer into the law enforcement officer's vehicle. "Okay, Wirt. I'll be ready when she gets here."

It took just a few minutes for Millie to fold the space blanket and stow it along with the other gear back into the emergency supply box. Making a mental note to resupply the box on the weekend, she shouldered her backpack and set off for the San Juan cactus plot. Since Wirt said it would be mid-morning before the landslide would be cleared, she was intent on finishing the GPS readings along the perimeter that the sudden thunderstorm interrupted. After ten steps into the sagebrush, she returned to grab the makeshift walking stick.

Setting the backpack in the usual place next to the boulder, Millie gazed up at the petroglyph about two feet above her head. Now spotlighted by early morning sun, the incised stone revealed a perfect spiral that spanned the width of her up-stretched hands.

How many centuries of sunrises had illuminated the icon, she wondered. Who took such pains to carve it in just this particular location? Had the artist anticipated her current task of circling within its view? Perhaps, like hers, the maker's world was spiraling out of control.

Shaking her head at the never-ending revelations she encountered in this high desert land, she got out the GPS and camera, picked up the walking stick and went to work. She punched a mark in the GPS at each flag she had placed the day before. At every three flags, she took a picture to provide a thorough overview of the area.

When she came to her tracks from yesterday's mad dash triggered by the rattlesnake, she spent several minutes inspecting the ground for damage to the small cactus plants. She winced at seeing one where her foot crushed an outer stem. Its three remaining stems showed little damage. It looked no worse than the surrounding plants she could see. Some showed evidence of being chewed by mice or insects. Some were pinched and distorted where seeds had pushed up too close to a stone or a fallen tree branch. A few were dead and dried up, naturally succumbing to a harsh environment.

Halfway around the plot, her body was ready for a break. About to take a sip of water, Millie saw a flash of light on top of the mesa beyond the petroglyph boulder. The sun, still only midway up in the eastern sky, outlined a human figure holding binoculars. The flash came again from the sun's reflection off the lenses. Millie waved. The figure retreated backwards and disappeared.

Even in the warming sunlight, Millie shivered. Someone was watching her. For how long? Why? Was it the same person driving through the dark last night?

A loud crash of rocks came from the direction of the pass. Millie had been hearing the hum of heavy machinery working on the landslide for the past hour. She figured it wouldn't be long now before the pass was cleared. With one last look along the top of the mesa, she refocused attention on marking the rest of the way around the perimeter, hoping she'd encounter no more intrusions.

* * *

When she pulled up to the blocked pass, Millie saw several trucks and one long-bed trailer parked willy-nilly on the opposite side. A bulldozer ground back and forth, the driver manipulating gears with precision, nudging a few remaining rocks to each side of the road. The enormous boulder that teetered over the road the previous night was nowhere in sight, apparently already pushed over the cliff.

After a few more runs, the bulldozer driver pulled to one side and nodded to Millie. The way was clear. Until, that is, she reached the cluster of trucks. She could not see a way to thread through them, so she parked and walked toward a small group of men. She wasn't surprised to see that they were gathered around Buddy Maddox's truck.

The men were in a jovial mood, perhaps because of this break in routine or because of the fresh, rain-washed air. One greeted her with, "So, you got caught out by that storm. I've had to spend a couple nights in the field like that myself."

Buddy was perched on the passenger's side seat of his truck, the door hanging open, as good as a welcome mat for folks to stop and visit. "Yup, that was a real toad-choker, all right."

Another man chimed in, "My neighbor calls them 'wash-washers.' When the rain comes slammin' down like that, it washes out all the trash and junk down the wash."

A tall Navajo man, pulling on a pair of yellow leather gloves, said, "My people call that a male rain. Those hard ones you get in summer. Not like a gentle female rain that comes in the spring." He nodded to the others and said,

"Time to get to work, men. Grab a rake and get the rest of those little rocks off the road."

Buddy stayed put, not being part of the road maintenance crew. He reached behind him and brought out his thermos. "Bet you could use a cup of coffee, Miss."

"Could I ever!" Millie reached for the silver cup of lukewarm coffee.

Buddy got out, stomped a few clods of mud off his shoes, and strolled around his truck. He settled himself on the back bumper, brushing off a space next to him for Millie to sit down.

Millie remembered what Wirt had said about Buddy, wondering how he ever got any work done because he always seemed to be socializing, like the times he turned up when she was checking San Juan cactus plots. Still, she was glad for his hospitality, offering her his last cup of coffee.

"I'm waiting for the BLM techs. Wirt is sending them to check on whether the road will need more repair. Hard to believe there was a wall here yesterday compared to what's left now."

"If you need a ride to town, Miss Millie, I'd be glad to give you a lift in. I know the boss wouldn't mind. Out here, we help each other out. Don't matter what logo you got on the side of your truck."

Millie assured him that arrangements were all worked out, the techs would take the Suburban, and she'd ride with Robby Ramirez. Just as Buddy was inquiring who the techs were, Robby's Chevy Tahoe came into sight.

In no time, Buddy was gabbing with the engineering techs and Millie had backpack and maps transferred to Robby's vehicle. The crew leader motioned for a man to move a truck, which opened a path for Robby and Millie to drive through the newly cleared pass.

23. Too Tidy

Nature abhors a vacuum.
—*Attributed to Aristotle*

"Bummer to get stuck out all night," Robby said, "but there's nothing you can do when it rains like that. You've got to bring donuts in for the office, you know. It's an office tradition. Whoever gets stuck out in the field supplies donuts the next day."

"Geez louise, some tradition. It wasn't even my fault. But I'm kind of glad it happened," Millie admitted. "Once the storm was over, there was the most beautiful sunset you could imagine."

"Atta' girl, Millie. I guess once that pass got blocked, there wouldn't be anybody around to bother you."

"Actually," Millie said, "there was somebody out here last night. I saw lights way across the road, in the direction of the T-one plot."

"Last night? Who'd be driving around then?"

"It was kind of spooky. All I could see were dim running lights. Then the lights went out, like somebody didn't want to be seen."

"We'd better take a look around there, before going to the T-two plot."

Robby turned onto the side road leading to the T-one

cactus plot. Neither spoke when they came to the spot where Herb's truck ran off the road. The erratic path was even more distinct since the tow truck had backed in, crushing additional sage and rabbitbrush, in order to take the vehicle back to Wellstown. Vegetation along the road-side where emergency vehicles had parked still showed trampling as well.

Robby slowed and pointed to the opposite side of the road "Look at that. Those muddy ruts are recent. Somebody pulled over here since that rainstorm hit."

Not sure whether it mattered and more to make con-versation, Millie told Robby about being watched this morning. "It had to be someone on the same side of the landslide. Maybe it was the same person driving around last night."

"You think somebody was spying on you?"

"I don't know, maybe. It gave me the creeps."

Robby parked a short distance from the T-one plot and got out of the vehicle. "Look at this," she dropped to one knee. "You were right, there was a vehicle here sometime after the rainstorm yesterday afternoon. The tracks don't show much on the road, but you can see where they backed a few inches into this soft sand. That might have been why you saw the lights. Had them on just long enough to see to get turned around."

Robby was stepping slowly, cat-like, paralleling the road about 10 feet into the brush. "One person came through here. And it looks to me like he—or she—took a lot of trouble to hide their tracks. Must have been wearing moccasins or something. No tread, no heel marks, barely made any impression."

Millie walked along the road, paralleling Robby, heed-ful of the ranger's vigilance. If it hadn't been for Robby observing a few inches of disturbed sand, they might not have noticed the footprints. Millie had the fleeting thought that she was glad her training involved working with plants, rather than living with the suspiciousness that Robby carried with her.

Halfway around the plot's perimeter, Robby threw up her arms. "I can't believe our luck. That rain softened the ground enough to show tracks even from soft soles. If whoever it was didn't want to be seen, they sure chose the wrong time to be here. You can see where the sand is smoothed over here and there. Looks like somebody stopped, put down a cloth or something, then moved on."

Millie's focus was on the cactus, more than on human tracks. "I'm pretty sure one of the biggest cactus was growing right here." Millie pointed the toe of her boot toward one of the smoothed over spots. Her voice wavered. "It's gone. I remember it because it had nine stems, making it one of the oldest I've found."

Robby looked at the bare ground where Millie was pointing, then looked into Millie's pale face. "*This* is what Herb was telling you in that note. Somebody's removing these cactus. The more rare they are, the more they're worth to outlaw collectors."

Skirting even wider around the plot, Robby hiked back to the vehicle to get her camera. Millie called after her to bring the one from her backpack as well.

Millie stood in silence, head bowed, looking at the ground, noting how it seemed barely disturbed. Cacti survive because they put roots deep into the ground and also spread out close to the surface, to absorb every bit of available moisture. It would take a deep excavation to extract such a long-lived cactus. Millie's heart sank. That didn't happen here. It couldn't have been dug more than two spades deep. The lower roots would have been cut off. The cactus might live for a few months with truncated roots, might even manage to survive if it re-rooted in stabilized soil, but not likely. It would stay green just long enough to look good to a willing buyer, who wasn't going to ask too many questions or dare complain later.

The more she looked, the more her systematic mind analyzed the ground extending beyond the smoothed-over spot. It looked different from the ground she had walked just this morning taking GPS readings. At "her" plot, the cactus looked, somehow, more natural.

When Robby returned with both cameras, Millie tried to explain what was niggling at her thoughts. "Remember, Robby, when we were here yesterday morning before that rainstorm, you said the ground looked clean, like it had been swept? You saw faint tracks from Herb's truck tires here and we stopped to pick up the yellow tape where we found his truck."

"Yeah, Belva came by and actually said something nice about BLM."

"You might have been partly right. There's no loose sticks here, no grass stems lying on top of any of these cactus. It just looks different from that new colony across the wash we looked at with Dr. Arnold. I don't see any insect damage or cactus pads chewed by mice either."

"If you say so." Robby shrugged. "Let's get photos all along here. I hope you took some when you first came out here. They'll be invaluable for comparison. Then I want you to take me to that T-two location that Dr. Arnold said is farther down the road. Maybe this jerk did some digging there last night, too."

* * *

Robby stopped at the place where Herb died and photographed the ruts she had spotted earlier. Millie remained in the passenger's seat, scrolling through the images on her camera. She didn't like the memories this place brought back.

Back on the road, heading to the T-two site, Robby reported, "It's iffy whether there are enough tire impressions at the T-one plot to compare to those back there, but maybe enlarging the photos might show something. It's got to be the same vehicle, out after dark last night, on this side of the landslide."

Neither tire tracks nor human tracks were evident at the T-two plot. Millie felt a modicum of relief. Still, she sensed a difference at this plot also, compared to her newly discovered one.

Hot and tired after a long day, their slow pace around the plot did not change as they walked back to the Chevy Tahoe. Millie's compulsive nature wouldn't let her bypass a piece of brightly colored cardboard lying next to the road. She bent down and picked it up.

"What's that?" Robby asked.

Millie turned the ripped cardboard around and read the partial lettering, "d-CON, kills mice, *mata ratones*, solves mouse problems fast."

Robby chuckled, "I remember my uncle used that on his ranch back in Texas. It's from a d-CON package, contains mouse poison. How'd that get here? No ranches anywhere around."

"Maybe the wind blew it here."

"Wait a minute," Robby stopped, reaching for the partial carton, which Millie considered a piece of trash. "You say it's normal to see some cactus chewed on by mice or insects or something. We didn't see anything like that here."

Now Millie stopped, stepping to face Robby. "Could somebody be poisoning mice that might be damaging the cactus?"

They both stared at the red and yellow cardboard. Millie spoke first. "I can't imagine anybody putting out poison here. There're rabbits, ground squirrels, all kinds of animals that might get into it."

Robby didn't reply, but her look shouted the message as clearly as words spoken out loud. "*Boy, are you naïve.*"

24. Evidence

There's family you're born to and the family you choose.
—Barbara K. Richardson, *Tributary*

The next morning, Millie dutifully laid out four dozen donuts in the break room. She hoped that was enough to comply with office tradition. Only crumbs and powdered sugar remained by the time Millie joined the other BLM staff in the warehouse for an All Employees Meeting.

The chatter in the warehouse was especially animated. The area manager rarely called an All Employees Meeting during the middle of the week. Nervous anticipation was high by the time Wirt stepped to the front. "You've probably heard about the landslide on the Lejos Canyon Road. Closed the pass overnight. Miss Whitehall got to spend the night on the other side. You can thank her for the donuts."

Millie gave a wave left and right. Cheers of "yeah, Millie" and "thank you" made her feel like one of the crew.

Wirt's voice became somber. "I called this meeting because I know there are a lot of rumors and misinformation going around about what happened to Herb Thompson. I'm going to tell you straight out as many details as I can about it." He recounted their day in the field, giving vague mention that Dr. Arnold and Millie were checking on cactus locations, and that Officer Ramirez was along. He moved right into the grim information about finding Herb Thompson's body. He described the death scene in detail, from the time Robby spotted the truck off the road to the time when the body was loaded into the ambulance. Millie wished he would stop; she saw the dangling leg in her mind again.

There was hardly a wiggle or a chair scrape among the employees. Most had worked with Herb before he retired. Wirt finished with, "I'm telling you all this because I want everybody to know as much as I do about this situation. Otherwise, people tend to speculate about what happened, make up their own versions. I even heard somebody say the Piñon Resource Area is jinxed."

This seemed to open the floodgates. A few voices could be heard over the general murmurings.

"Yeah, I heard he'd been run off the road by a water tanker."

"Somebody said it was suicide, that he couldn't stand being retired with nothing to do."

"I heard that old truck of his blew a tire, careened off the road, and that he hit his head on the windshield."

Wirt paused, letting the gossip play itself out.

Someone in the second row called out, "What about Harrison Howdy, that BIA archaeologist? Know anything more on him? That makes two good field men found dead." Wirt held up a hand in a wait-a-minute signal and called Robby Ramirez to the front.

Although medium in stature, the uniformed Robby carried a presence that caused people to pay attention when she spoke. "I know, I know, you guys, this isn't something that happens in our part of the world. But it did, and we're still investigating both deaths."

The same person in the second row called out, "Any more and you'll have to put in a requisition for a hearse.

Go driving around to pick up dead bodies."

"All right, I'll pretend I didn't hear that. Here's what we know so far." Robby relayed the same information that she had told Millie earlier. Herb was known to have heart problems and nitroglycerin pills were found on the scene.

There were details, though, that Millie knew Robby was leaving out. The Law Enforcement Officer did not mention the note that the retired botanist scribbled just before he died. A note which added a very different dimension to the story.

Wirt moved to the front and thanked Robby. "Now, you all know what happened. I don't want to hear anymore crazy rumors or talk about being cursed. That's all I have to say. So get back to work."

* * *

The office atmosphere brightened after the morning's meeting. Wirt's and Robby's account of the circumstances surrounding finding Herb Thompson's body seemed to help the staff wrestle with their anxiety over the abnormal incidents.

The range con, Linda, next to Millie's cubicle, popped her head in to say a few folks were going out to lunch and would she like to come along?

"Love to. After this morning, I'm ready for a break."

At the busy restaurant, Millie slid into the booth next to Linda, and four more fellow workers squeezed in after her. This time, Millie was ready to call out "green" when the waitress asked which chile sauce. The conversation revolved around Herb-stories, the time he stood up to the bulldozer driver and the fishing expeditions shared by two of those at the table. There was no need for more speculation on what happened that day. The retired botanist had a bad heart; they all knew that.

Millie enjoyed the camaraderie. She contributed to the conversation by describing the bizarre cartoons she had unearthed in Herb's office. She realized this is how community is built in the West, breaking bread together with co-workers. Like herself, most had moved to Wellstown for the job, exchanging family ties for career adventures.

* * *

Millie returned from lunch to find Robby pacing the hallway outside of her cubicle, waiting for her. Millie sat down and motioned to the chair by the desk. Robby shook her head, and leaned against the doorway. "Can you get those pictures we took at the T-one plot yesterday, so I can take a look at them, along with any photos you have from prior to the night of the rainstorm?"

Millie nodded, "No problem. I have the previous ones all labeled and organized by date of site visits. I'll get started on our new ones, but it'll take some time to sort and categorize them."

"Good. I'll come by first thing Friday morning."

Millie was arranging eighteen photographs across her desk when Robby arrived. She had marked the bottom of each eight by ten glossy color print with date and location using the wax pencil she kept specifically for labeling photos.

Robby began with images from the T-one plot, since it was closest to where they found Herb Thompson's body and the scribbled note. She compared the photographs taken in late May with their counterparts taken after the storm. By the time she scrutinized the third set she said, "We've got to show these to Wirt."

She used the phone in Millie's office to call Momma Agnes. The area manager was attending a Wellstown Chamber of Commerce meeting and wouldn't be back until late afternoon. Millie could overhear Momma Agnes's assurances that she would inform them as soon as Wirt returned.

Robby continued examining paired photos from the T-two plot, where Millie had picked up the d-CON box. "I can't make out any missing plants here. I hope they took photographs when they did the original T-two inventory. We'll need to search the archive files. Herb was in on both surveys. He could have told us, if only... All he was able to do was write those three words on that note."

Sinking into the extra chair by Millie's desk, Robby said, "I keep thinking that whoever made those tracks after the storm at the T-one plot had to be on the other side of that landslide, just like you were. That's all Piñon Resource Area land. There aren't any residences or ranches anywhere around there."

Millie, unsettled by Robby's belief that someone was stealing San Juan cactus, dropped into her chair. "And I keep thinking it was the same person watching me with binoculars the next morning."

"I've got to wonder about that cowboy you said almost rode his mustang across the T-one plot. I've seen him, off and on, riding out in the junipers, poking along after a stray cow. He could have been around there. But I've never noticed a pair of binoculars hanging on his saddle."

Robby seemed to be talking to herself as much as to Millie. "It wouldn't take a lot of effort for someone that morning to get around the landslide. If they dropped down into the wash somewhere before the pass, they could hike around the slide."

The law enforcement officer stared at the floor, seeming to search for a course of action. "Last summer, I saw Belva Banks walking along that wash. She walks all over out there. She could easily hike up that mesa. She's likely to carry binoculars, too."

Robby leaned forward, about to leave, but settled back in the chair. "But those tire tracks by the T-one plot after the rain, that wasn't somebody hiking around or on horseback. Anybody could have still gotten there by taking back roads, if they were familiar with how to access all the well sites in the north unit."

"I heard TJ bragging about how he knows every inch of the Piñon Resource Area." Millie offered. "He was at the copy machine, making maps for Fritz Müller."

"That clown. I sometimes wonder what he really thinks about working for BLM."

Millie hesitated, but felt compelled to add, "You know that morning you brought the engineering techs out and met me at the slide? Buddy Maddox had gobs of mud on his shoes. I noticed it when he gave me a cup of coffee."

"Hmm. Those rare little cactus would bring a pretty penny on the open market." Robby slapped her knees, sprang up and said, "I'll hold on to these. They're evidence." She gathered the prints, keeping them in Millie's organized groupings. Starting down the hallway, she called back to Millie, "After we meet with Wirt, I'll have a few people to visit with. Find out where they were the night of that storm."

Millie was left staring at the empty desktop. Musings and speculations, just what Wirt was trying to avoid. She was glad her research came from field guides and journals, not from interrogating people that she had come to think of as friends.

She scanned the bookshelves lining the cubicle and pulled out a stack of references that might shed more light on San Juan cactus ecology. Spreading them across the desk, she pulled a soft-cover, spiral-bound document closer, *Southwest Native Plant Society Symposium*, Wellstown,

New Mexico. A gathering of amateur and professional botanists would be likely to cover local, rare species.

She flipped to the index in the back of the book for *Sclerocactus sanjuanensis.* She found that Dr. Arnold, Herb Thompson, and two others had presented a panel discussion on the first day of the meeting.

The pages listing conference participants flipped open. One name, Fritz Müller, caught her eye. Millie considered whether this might be the same Fritz Müller, the photographer.

She looked through other names on the list, seeing Harvey Sageman's name just before Herb Thompson's. *Now that can't be a common name,* she thought, *this must be Ben's grandfather.* She was surprised that the list contained names of people she knew after being in New Mexico for just a few months, but concluded that it wasn't such a coincidence. People with common interests seek out and network with each other.

She read the four pages of text covering the panel discussion, which even included the questions and answers at the end of the session. It appeared that Dr. Arnold and Herb took turns responding to questions from the audience—yes, there were only two known locations of San Juan cactus, and yes, that made it one of the rarest cacti in the western hemisphere.

This was information that needed to be added to Millie's research. She carried the conference report to the copy machine, holding it open at the page where the panel discussion section began. She was about to copy the participant list as well, when the smell of popcorn reached her.

She glanced up to see TJ exit the break room, holding a microwaveable bag in one hand and scooping a handful of popcorn into his mouth with the other.

"What 'cha lookin' at?"

The last time she encountered TJ at the copy machine, Fritz Müller was with him. Millie pointed to the name near the bottom of the page. "I wonder if this is the same Fritz who is the photographer."

"Oh sure, he comes here every two or three years. Kind of cozies up to me, you know. He likes it when I show him my knife collection out in the motor pool yard. Comes right into the yard, don't even bother to stop at the front desk. Says I'm the real deal, a real *westerner*. Always pumping me to show him places I go hunting. How do you get to this canyon, or any way to get over there? Things like that."

Millie nodded, declined TJ's offer to grab a handful of popcorn, and gathered up the copies. She returned to her cubicle to mull over these puzzling pieces of information.

25. Vegetal Matter

The value of botanical trace evidence in criminal and civil cases has been clearly demonstrated and is accepted by the courts.
—Botanical Society of America, *Plant Science Bulletin, Fall 2006*

Millie didn't know whether Momma Agnes called her or Robby first to say the area manager was available, but they arrived at the same time at Wirt's office door.

Wirt leaned back in his chair, not making any move to get up. "Come on in. From the looks on your faces, I'm guessing this won't be good news. Well, pile it on—it's been one of those days. The Chamber of Commerce folks think it would be a grand idea to have horse and camel races in Lejos wash. They found some old newspaper clippings that talked about a camel race in 1903. Seems traveling shows put on such races back then. Camels, for Pete's sake!"

Robby was blunt. "You're right, this isn't happy news. We have evidence that someone is stealing San Juan cactus on the Resource Area."

Wirt looked at Robbie, then fixed his stare on Millie. "First you find an unrecorded site for an endangered cactus right where there's an Application for Permit to Drill.

Now you decide somebody's stealing them. And two dead bodies show up on the RA. This summer can't get any worse." He sighed and said, "Tell me what you've got."

Robby said, "We've got photographic documentation that cactus were removed from the T-one plot. Come on to the conference room and we can show you what we're talking about." They reached the conference room and Robbie began to lay out the photos in the same order they had been on Millie's desk.

Millie spread her map of the T-one plot on an adjoining table. She also had prints of photos she took at her newly discovered plot. She selected ones that particularly showed the raggedness of bunch grass and loose sticks on the plot and surrounding area. She included two close-ups of cactus stems chewed by hungry mice or rabbits. They showed grooves where teeth cut through the green outer cactus pad to its white core.

Robby laid out the plastic bag containing the cardboard d-CON package that Millie picked up near the T-two plot.

Wirt made few comments, absorbing the information Robby and Millie relayed about what they found the day after the rainstorm.

"Somebody was on the back side of that landslide, at the T-one plot, the night of the big storm." She was sticking to the facts. She did not repeat their deliberations shared earlier in Millie's office, except to add, "Millie thinks it may be the same person that was watching her the next morning at her new plot."

At Wirt's questioning stare, Millie filled him in how she had looked up, saw a reflection from binoculars, and realized she was being watched.

"All right, some strange things are going on out there. These pictures back-up what you're saying. Let's go back to my office and deal with this." Wirt led the way to his office and waited for Robby and Millie to take a seat before he shut the door. As soon as he sat down, he began giving instructions to Robby to contact the US Fish and Wildlife Service. Investigating poaching of federally endangered species came under that agency's jurisdiction.

"Robby, I meant to call you in today anyway. The State Medical Investigator's Office delivered the preliminary autopsy reports this morning. Look them over while I go help Momma Agnes close up for the day."

Wirt handed one legal-sized manila envelope to Robby and the other one to Millie. "Here, you're the plant specialist. Both reports on Harrison Howdy and Herb Thompson put a lot of attention on plants. Maybe you can make some sense out of this."

A bit startled, Millie opened the report on Herb Thompson while Robby started perusing the other document.

Robby read snatches of the report out loud. "This puts cause of death as 'skull fracture, causing immediate cessation of brain function.'"

Her voice rose almost to a shriek. "Millie, hold onto your seat. This says 'manner of death was probably homicide.'"

"How could that be? Wirt, you, everybody said Harrison Howdy walked off that cliff."

"Well, shut my mouth. Here's how that's explained. 'Significant abrasions evident, consistent with striking hard surfaces such as caused by fall from cliff, as described for location of discovery per report by MI at the scene. However, noticeable lack of perimortem contusions indicates subject already deceased prior to fall.'"

"Already deceased?" Millie said. "Hmmm, contusions mean bruises, so there's got to be blood flow in order for bruises to form, and that says they were lacking. What about him being blinded by a yucca, the reason I heard for why he fell?"

Robby flipped over a page. "Here it is. '...particles of plant material lodged in right eye socket. Material matched plant specimen collected by field medical investigator at location deceased found. Per MI's notes, the individual who discovered the body, Mr. Buddy Maddox, provided verbal account that he extracted a 'big, fat yucca spike' from the eye immediately after he called 911.'

"All kinds of details here: depth of penetration and angle of entry for 'pointed, vegetable matter'...'Specimen collected at scene—oblong in form, sixteen point nine centimeters in length, five centimeters at widest section'...'The plant species is identified as *Yucca baccata.*'"

Robby interjected a drawn-out "ewww." "It describes liquids found on the sample. Glad I don't have that job."

Millie rolled her eyes upward, doing calculations in her mind. "That would be a yucca leaf about five, maybe five and a half inches long and about two inches wide. The liquids, well, that's what your eye is composed of."

Robby flipped over a couple more pages. "Here, in the remarks, it says 'configuration of severely depressed skull fracture suggests forceful blow by linear, convex instrument.'" Robby laid the report face down on her lap. "It was brain injury, Millie, not stumbling off that cliff."

She leaned toward Millie's chair, "What did Wirt mean about plants and Herb's autopsy?"

Millie was swishing an index finger back and forth on the third page of the document she held. "I just found it. 'A three-millimeter specimen of vegetal matter lodged between second and third molars. Initial microscopic analysis indicates likelihood matter is from the genus *Ephedra*. Samples being sent to FBI Forensic Botany

Laboratory for further identification.'"

"Forensic Botany, I know a little about that," Robby was nodding. "We had a session on it during law enforcement training. They look for such things as vegetable matter under fingernails, analyze stomach contents of people who might have eaten poisonous plants, and even look for pollen or spores on shoes to pin down locations where a person had walked. All in a day's work for a forensic botanist. Not a job for me, though, they spend most of their time in a lab looking through a microscope."

Millie flipped back and read highlights of the report's early statements. "'Cause of death—fatal arrhythmia. Time of death—approximately between one-thirty and three-thirty p.m. as indicated by lack of onset of rigor mortis at time of MI's arrival.' I think it was about four o'clock when we found his truck off the road."

Millie squeezed her eyes shut. How could that scene, still hovering in her memory, be distilled into impersonal black marks on white pages? Forcing her eyes and mind back to the information in front of her, Millie read a few more statements to Robby.

"In the remarks, it says, 'inspection of the heart muscle indicates deceased had early, acute damage to the heart muscle. Nitroglycerin tablets found at scene denote under treatment for prior coronary vessel narrowing... contorted limbs indicate decedent was experiencing pain prior to death.'"

Robby groaned.

"It goes on to say 'cyanosis of the skin evident due to insufficient oxygenation to heart muscle.' Cyanosis—I don't know what that means." Millie pulled her phone from a pocket and punched in a search for the term. "Okay, here it is. Cyanosis means a bluish cast to the skin."

"That's why his face looked so ghastly," Robby said.

"This is interesting. 'Manner of death, preliminary determination, possibly accidental due to ingestion of toxic substance causing severe cardiac arrhythmia... Further toxicology analysis of gastric contents pending.'"

Millie slapped the report down on her knees. "You know what, Robby? Ephedra plant parts, that's what everybody calls Mormon tea. The Food and Drug Administration banned ephedra supplements years ago. It was causing problems for people taking it to lose weight. It speeds up metabolism. There's something about athletes, too, if I remember right. Wirt and I talked about it when he showed me around the Piñon Resource Area the first week I started. He said it tastes awful."

"Figured you'd know something about that, Millie," Wirt said, as he stepped back into his office, leaving the door open this time. "But I don't see how it makes any difference. There's yucca and Mormon tea all over Piñon Resource Area." The reception area beyond his office was dim, the only light coming from windows. The building was quiet at the end of the week, all the staff had left for the weekend.

Millie was about to hand the Thompson autopsy report to the area manager, but he indicated that it should go to Robby. "Remember, this information is preliminary, and of course, confidential. Robby, put that call into the Fish and Wildlife Service before you leave, but I doubt that they'll take any action until Monday." He sat down and picked up the day's mail.

Robby headed for her office, juggling the two manila envelopes on top of the stack of the incriminating photographs. Millie secured her photo prints in her desk's bottom drawer and drove home, feeling exhausted, lonely, and let down. Her hopes for a tranquil season in the high desert were shrinking like cactus in a drought.

26. Yarn and Yucca Fiber

As the bearers of children, Navajo weavers often say, 'the rugs are like our children.' Traditional Navajo look at their weaving as an expression of the essence of being Navajo, almost comparable to a permanent written record.
—William Dunmire & Gail Tierney, *Wild Plants and Native Peoples of the Four Corners*

Millie planned the call home carefully, taking into account the East Coast two-hour time zone difference. She needed to unload to somebody. Her mother should be home and tidying up around the house on a late Saturday morning.

Millie tried to sound calm on the phone but was unable to control her wavering voice, jumbling together the recent events—a dead man, autopsy reports, a rattlesnake encounter, and drilling threatening her cactus.

Her mother said little until Millie finished her litany of troubles. "Well, what did you expect? You run off and do this dangerous job. Just like that summer you spent traipsing around Germany with that, that... what's-his-name."

"I didn't run off. It was an internship, a chance of a lifetime to go to Europe." Why is it that, no matter how old you are, bickering with your mother makes you feel like a naughty child.

Her mother tried changing tactics. "You know, dear, we really need your organizational abilities." Her tone became soothing. "I've been thinking about adding a plant care service to the cleaning business. It's a perfect fit. The buildings we contract for custodial services often have decorative plants. You'd do a great job with those."

Then she hit her overly responsible daughter with the clincher, "Come home, Millie, we need you here."

"I can't just quit. I've got a job to do here. Goodbye, Mom." There was nothing more to say. Millie felt drained. She had hoped for empathy on her call home.

This was Millie's third call home since she arrived in New Mexico. The first one was to tell her folks she was in Wellstown and found the rental was OK. The second call was about her terrific discovery of the San Juan cactus plot. They didn't seem a bit impressed, just talked about the heat wave that was making everybody miserable. A few emails in between these conversations had been enough to keep in touch.

Now Millie wished she'd never made the call. She felt caught between duty to family and doing botany work that drew a compliment even from Dr. Arnold. She couldn't stop the angry tears, and she'd never felt so lonely.

'Come home, Millie, we need you here,' her mother had pleaded. Millie knew it was the truth. *Why don't I just do that? Give up and go home. I'm needed there and...here I seem to either be making trouble or getting involved in situations I never thought could happen to me.*

She dropped the phone next to Ragged Ear, settled in his usual meatloaf position on the desk in the living room. "Sorry to disturb your nap, old boy." The cat flicked his tail and draped it across the laptop. He'd been scolded several times for perching on top of the silver square, but he had a rebellious streak, which mirrored Millie's mood.

She looked into the cat's golden eyes, but in her mind's eye, Millie saw fuchsia cactus blossoms, felt the tingling aroma of crushed sagebrush, and heard the raven's call.

Millie leaned back in her chair, and wiped the back of her hand across her eyes. "Don't worry, fuzz ball. I'll be okay. I'll keep feeding you and somebody's got to make sure a well doesn't take out my San Juan cactus." Ragged Ear pushed his face against her chin and revved up a comforting purr. Millie tapped a bit of cottonwood fluff off the cat's whiskers.

The screen door rattled to the tune of *dum-dum-da-dum-dum ...tum-tum*.

Ragged Ear jumped down from the desk and crouched behind the front door. As soon as Millie opened the door a crack, the cat sprang outside in a yellow flash.

Ben Benallee jumped aside. "Geez, what was that? Say, I heard you got stuck out in that storm. Thought I'd take you to breakfast and we could cruise the flea market in Shiprock. It's the best flea market in the Four Corners. It'll take your mind off all that crazy stuff happening on the Piñon Resource Area."

The tips of Ben's shoulder-length hair still swung with moisture from a morning shower. She couldn't resist his expectant eyes and carefree smile. "Watch it, Ben, this almost sounds like you are asking me out."

"Well, I was thinking we could split breakfast, then maybe I can buy a couple CDs at the flea market. I've got enough gas to make it to Shiprock and back."

"Enough gas? You'd better have. I'll buy my breakfast and you buy yours, wouldn't want you to pass up a good deal on CDs just for my sake."

Ben shrugged. "How soon can you get ready? I'll be in the car."

* * *

185

Ben nosed the Miata between a horse trailer and an aged car that would be considered a classic in some areas, but was currently disgorging three adults and five children. Millie unfolded herself from the passenger's seat, stepped onto the hard-packed dirt parking area, and slipped on a sun visor. She hoped to blend in by dressing in tan shorts and casual T-shirt, but could not overcome the fact that she was a head taller than almost everyone in sight. Her long legs and shining chestnut hair made her as conspicuous as a tulip growing in the desert.

Ben led the way toward rows of booths and stopped at the very first one. Its three tables placed in a U-shape were crowded with boxes of new and used CDs; one of the tables featured dozens of pow wow recordings. Ben struck up a conversation with the booth's young proprietor.

Millie continued strolling among the vendors offering everything from toys to used tools and tires. Clothing booths showed off jackets, vests, purses, and pillows fashioned from Pendleton wool blankets. One booth had vivid blouses and skirts sewn from forest-green, midnight-blue, or tawny-gold velvet that flashed and winked with the slightest breeze. Miniature versions to fit elementary-age girls hung from lower racks.

Every third booth, it seemed to Millie, displayed jewelry. Some featured beadwork made into colorful bracelets and little girls' hair barrettes. Others showed off the work of silversmiths, with fine necklaces, heavy bracelets encrusted with massive turquoise nuggets, money clips, and child- to adult-sized rings.

Millie fingered a rack of earrings. Her mother would never have let her out of the house as a teenager wearing such showy, dangling jewelry. A short woman slid off a stool at the back of the booth, went to a table draped with a red and yellow striped cloth, and ran her hand over a collection of thirty or so silver bracelets. She lifted one to eye level, nodded, and handed it to Millie. Finely incised lines formed the outlines of mesas, raincloud symbols, and a trio of yucca plants, one with blossoms. Millie was speechless. How did this woman know that the iconic yucca captivated her? Millie slipped the bracelet around her wrist, felt the perfect embrace, and extracted her wallet from a pocket.

Stepping back among the passing shoppers, Millie was still admiring the bracelet when Ben appeared at her side. "Knew you'd find something like that." He motioned toward a cluster of food trucks enticing customers with aromas of roasted turkey legs, corn on the cob, cotton candy, and popcorn. "Come on, I'll treat you to the best Navajo cuisine."

Taking his turn, Ben stepped up to the window and ordered fry bread and coffee for two.

When the order came, Ben slid the paper plates onto Millie's upturned hands. She carried the delicious smelling, still-sizzling fried dough to one of the picnic tables scattered among the food trucks. Ben followed, using both hands to carry the coffee. He darted back to the window, returned with a plastic bottle, and squeezed honey around and around over each fry bread.

Fried dough slathered with honey—contrary to every healthy eating principle Millie ever heard. She savored it.

Still licking honey from fingers and carrying coffee cups, Millie and Ben strolled among the vendors, occasionally stepping around a stray dog, and dodging laughing, racing children—girls with braids flying and boys wearing flapping, oversized, go-to-town cowboy boots.

At the end of a row, tables covered with dried plants drew Millie's attention. One table had a sign, "NATURAL DYES." Skeins of yarn were arranged from one end of the table to the other, in ascending shades from pure white, through yellows, tans, greens to deepest browns. In front of each grouping of yarns was a neatly labeled packet of dried stems, leaves or blossoms in re-closeable plastic bags or tied into bundles with white string.

Millie moved along the table, reading each label— purple bee plant flowers next to light gray skeins, Mormon tea stems made light tan skeins, and cliffrose leaves for a deep-brown-colored yarn.

Millie fingered a reddish-brown skein dyed with globe mallow. She lowered her head to lay a strand of her own hair next to it. The yarn made a perfect match.

One yarn skein, noticeably smaller, was a stunning scarlet color. Its dye was in a round, plastic container labeled "cochineal." Millie looked closer and saw what looked like bits of insect parts.

"They're bugs," a woman said, pushing dollar bills from her last customer into her apron pocket. "That's the hardest one to collect. It costs a lot, but makes the best dye for producing shades of reds."

"Oh yeah, I know about them," Ben chimed in, "they're those squishy scale insects that live in clusters on prickly pear cactus. They're only found on *Opuntia* cactus."

"I give any extra I can't sell to my mother. She's a weaver," the woman said with pride. "Here, look at this rug my mom made," she waived Millie and Ben into her booth bordered by tables. She picked up a woven rug, about three feet long and nearly as wide. It had layers of rose interspersed with muted gray and soft yellow. "That pink is from cochineal, the gray is natural from the sheep, and that yellow one is dyed with snake weed."

"It looks like a sunrise. It's just like a New Mexico sunrise!" Millie blurted out.

The woman draped the rug back over a chair and

picked up a handful of twisted fibers. "See, this is what I make. Hardly anyone does this anymore, but I like to keep the traditional crafts alive. I'm a teacher during the year and summers I go around and show people how the elders use what nature has given us. It's important to share this knowledge. Mother Earth always gives what we need. Too many people try to replace our traditional knowledge of medicines and healing practices with Western ways."

The teacher laid the fibers over Millie's hand and turned to pick up a sandal made from similar strands sewn together. "Takes forever to make yucca sandals like this, but archaeologists have found hundreds in caves and ruins of the ancients."

"These are made from yucca?" Millie asked, not able to translate the green, leathery leaves she'd seen into this strong, tan string.

"It's a lot of work," the teacher went on, "but I do demonstrations at fairs and festivals. I keep a tub of yucca leaves soaking all the time at home. You just leave them in water for a couple of weeks, swish it around, and all that's left are these long fibers. Once you got that, you twist a few together, adding and overlapping a few more, and in no time you've got a long, long rope. You can make a rabbit snare, a medicine pouch, or weave in turkey feathers for the softest blanket ever—all kinds of things."

Like any good teacher, the woman acted out each of these steps with exaggerated body movement, letting her students practically feel stirring the wet fibers, twisting the strands, and sewing them together.

Millie handed the strands to Ben. "I was taking pictures of yucca flowers up in that ponderosa pine stand that day you were chasing the deer."

The teacher waved Millie's words away. "Oh, that wouldn't be the kind of yucca to use for making string.

That yucca that grows up high—the one with big, fat leaves, that's not so good for rope. Too fleshy. You only want to use narrowleaf yucca. But you can eat the flowers of either one. I have a recipe for yucca soup."

Ben moved toward a table with a sign, "GOOD FOR YOU PLANTS," and picked up a bundle of leaves and stems that filled the palm of his hand. "I'll take this Navajo tea to sheep camp. Grandmother Sageman likes it." He picked up two more rolls of the tightly wrapped herbs and counted out six dollars. The teacher stuffed the money into her apron pocket, already turning her attention to the next customer, assuring a wobbly, ancient man wearing a cowboy hat, that yes, indeed, she had fourwing saltbush root for toothache.

27. Map Art

The question is not what you look at, but what you see.
—*Henry David Thoreau, 1851*

Millie's stomach grumbled as she started up the trail to Split Lip Canyon Overlook. The lunch spot would provide a welcome respite after last week's meetings and the dusty flea market trip. She smiled, Ben was right, the trip to the flea market was the get-away she needed from her mother's appeal to come home, from dwelling on autopsy reports, and worrying about the fate of *her* cactus.

She stopped by the banana yucca. Its flower stalk was now a dried stick. She ran her hand up the stalk, making the desiccated blossoms pop off and flutter to the ground like bits of parchment paper. She touched her face, now rougher and shades darker than the first time she stopped here. "Big yucca, you look as ragged as I feel. But I know you make lovely flowers." She extended her wrist to catch a shaft of sunlight that penetrated the ponderosa pine branches, making the silver bracelet sparkle.

When Millie got to the overlook, she gave a brief look up and down the canyon, and plopped down at the flat rock table. She was starving, but satisfied with her accomplishments so far this week. She had walked three ever-widening circles around the San Juan cactus plot. She could report to Wirt that no other specimens occurred within 500, 1,000, and 1,500 meters beyond the perimeter she had marked with GPS points on her map.

She dumped out the lunch she threw together at dawn this morning—a roll of crackers, a snack-size peanut butter container, a bag of pre-washed baby carrots, and a plastic knife. She shook her head, thinking how far she was from the strictures of her upbringing—licking honey off her fingers in public at the flea market, gobbling a haphazard lunch dropped on a rock today.

I can see miles from this spot. My view is so much broader than the circle of a microscope. This land—what happens to it—hinges on conflicting laws, demand for energy, politics, and stakeholder users like Buddy, Belva, Fritz, and Cowboy. Thank heavens there's a law that protects the humble, endangered San Juan cactus, a product of geology, elevation, soil conditions, and millennia of changing seasons. My mind and heart tell me this is where I need to be.

A cliffrose bush next to the ponderosa reminded Millie of the natural dyed yarns at the traditional plants booth. How proud the Navajo woman was of her mother's exquisitely woven rug and of her own handiwork fashioning products from yucca fiber.

Millie quieted her thoughts and listened to the silence. But Robby's voice reading lines from the autopsy report echoed in Millie's mind—plant matter, *Yucca baccata*, in the eye socket. The kind of fat-leaved yucca the Navajo woman said was no good for sandal making.

Millie snapped her fingers, dropping a carrot which rolled off the stone. Bits of information suddenly fused in her mind. "Wirt was wrong when he said yucca and Mormon tea are all over Piñon Resource Area. That archaeologist's body was found at the base of the cliff. It's not likely that he stumbled onto a banana yucca. That type of yucca mainly grows at *higher* elevations. Something must have already happened to him, and not at that place."

A raven was gliding along the canyon, just beyond the rim, its outstretched wings seizing the slightest air current. Millie stood, placed her feet and raised her arms in ballet's second position, imitating the raven's glide. The raven circled, flapping low over her head, and made a throaty gurgling sound. Then it caught updrafts from the canyon and rose higher and higher until its form merged with the sky. "Nice to see you again, Raven."

If it hadn't been for overhearing her first conversation with the raven, Ben might never have stumbled on to her lunch spot. She would never have slapped fry bread between her hands, laughed with his family, and listened to the elders' stories.

Stomach rumbles now satisfied, surrounded by quiet and relaxed under the ponderosa's shade, Millie let her mind flow. *Could there be a link among the awful events happening on Piñon Resource Area—the missing cactus plants and two men found dead?* Grandfather Sageman said nothing happens in isolation, there's always a cause for something good and for something bad to happen.

Tapping the chestnut hair looped over her temple, she mumbled, "Think, Millie, think, use your little gray cells. There must be a way to key out the cause of these evil occurrences. What is the key?

"What would Anna Pigeon do to track down a murderer in her national park? Hmm... she'd probably blunder through the woods until she crashed into the suspect. What would Joe Leaphorn do? He could always find the answer. He'd put pins in a map, he always started by sticking pins in a map on his wall. Well, I have maps."

She reached for the backpack and found the folded BLM map tucked in the back pocket. The more cumbersome 20-foot contour interval maps marked with GPS readings for the San Juan cactus plots were rolled up on the back seat of the Suburban parked below.

Guess I can plot people just the same as plants. She smiled and drew a cowboy hat on the spot where she met Cowboy at the T-one plot. Laughing, she drew a music note at the well site where Buddy Maddox's whistling was interrupted by a rattlesnake. Their first encounter with Belva Banks was marked with a crooked walking stick. After a moment's debate, she penciled in the shape of a pipe by the overlook trail where she met Fritz Müller.

Who else? She blew a strand of hair aside. She drew a dollar sign near the map's upper margin to indicate the clearing where Ben's Grandfather Sageman collected plants to sell.

Those were beneficial uses of plants, not what forensic botanists deal with like Robby talked about. *Do people really use plants to commit crimes? Of course, what would the venerable Agatha Christie mysteries be without deadly nightshade?*

* * *

Leaving the ponderosa pines' coolness and scuffling down the trail through dense P-J, Millie realized how absorbed with her thoughts she had been over lunch. Fritz Müller's green camper was parked near the Suburban, the awning already stretched out and two chairs set up under its shade. She had not even heard a vehicle arrive.

Millie stopped short. Fritz's back blocked the Suburban's side window. One hand was above his shoulder, sliding something into the gap where the top of the window met the door's rubber gasket.

He must have caught her reflection in the window, because he wheeled around with a start. A bent wire extended from the window. He called out. "There you are, Madam Millie. I became worried about you." He put on a broad smile. "I thought perhaps there would be something in your car that would say where you had gone." He took a step toward her, but turned back and eased the wire up and out of the gap.

"I wasn't gone that long, Fritz. And you know the most likely place anybody parked here would be hiking the trail to Split Lip Canyon Overlook."

He strode over to where she stood. "You should be careful, young lady, it is not wise to hike in the New Mexico hot summer sun."

She did have a headache, not from the sun but from her unwanted thoughts that kept linking the disappearing cactus to the puzzling deaths.

He clasped her upper arm and started toward the awning. "You must join me for a cold drink." Millie pulled away, but welcoming a cool drink, followed him to the awning's shade.

She took a sip of iced tea from a tall glass and called out, "Earl Gray?"

"You are right again, Madam Millie." Her host was scooping a third teaspoonful of sugar into his glass, which dripped moisture on the tea set he had carried out of the camper's dark interior.

"I've just returned from a few days in Wellstown. The Bureau of Land Management frowns on camping in one place for too many days, so, I move from this or that canyon to a different scenic spot. Camping is delightful, *Ja*, but a few days experiencing restaurant meals, a comfortable bed, and nice shower is also a very welcome thing."

Fritz stopped stirring, satisfied that the sugar was dissolved, and let the swirling ice cubes slow. "And you, Madam Millie, where have you been?"

She related that the plant monitoring was about half done for the season, without mentioning her many days focused solely on San Juan cactus. No way was she going say a word about the cactus, after Wirt's dressing-down about keeping quiet about the new plot.

"You did not say one very important thing. My old friend, Herb Thompson, is no longer on this earth."

Millie nodded. The efficiency with which information was broadcast in this remote region continued to amaze her.

"I met Herb just once, at the office. He was popular among the staff. Everybody misses him."

The mention of Herb's name reminded Millie of the list of symposium participants that she had come across. "Were you at the Native Plant Society Symposium in Wellstown two years ago? I saw your name on the proceedings report."

"Ah, you were reading about what Mr. Thompson and the others said about the little San Juan cactus. Yes, I was there. They were very enthusiastic about their work."

Tea dribbled from the glass Fritz was holding, he was leaning toward her with such intensity. "Did Mr. Thompson like that you found more of the little cactus, as you told me about?"

"No, I never got the chance to talk to Herb again, after I looked at the location," Millie's voice trailed off.

"But you knew it was the little cactus, didn't you? You said to me that you discovered another place where the cactus lives. That is a very nice map you have by your chair. Show me where you found it."

Fritz, already leaning forward, took one step and plucked the map from the backpack so quickly Millie did not have time to react.

"That map is what I use to get around the Piñon

Resource Area, Fritz. It has nothing to do with vegetation communities."

Fritz sat back down and lightning quick, unfolded the map. "I see no marks on this except for doodling. Is this your artwork, girl?"

Millie nodded and held out a hand to retrieve the map.

"That is charming, your map. I consider it an example of western folk art. I collect such things. May I have it? I must look at it more closely."

"No way this is folk art, and I need it, Fritz."

"In my country it is common for friends to exchange one thing for another. You liked my sunset photograph of the mustang. I would be happy for you to have that photograph and I would like to have your map."

Millie stood, hands on hips, "Give me the map, Fritz. You can get your own at the BLM office next time you're in town."

A snort and sound of a horse blowing dust out of its nose startled them both. Cowboy guided Dunnie between the Suburban and the camper.

"Are you trying to pass off a photo of this old wreck and a scrawny mustang to this fine lady here, Fritz?" Cowboy only reined in the horse after it was close enough for Millie to scratch Dunnie's muzzle. "Glad to find you here, Fritz, there's some business I need to talk to you about."

Millie picked up her map where Fritz dropped it when he grabbed the tea tray away from Dunnie nuzzling the sugar container. Fritz backed against the camper, the cups on the silver tray rattled in his shaking hands. "Take that beast away."

Millie stood, slung the pack over one shoulder, and said, "Glad to see you again, Cowboy. I need to get on the road." She nodded toward the tea tray Fritz was holding, called out, "*Danke*," and waved goodbye to the two men.

28. Tossing and Turning

Mapping is fundamental to the process of lending order to the world.
—*Robert Rundstrum, 1926*

"Evaporative coolers don't cool worth squat when it's ninety degrees," Millie grumbled. Tossing and turning, pushing blankets and sheets off, she wanted to blame the hot summer night for her restlessness. She finally admitted it was the thoughts swirling in her mind and climbed out of bed at 2:00 a.m. The only way to quell them was to get up and organize them on paper.

She padded barefoot to the living room and found Ragged Ear fast asleep, curled up on the top of the laptop computer. She pushed him off and received a vexed look from golden eyes.

Millie opened her field notebook and spread out the BLM map. Her "doodles," as Fritz had called them, did not look anything like art to her. Flipping through field notes, Millie decided to continue plotting people sightings, just like she recorded plant locations. She penciled in Belva's walking stick where Herb Thompson's truck ran off the road and at a well pad where Millie had seen the faded green Subaru parked. Millie remembered another day when she watched the public lands protection Old Broad bounding up a distant, steep hillside like a desert bighorn.

It took longer to draw a music note in the several places where Millie had crossed paths with Buddy. By 3:30 a.m., marks of a cowboy hat, walking stick, pipe, and music notes were scattered across the map. She darkened the dollar sign, making it more distinct on the edge of the map. No doubt Mr. Sageman had been in some of these same locations.

Millie leaned back in her chair, finally feeling sleepy. Map details blurred. Certain clusters of figures emerged. Almost every time the music note or cowboy hat occurred, it was near San Juan cactus locations.

* * *

Millie was only a few minutes late getting to the office, despite being awake most of the night. She took one more look at the marked-up map and reached for the phone to call Robby, who was becoming more of a friend and confidant than Millie ever expected.

Robby answered on the first ring and suggested they meet in the conference room. Robby arrived carrying the two manila envelopes containing the preliminary autopsy reports.

"I've got something to tell you about that report," Millie said, "the one on the BIA archaeologist. Remember it identified the spike in his eye as *Yucca baccata*?" At Robby's nod, Millie continued, "Banana yucca grows mainly at high elevations. It's not likely to be down around that area where his body was found."

Robby pulled the autopsy report out of its envelope. "We just assumed Harrison Howdy walked off that cliff. The head injury could have happened someplace else, and his body thrown off the cliff to disguise it... the yucca put in his eye to make it look like an accident.

"When I found his truck the next day, it was all catawampus, run up on slick-rock. I suppose somebody else could have driven it there and wouldn't have left any tracks on that smooth rock. It never occurred to me to look farther beyond the truck, it seemed so plain what happened. It rained right after that, too, so tracks wouldn't show up anyway."

Millie unfolded the map on the table between them. "Don't laugh, I'm not the best artist in the world, but I see a pattern here of either Buddy or Cowboy showing up close to where the San Juan cactus are." Millie had to draw a legend at the bottom of the map for the symbols before Robby got the gist of what Millie was saying. "See? The hat equals Cowboy, the pipe is Fritz..."

Robby gave her a *what-the-hell* look and said, "Couldn't you just put their initials or something?"

"Oh, I didn't think of that."

Robby shifted her attention to the map. "We know for a fact that Cowboy is familiar with the T-one plot since he nearly rode his horse through it."

"And he told me about the new plot," Millie didn't want to admit it, but said, "I actually told Cowboy and Buddy that I keyed it out as bona fide San Juan cactus when I first looked at it."

"Who else would know where that San Juan cactus grows?" Robby asked, and then answered her own question. "Anybody in the office would have access to those original T and E surveys. Just snooping through that rat's nest that Herb called his office, anybody could have found that information."

"I might have mentioned finding the new one to Ben Benallee, too."

"Don't know him, but Momma Agnes told me you were hanging out with somebody on weekends. Pretty fast work, New Jersey girl. Why don't you have him on here? Maybe with a little heart symbol?" Robbie teased.

Millie groaned. "Momma Agnes is way too involved in other people's lives. Give me a break. Ben's just a friend. He told me he works for the Jicarilla Tribe. I only saw him once on BLM land. I was eating lunch at Split Lip overlook, and he'd been tracking a radio-collared deer. And, no, I'm not putting a little heart on this map."

Millie tapped the symbol on the top margin of the map, to take attention away from her reddening face. "You see this dollar sign here. Ben's grandfather, Harvey Sageman, gathers native plants for a living. He sells herbs and stuff. Ben says he goes all around here collecting plants. He even has a website where people can order from him."

"Tradition meets technology, I guess," Robby said. "Lots of people want cactus. The rare ones can bring a lot of money."

After studying the map a little longer, Robby picked up the other manila envelope. "I've been thinking about this report on Herb Thompson. The other day, Millie, you said ephedra is a stimulant, that it can speed up the heart. I wonder if it could have caused Herb's heart failure."

Comprehension spread across Millie's face. "Ephedra, the report said they found a particle of it in his mouth. I remember drinking Navajo tea when Ben took me to his family's sheep camp. There were little bits of the herb floating in the cup. If somebody drank Mormon tea made out of either fresh or dried stems, a little piece could get stuck between their teeth."

Robby stood and picked up the two envelopes. "I'll let you and Wirt know when I hear further. Meanwhile, keep your schedule open toward the end of the week. Fish and Wildlife Service is sending a Special Agent to investigate whether there's cactus rustling going on. Whoever they send won't just take our word for it. The agent will want to go through everything we showed Wirt and then go look at each of the plots."

Millie rubbed her eyes with the palms of her hands. She wanted all of this to go away.

"I know this isn't what you expected, plant lady."

29. Fascinating Four Corners Plants

Regional and national meetings of cactus and succulent societies result in a concentration of individuals who may, if unscrupulous, seriously deplete populations along their route to, or in the vicinity of, the convention.
—Richard Spellenberg, in *William A. Dick-Peddie, New Mexico Vegetation*

Millie trudged back to her cubicle, dropped the map on the desk, and slumped into the chair.

Trying to ease the throbbing in her head, Millie shoved a hand beneath her drooping hair to message her right temple. *Why don't I just pack up and go home? Robby is right, being in the middle of this crazy mess isn't what I signed up for. All I wanted to do was survey plants, not be told to guard a corpse or be at the disposal of federal agents investigating cactus stealing.*

This only seemed to drive the throbbing deeper. Millie switched hands to rub her left temple. Ephedra, Robby said, maybe that stimulated Herb Thompson's heart too much. If the yucca spike in that first guy's eye didn't get there by itself, maybe there was more to Herb's twisted body than just a heart attack.

Millie tapped her computer awake and connected to the Internet. She typed "Ephedra" in the search box. Confronted with thousands of results, Millie picked the Wikipedia link as a start, ignoring memories of her professors scolding students for relying on this non-refereed source.

She skimmed the text and began jotting notes on a yellow pad. As she jumped to related links, her fact-finding list grew:

-the genus Ephedra includes several species traditionally used for a variety of medicinal purposes

-Ephedra sinica has been used in China for more than 2,000 years

-the Chinese remedy, ma huang, is widely touted as a supplement for rapid weight-loss and improving athletic performance

-commercial distributors and Food and Drug Administration received thousands of reports of side effects from concoctions containing ephedrine, an extract from Ephedra sinica

-Food and Drug Administration banned supplements containing ephedrine in 2004

-side effects include anxiety, hallucinations, high blood pressure, fast heart rate, stroke. In severe cases, long-term disability or even sudden cardiac arrest may occur.

Millie sighed and grumped, "I'm missing something here. Wirt said he drank Mormon tea as a kid and he seems to be all right. Ben's grandfather sells bunches of it for tea."

"Who are you talking to?" A fluff of frizzy hair and curious eyes peeked over the top of the cubicle's divider.

"Oh, sorry. Was I talking out loud? Didn't mean to disturb you." She always welcomed a visit from Linda, the range conservationist who took Millie under her wing that first day on the job. They'd gone out to lunch a few times since. Linda had been with the Piñon Resource Area longer than any other staff, except for Momma Agnes. She seemed to take it upon herself to make everybody feel a part of BLM.

Linda came around the divider to Millie's cubicle and sat in the other chair. "I thought you had an angry rancher in here or something. Sounded like you were arguing."

"Guess I'm arguing with myself, common sense versus what I'm reading. What do you know about drinking Mormon tea?"

"Mormon tea? Ephedra? It's all over the place. Early Mormon settlers along the San Juan River used it as a spring tonic. Maybe because it stays green all winter and puts out fresh shoots in the spring."

"Then how come it was banned for diet pills?"

Linda laughed. "I know what your problem is. Look at the species, that harmful stuff comes from China. See, you wrote it right there, *Ephedra sinica*. What we have around here most commonly is *Ephedra viridis*. Same genus, different species. And you call yourself a botanist!"

Millie popped her forehead with the palm of her hand. "Linda, if you tell anyone I screwed up on this, I'll... I'll..."

"Ha, you're not the only person to make *that* mistake. When I first started working here, Momma Agnes called me up to the front desk. This scruffy looking dude was asking where he could find that 'bodacious Ephedra plant.' It was just about the time the FDA was looking at banning it. Seems he was going to stuff the trunk of his car with it, take it back to California and make his fortune selling it to fat ladies. That's what he said, 'fat ladies,'—the stupid idiot."

By the time they both stopped laughing, the pink was nearly gone from Millie's cheeks. Linda stood up to leave, saying, "You'd better be nice to me, or I'll add you to my *Ephedra* tales list."

"Deal, next lunch is on me. I'll take you to a world-famous restaurant."

"Yeah, like you're going to fly me to Paris or something."

"No, no... there's a McDonald's just three blocks from here."

"Smartass city kid, you got me." Linda stomped back to her cubicle.

Digging her heels into the carpet to propel the chair, Millie rolled over to the bookcase. She pulled out the massive taxonomic guide, *Flora of the Four Corners Region*, and rolled back to the desk. She found the genus *Ephedra* in the index and flipped to the pages describing species that occur in the San Juan River Basin.

Millie nodded as she read the detailed description. "*E. viridis* is... the source of Mormon tea... a yellowish drink made by steeping the branchlets in hot water."

When she came to the next sentence, Millie lifted the heavy tome with both hands and carried it to Linda's cubicle. "You've got to see this."

Linda read aloud the words above Millie's index finger. "'The tea has the flavor of an old stocking soaked in hot water.' Yuck. Only a smart-ass city kid could find something like that in a book that's a thousand pages long. Go back to your own tidy little office."

That settles that. Millie replaced the taxonomic guide on the bookshelf. That bit of Ephedra, that the autopsy said was caught in Herb's teeth, probably meant he drank some home-brewed Mormon tea. Just like that tea at Ben's grandparents' Sheep Camp. There were particles of leaves floating on the top. But it shouldn't have caused heart failure, even if he drank a gallon of it.

Straightening up the adjacent books, she came to the *Southwest Native Plant Symposium* publication, the same one that contained Dr. Arnold's and Herb Thompson's panel discussion on San Juan cactus. The volume bothered her sense of order because its oversized pages and spiral binding kept it from aligning evenly with other references on the shelf. When she pulled it out, it fell open on her lap. Dr. Arnold's name caught her eye. He had given a second presentation titled, "Fascinating Plants of the Four Corners." Intrigued, Millie skimmed the abstract.

> *Rare, poisonous and unexpected plants can be found along roadsides, in our parks, on stream banks of favorite fishing spots, and sometimes even on playgrounds. Other species grow only in the most inaccessible canyons, hide under rock overhangs, or cling to life on smooth slickrock.*

Millie continued reading the text of Dr. Arnold's presentation. She could almost hear his animated voice and wished she had been in the audience that day. His introduction started with, "Can you believe that orchids grow in New Mexico?" Millie shook her head in disbelief, but his talk went on to affirm this fact.

Dr. Arnold's longest discussion concerned poisonous plants. He started out with loco weed, *Oxytropis*, as causing problems for cattle and horses, tempting to the animals because it is one of the earliest green plants to come up in the spring. Next, he covered *Halogeton*, a particularly noxious invasive weed. If sufficient quantities are ingested to cause urinary damage, it can be fatal to sheep, an important economic resource for the Navajo.

The text continued:

> *Most important to recognize are those poisonous species that humans confuse with edible or medicinal plants. If you really want to do away with someone, there are some options growing within a fifty-mile radius of where we stand. Water hemlock, for example,* Cicuta maculata, *grows in wet areas along streams and irrigation ditches. It looks similar to other members of the* Apiaceae— *that's the Parsley Family—such as angelica and water parsnip, which Native American tribes and early settlers have long used as a food source and for medicinal purposes.*

The next sentence made Millie's hands start to shake.

> *Ingesting even small quantities of water hemlock can cause seizures. It stimulates the nervous system to the point that it can cause irregular heart function and respiratory failure. A lack of oxygen in the blood flow can produce a blue cast to the victim's skin.*

It was as if the passage was describing the image burned into Millie's mind of Herb's twisted body and ashen face in the gloom of the pickup's cab.

Water hemlock! I've got to find out whether it grows anywhere around where Herb Thompson was that day.

30. Warning

A friend may well be reckoned the masterpiece of nature.
—*Ralph Waldo Emerson, 1841*

Millie unrolled the GIS map Wirt gave her during their meeting on her first day at BLM. She scanned it for riparian areas, indicated by squiggly hash marks on the map. Then she spent several minutes looking for roads leading to the wetland areas. There weren't many, since BLM holdings consist of land that, historically, nobody wanted—the leftovers after settlers and ranchers claimed good agricultural land, Indian reservations were established, and railroad right-of-ways carved out.

She began with familiar roads, locating and drawing small circles around the T-one, T-two, and the Millie cactus locations. Expanding from these, she memorized the turn-offs that would take her to the longest strip of wetland shown on the map. It was at the bottom of Split Lip Canyon, where enough runoff moisture collected into a small stream to support water-dependent riparian vegetation year-round.

After making a quick trip to the copy machine to have the water hemlock taxonomic description in hand, Millie gathered up maps, passed by Momma Agnes's desk to sign out, and headed to the motor vehicle yard.

By late morning, she was maneuvering the Suburban along the bumpy road that snaked between the green belt of riparian vegetation and the towering walls of Split Lip Canyon.

Estimating that she was about mid-way up the canyon, Millie watched for a place where the road broadened. She made a three-point turn, which required nudging the front bumper, then the back bumper into the sagebrush that lined the narrow road. Now facing in the direction she came, she pulled into a spot wide enough that someone could pass by, in the unlikely event of another vehicle traveling this road.

Millie made sure the pages describing water hemlock were safely tucked into her pack and shoved a water bottle deeper into the side pocket before locking the Suburban. The narrow column of greenery beckoned just a half-football-field hike away.

Rabbitbrush grew taller and denser here, causing Millie to hold an arm in front of her face to deflect bits of chaff. Its branches terminated in clusters of bright yellow flowers, an early harbinger of the coming fall season.

Soon she was pushing through supple willow branches. She sniffed the air. The willows' fecund aroma, combined with the soil's dampness, brought back the sensation of walking with Aunt Nina inside an eastern deciduous forest. She stopped by the first cottonwood tree she came to, and ran a hand over the deep diamond shaped crevices along its massive trunk.

Seeking a standing pool of water, she continued weaving through the widely spaced cottonwoods. Some of the gnarly ancient sentinels had trunks broader than she could encircle with her arms. Young seedlings brushed her knees with shiny serrated leaves.

Lying in a curve along the bank and shaded by a sturdy cottonwood branch, a mossy basin cradled a child's swimming pool amount of water. Millie crouched down to watch a whirligig beetle making its erratic passage along the water's surface.

"You're lucky, little bug. This being August, most pools are gone along here, I hope the monsoon summer rains come before your little hot tub dries up."

Still in a crouch, Millie inspected the surrounding flora. This was the densest plant life she had seen on the Piñon Resource Area; leaves of saltgrass crowded among stems of tri-cornered rush.

There, just an arm's length away, she saw an umbel of puffy white flowers. Definitely an Apiaceae, member of the Parsley Family. It looked somewhat like the flat-topped, beautiful Queen Anne's lace that she had gathered with Aunt Nina, but this plant was taller and its flowers not so evenly arranged.

She estimated that it would take two cupped hands to surround one of the flower clusters, but had no intention of doing so. Even though descriptions of *Cicuta maculata* said the most poisonous part of the plant was the yellowish liquid found in its roots, the literature cited numerous cases of poisoning caused by people mistaking the leaves for an edible green.

Millie opened the copied pages and held the leaf diagram next to the plant. The leaves, with narrow, deeply toothed leaflets, matched. She fished under her hair for the magnifying loupe's string and pulled the small, silver instrument from under her shirt. Lifting it to her eye, she bent close to the leaf until its one distinguishing attribute came into focus. Veins extended from the center of each leaflet, not to the tips of its toothed edges, but to the notches in between the tips.

Millie took a few steps back from where the whirligig

beetle was mindlessly bumping against a tangle of stalks. She looked along the water's edge and counted four more flowery tops of the plant. *Confirmed, poison water hemlock occurs on the Piñon Resource Area.*

The text of Dr. Arnold's presentation materialized in her mind. *Anyone wanting to do away with someone could find the extremely poisonous plants nearby.* "I've got to tell Robby and Wirt about this."

* * *

On the way out of the riparian zone's cooling environment, Millie stopped and reached for the water bottle that always seemed to dodge her grasp. She caught a willow branch in the other hand, whipped it back and forth, then bent the pliable stem double. *That's how I was until this summer. I bent to the family's wishes, to the professors' demands.*

She twined the stem over and under her fingers. This was the coyote willow that formed the strong basket Grandmother Sageman gave her. Shaped by caring hands, cured by desert sun, and woven together for a purpose, the basket was strong, enduring. With Wirt, Robby, and Belva, she was part of the brotherhood and sisterhood holding the line for conservation. *Together we must stop cactus being murdered by shovel.*

Back at the Suburban, Millie checked her watch. She needed to return directly to the office in order to catch Robby before quitting time. She ducked under the uplifted rear hatch to get a granola bar out of the stash of snacks. A familiar shadow glided overhead, followed by a demanding shriek.

Millie waved to the raven. The bird's back flashed silver as it circled and made another low pass. She wondered if it was eyeing the granola bar in her hand. But it flapped hard, cackling in its raspy voice, and flew toward the cliff, pulling her attention in that direction.

She was directly below the Split Lip Canyon Overlook, looking up at the spot where she and Wirt had lunch and where she first laid eyes on Ben Benallee. That seemed a lifetime ago.

The raven made a tight circle around the lunch spot just above the ponderosa treetops. Emitting another scream, it plunged downward, barely missing the cliff's edge. Millie saw movement at the overlook. A figure stood up, binoculars obscuring the face.

Millie gave a hesitant wave. The figure stepped backward, leaving only the uncompromising rock face in view. *This is unreal. I'm being watched, just like before.*

She slammed the rear hatch closed and ran to the driver's side door. For the first half mile, the raven flew in front of the vehicle, low over the road. Gradually it flapped higher and higher as it escorted her out of the canyon.

When it whirled away, Millie's eyes followed. *Thank you, Raven. You were warning me.*

* * *

By the time Millie reached the intersection with Lejos Canyon Road, she had pretty well talked herself out of the farcical notion that a bird guided her out of harm's way. *Why wouldn't somebody at a scenic outlook have binoculars? But why did the person retreat so fast?*

After a quick glance to check for oncoming vehicles, Millie veered onto Lejos Canyon Road in the direction of Wellstown. A vehicle suddenly appeared just inches from the Suburban's back bumper. *You must be in an awful hurry, dude.* She tapped the brake and pulled over to let the nudnik pass. Instead, the vehicle came along side, and then angled ahead, leaving Millie no choice but to slow down or drive into the sagebrush. The raven's scream rang again in her mind.

The bulky shape coalesced into the familiar green camper. She slowed to a stop and sighed. *Fritz Müller again. He can't be expecting me to sit and gossip right here.*

Hoping he'd get the hint, she did not stir more than to roll down the window.

"Were you looking for anything special today, Madam Millie?" There were underarm sweat rings on his usually pristine white shirt.

At first, she could not grasp this abrupt greeting. "It was you, wasn't it, with the binoculars at the overlook."

"You were at one of the few places with water here." His stern face obscured the sky. "What were you looking for?"

"Looking for?... I was, ah, examining different plant habitats."

"What were you looking for?" His voice was louder, menacing.

She had made a mistake before of talking about finding the new cactus location. She wasn't about to mention finding a poisonous plant. "Why wouldn't I be surveying there. That's my job, Fritz, cataloging plants on BLM land. So why were you watching me?"

"Give me the map you kept from me at my camp." There was no asking in his voice. It was a demand.

Millie glanced in her rearview mirror, about to shift into reverse. Fritz, anticipating her intent, wrenched open the door and yanked her arm, trying to pull her from the vehicle.

"Stop it, Fritz. What's wrong with you!"

Feeling his grip suddenly release, she dropped back onto the seat. Then she saw why Fritz was backing away. Buddy stepped next to the open door. The Dagun logo showed through the dust cloud kicked up by the vehicles.

"Is everything all right here?" His affable voice was directed at Millie, but he was eyeing Fritz.

"Of course. I was just saying goodbye to Madam Millie." With that, Fritz strode to his camper, started the engine, and made a tight turn around in the road. He did not look in their direction as he sped past.

"What was that all about?"

Millie unbuckled the seatbelt and stood up, steadying herself with one hand on the doorframe. "I don't know, Buddy, but I know I'm glad you came along just now. Fritz is acting like a jerk. He keeps trying to get at my maps."

"Why? All he's interested in is mustangs and taking pretty pictures."

Millie drew a long, slow breath and stepped back from Buddy. The music note symbol on the map—why was it that Buddy always seemed to show up around locations of certain uncommon plants.

"I can only guess. Fritz told me that Herb used to show him places to photograph cactus flowers. Maybe he wants to get photos of the rarer ones, like San Juan cactus, and thinks he could find them on his own if he had the maps."

Buddy pulled off his cap and rubbed his palm across his forehead, removing a rim of sweat. "Maybe so. He seems like a pretty determined fellow, wanting to get pictures of anything western. I know about where those cactus are, because I saw you come down the trail from the petroglyph boulder, but I never told Fritz about it." He turned and looked in the direction the green camper disappeared. "Of course, I did mention it to our drilling foreman, because I know we can't do anything anywhere near archeological ruins or endangered plants on BLM land."

Millie dropped back onto the seat and rubbed an index finger back and forth over her lips, wishing she'd been a more circumspect about announcing her find that day to Buddy and Cowboy. How many more people know about the location? She felt herself swaying on Wirt's tightrope.

Buddy put a calloused hand on the door and gently eased it closed. "You go on ahead, Miss Millie. I'll just follow along behind, make sure no one bothers you again."

Every now and then, Millie checked the rear view mirror, getting reassuring glimpses of the orange flag flying over Buddy's truck. It would be past quitting time when she got back to the office. She focused on formulating the messages that she would leave on Wirt's and Robby's voice mail. The memory of the raven leading her out of the canyon was mystifying, but its warning was real.

31. Transformation

Mission - protect wildlife and plant resources.
—U.S. Fish & Wildlife Service Office of Law Enforcement

When Millie arrived at the office the next morning, her phone was blinking with two messages. Robby's was concise. "Next time you get harassed on BLM land anywhere, anytime, you call me. Use my cell phone. Doesn't matter if it's after hours."

The second message from Wirt was similar, except he added, "Meet me and Robby in my office at 9:00 a.m. The Fish and Wildlife Service Special Agent is here and wants to talk to you."

Millie approached Wirt's office with head down. The meeting had to be about her screwing up by not immediately reporting yesterday's incident.

She nearly tripped over the blue-jeans-clad legs stretched out just inside Wirt's office. Her eyes traveled from the man's scuffed boots to the cowboy hat resting on his lap to his blue-gray eyes. The slim figure appeared totally at ease in the same chair Millie had occupied on her first meeting with the area manager.

"Excuse me, ma'am," he said, drawing his legs back so she could pass. His voice was familiar, as well as his demeanor—exuding self-confidence.

Millie saw Robby sitting in one of the two folding chairs brought in for the meeting. She eased into the nearer one, putting herself between Robby and the visitor, all facing the AM's desk.

Robby shuffled her chair over a little to give Millie more room, but she, too, was staring at the man. *Why would Cowboy be in Wirt's office?*

Wirt appeared relaxed, leaning back in his chair. "Millie, let's hear about your run-in with Fritz Müller yesterday."

Millie heard Robby's intake of breath. "Wirt, maybe I should debrief Millie in the conference room first." Robby's nod toward the visitor could not be more telling—*let's not discuss BLM affairs in front of this outsider.*

Momma Agnes's plump figure filled the doorway, hands on her hips. "Wirt, where are your manners. Agent Anderson, would you like some coffee?"

"Sorry, Andy, would you like coffee?"

"Not now, but thank you kindly."

Momma Agnes gave a disappointed "harrumph" and retreated after giving a message to the Agent. "Tell your Tio Eladio his aunt's cousin's mother-in-law sends her regards."

"I guess I have neglected my manners," Wirt said. "I haven't done proper introductions. Officer Roberta Ramirez, meet Special Agent Andrew Anderson. And I know you've already met Miss Millicent Whitehall."

Robby recovered first, "You're shittin' me! *You're* with Fish and Wildlife?"

With the grace of a mountain lion, Cowboy rose and bowed low, making a sweeping gesture with his hat. "Special Agent Andrew Anderson, US Fish and Wildlife Service, Southwest region, at your service. Call me Andy."

Wirt's grin revealed his delight at getting one over on his law enforcement officer. "Now, Andy, if you'd pull the door closed, we can get back to what happened yesterday."

"Hold on," Robby broke in, "you can't just stop there. I've seen you riding some nag on the Piñon Resource Area off and on for the last few years. What's up with that?"

"You've got me there. Okay, here's my story in a nutshell. When I finished up my service in Iraq, I went through kind of a hard readjustment when I got back to the States. My uncle, Eladio Gomez, took me in. He has a ranch and runs a few cattle on a BLM grazing allotment. Worked me to the bone, he did."

"So, what that got to do with being a Special Agent?" Robby snapped.

"Uncle Eladio had me gentle his horses, and in time, the cruelty I saw over there... the memories. I guess they just got sweated out of my system. Once I got my head straight, I decided more structure in my life would keep me on the straight and narrow. I looked into law enforcement, but couldn't see myself as a city cop. To make a long story short, I pursued law enforcement with the Fish and Wildlife Service, maybe because I wanted to protect what I loved about the West and I had the right training.

"So, yes," he addressed Robby, "you've seen me every once in a while. Whenever I get any length of time off between assignments, I come up here to help out Uncle Eladio. He's getting on in years and can't keep track of his cattle like he used to."

Robby's voice still held a note of reservation. "Millie told me that you're the one that clued her in about that other cactus plot, that you hobbled a horse there overnight. That doesn't sound like an every once in a while visit to herd cattle."

He turned to Millie, "It's true, Miss Whitehall, I did hobble Dunnie near there. I was hoping you'd confirm what I thought was San Juan cactus. I didn't know it would

221

put you in danger."

Robby was like a bulldog. "That still doesn't explain why you've been hanging around where San Juan cactus happens to be located."

"Our Southwest Region sees the most cactus rustling. We've been watching this Fritz Müller for some time now. His pattern is to fly in every two or three years, rent a camper, and spread it around that he leads photography tours for foreign tourists. We had some evidence that it wasn't all on the up and up. Since I work out of the Albuquerque office, when he showed up again last month, I was requested to go undercover. I've been hanging around in the vicinity to track his movements."

Millie wasn't sure just when his manner had changed from aw-shucks cowboy to authoritative, but he was now sitting ramrod straight. Like herself, Wirt and Robby were leaning in his direction, listening intently.

Agent Anderson reached beneath his chair for a leather case. When he opened it, the zipping sound seemed loud in the closed office. He brought out a card that Millie recognized at once.

He handed the card to Wirt, who read it out loud. "Land of Enchantment Wild Horse Tours. Capture the Spirit of the West. Fantastic Images of Wild Mustangs Guaranteed. Frederick (Fritz) Müller Photographer, Exporter, Adventurer".

Wirt stretched over his desk to give it to Millie. She already knew what it said, so she passed it on to Robby. "Wild mustangs guaranteed, exporter... It ought to read 'sleezeball,' too."

"That part about wild mustangs is why it was so easy for me to slip into Müller's circle of criminal behavior." Agent Anderson secured the card back into the case. "Müller's cover of running photography trips seemed legit at first. Then when he was working this area two years ago, one of his so-called clients tried to sneak a San Juan cactus through airport screening. It was wrapped in tin-foil lodged between the legs of a tripod in the luggage."

He shook his head and broke into a Cheshire Cat grin. "If the lamebrain had only wrapped it in cloth, it might have passed as padding in the tripod case."

Robby laughed, but Millie spoke up, "It must have come from either the T-one or T-two plot. It could even have been one that Herb Thompson remembered being there, that he was referring to as 'gone.' It was probably dead within two months after the guy got back home."

"Actually, Miss Whitehall, it was a woman returning to Germany and the cactus never left the United States." He seemed a little perturbed at the suggestion that the Fish and Wildlife Service would let an endangered plant be transported out of the United States. "It was confiscat-ed and sent to an authorized Plant Rescue Center that's designated as a repository for seized plant material. They do their best to help any live specimen recover. But the good thing that came out of this was that, in exchange for not being fined, this pseudo-photographer gave us a lot of information about how one Mr. Müller operated.

"The woman said that during the day, Fritz would drive her and the three other so-called photographers around, looking for mustangs. She even griped that they never got close enough for a good shot of wild stallions fighting." Again, he shook his head, seeming to be incredulous about the tourists' gullibility.

"On two separate nights, she confessed, they went on what Fritz called 'his special capture.' That meant that they were going after cactus. She bragged that digging up the mini San Juan cactus was easy. It was ripping off pads of prickly pear and claret cup stems that hurt like the dickens. Seems the day after such raids, Fritz would pick them up at their hotel in Wellstown. He'd be carrying mailing boxes for them to pack their booty in and take them to the Post Office so they could mail souvenirs of the great American West to their home addresses."

"Son of a bitch," Robby blurted out, "he had it all planned."

"Except that one incident, the one we caught on to, with the tin foil woman. For some reason she didn't play by Fritz's rules, didn't send all her specimens in the mail. Gee, imagine that, a cactus thief not playing by the rules.

"After checking his entry tourist visa, it looks like this was Müller's sixth time coming to the US, half of them landing at Albuquerque's Sunport and half at the Phoenix Sky Harbor airport. My superiors want to nail this guy, but need to have hard evidence, catch him in possession. Since they knew I was familiar with this community, they put me on the detail.

"So, one day I just ambled up to Fritz's camp on Dunnie, and pretty soon I was feeding him a line that I knew all about mustangs, that I could make sure his clients would get up-close pictures."

"Wait a minute," Millie reared back in her chair, making it bump against the bookcase behind her. "That was a line you were giving me, too, about working for BLM on wild horse roundups?"

"Sort of." Andy put his hat on and did the cowboy thing of pulling it down to shade his eyes.

Wirt came to his rescue. "It's not so much 'works for' but 'coordinates with.' Fish and Wildlife contacted me about Agent Anderson's undercover assignment on the Piñon Resource Area. I gave permission for him to put hay out to bait a horse herd that roams that area."

Andy pushed his hat back and took up the story. "I told

Fritz how I could lure mustangs by putting a couple bales of hay and a salt lick in a clearing for a few days before his clients were due. He couldn't believe his good luck, a real cowboy making him look good. Said he'd give me a hundred dollars for helping with each group, more if they got pictures of foals. I'm pretty sure he wasn't planning to divvy up any of the under-the-table money he got for the cactus they'd dig up."

"So that was what you meant at his camp the day I was there? That was the 'business' you wanted to discuss?" Millie asked.

"Exactly. Müller told me he has a group arriving this week. He wants lots of horses showing up one hour before sunset to get photos in twilight. So I figure the night after that they'll go for cactus."

Millie noticed his hands clenching and unclenching the leather case. "To me, stealing our natural heritage is reprehensible, similar to sneaking sacred Native American artifacts out of the country. Both are national treasures, and our agencies are mandated to protect them."

No one was going to contradict that statement. Wirt snapped them back to the purpose of the meeting. "Tell us what happened yesterday, Millie."

She took a deep breath, deciding whether to start at the end or the beginning. It was what she first intended to communicate to Wirt and Robby that won out.

"Remember the way Herb Thompson looked that... that day?" None of them wanted to re-live that scene, so she rushed on with her findings. "It was water hemlock. He was poisoned with water hemlock."

"Wait a minute," Robby leaned aside to get a better read on Millie's face. "That preliminary autopsy report said he had taken in Ephedra, maybe from drinking Mormon tea. Ephedra was banned as a weight-loss miracle because it caused side effects, like speeding up the heart. We all knew he had heart problems."

"I was wrong. The most common species around here used for Mormon tea is *Ephedra viridis*. It's not the one that contains the ephedrine stimulant. That's *Ephedra sinica*. It comes from Asia. Linda straightened me out on that," Millie said, giving credit where credit was due.

"I did more research. Everything points to water hemlock, *Cicuta maculata*. It grows in Split Lip Canyon. I went there yesterday to find it."

"Girlfriend, I'd say you're pretty good on figuring out plants," Robby said. "*Cicuta*... what? Even sounds cruel."

"*Cicuta maculata.* It's one of the deadliest plants on this continent. Its toxin, cicutoxin, affects the nervous system and causes seizures that can interfere with heart function. When that happens, there's less oxygenation of the blood, which is what gave that bluish cast to... the skin." Millie avoided saying the dead man's name, it made these clinical terms too personal.

"You've got to be..." Robby started to say, got a stern look from Wirt, and quashed the expletive. "I thought he was all twisted like that and looked so bad because of a heart attack."

"I think that's why Fritz almost ran me off the road when I drove out of Split Lip Canyon yesterday. The raven showed me somebody was at the overlook watching me with binoculars. I'm pretty sure that it was Fritz because he looked like he'd run down the trail to his camper and waited for me by the intersection. His face was all red." Millie rushed on, not wanting to discuss the raven part. "Fritz tried to yank me out of the vehicle. Just then, Buddy Maddox drove up, got out and walked right over close to Fritz. Then Fritz got all smiley, like nothing happened, and took off.

"That's what I was heading back to tell you. It was water hemlock, it contains a yellowish liquid in its roots. Even if it has a strong taste, it wouldn't be noticeable mixed into Mormon tea."

Wirt nodded in agreement. "I think you've got something there. Good thing Buddy Maddox come along just then."

"There's more that I've figured out. Fritz camps around the Split Lips overlook. That's high up, you get that great view for miles. It's Ponderosa pine habitat up there, and that's where you usually see banana yucca, *Yucca baccata*."

"So...?" Robbie said.

"So, remember in the autopsy report? The yucca stalk in that guy's eye they analyzed? It was *Yucca baccata*."

"Right, I remember you saying that. That's the one that grows at higher elevations."

"I can see where you're going with this, Millie," Wirt said. "Where Harrison Howdy's body was, at the bottom of that cliff, is at a lower elevation. You'll see narrowleaf yucca around there, but that banana yucca spike probably came from somewhere around Fritz's camp."

"Well that clinches it for me. I had my suspicions about this guy after I talked to Belva Banks." Robby now had their full attention. "Remember, Millie, we talked about who could have been watching you with binoculars that morning after the landslide closed the road? So I had a casual conversation with Belva after that—just generally visiting about happenings on the Piñon Resource Area."

Robby glanced at the Special Agent. He nodded as if to indicate he understood her meaning of 'casual conversation' as pumping for information without the informant knowing it.

"Our favorite Old Broad for Public Lands Protection mentioned a very important piece of information. She said she was driving around a couple of months ago and saw Fritz walking along the road. He flagged her down. She said Fritz looked like hell, worn out. She drove him several miles back to his camper. Actually, she called him, 'that pantywaist German dude' and roundly cursed all tourists that go wandering around in the desert, thinking they can just flag down a taxi to get home."

Wirt didn't blink an eye, but Andy replied to Robby, "Sounds like you and this Belva would really hit it off."

Robby responded with a dismissive snort. She made a show of flipping open the stenographer's notebook she had brought along. "I remembered taking a call from an irate drilling foreman. He told me some crazy woman in a green Outback drove right up to the drill rig and started giving his crew hell about littering."

"So, we know Belva Banks was on the Resource Area that day," Wirt said.

Robby started chuckling as she quoted from her notes, "That foreman, he said, 'The hands just finished lunch and maybe there were a couple sandwich wrappers lying around, but that wasn't any cause for the kind of language she used.'" This got Wirt laughing, too.

"Anyway, he wanted me to know they had everything cleaned up and were in full compliance with every single regulation. If I got any complaints from some tree-hugger, well, 'it just wasn't fair, that's all.' I assured him that if any complaint came in, I'd talk to him first about it.

"Belva didn't remember just when she gave Fritz a ride to his camper, but she did say he made the weakest tea she ever tasted." Then Robby's voice dropped a notch. "That call from the drilling foreman—it came in the same day that Harrison Howdy's body showed up at the bottom of the cliff."

32. Back In The Saddle

The current estimated on-range wild horse and burro population is 81,951.
—Bureau Of Land Management Wild Horse and Burro Program, 2018

Part one of the plan was working. Cowboy pushed Dunnie out of the shade just as the two vehicles reached the designated meeting spot on Lejos Canyon Road. The saddle creaked when Andy leaned down over Dunnie's neck to look into the driver's side window. "Now remember, Millie, as soon as you get a few markers around the T-two plot, and show Robby where it's safe to hide vehicles without disturbing any cactus, you go directly back to the office. Wirt will be expecting you to check in with him."

Millie nodded, not sure whether to address him as Cowboy, Special Agent Anderson, or just Andy. She reached out and rubbed Dunnie's soft nose. She felt a blush on her cheeks at the memory of their first encounter when she scolded Cowboy for nearly riding across the T-one plot, when all along he knew about it and was bent on protecting the endangered San Juan cactus.

The Special Agent, now indistinguishable from a working cowboy, reined Dunnie toward Robby's vehicle. Millie watched in the rear view mirror as he reiterated the plan with Robby, who was parked directly behind her. When Cowboy pushed Dunnie into the sagebrush in the direction of Fritz's camp, Millie started the engine and proceeded to the T-two plot, with Robby following.

Millie was uneasy. There were too many unknowns here. Andy said he would ride up to Fritz's camp and keep him talking about when the next group of tourists would be arriving. This would ensure she and Robby had enough time to complete their task at the T-two plot. This she didn't mind. It was his uncertainty about the next steps that Millie found unsettling.

They had gone over and over this plan before leaving Wirt's office. Agent Anderson laid out his strategy of staking out the T-two plot for the next few nights. "I'm pretty certain Müller will target the T-two plot. He probably thinks he's covered his tracks by eliminating Harrison Howdy and Herb Thompson when they got on to him about raiding the T-one plot, but fears that returning to the same site might get noticed. I expect he will scope out the T-two plot and dig up a couple specimens just to whet his clients' appetites for one of his 'special capture' nighttime excursions."

His voice took on a hesitant tone, "I couldn't get Müller pinned down as to when his so-called photographers are to arrive. I just don't know if he'll hit tonight, tomorrow night, or when. I've alerted local law enforcement about the possible need for back up. They'll know where to come when I give the word."

Millie glanced in the rearview mirror and saw that Robby had dropped back about three car lengths, avoiding the worst of the dust cloud kicked up by the Suburban. Millie feared for her friend. Robby had insisted that no stakeout was going to take place on BLM land without her. Her dark eyes had flashed in anticipation and she rubbed her hands together. "We're going to nail that bastard red-handed."

Millie recalled Wirt's words that turned the morning's meeting from piecing together past events to laying out the current arrangements. His reaction to Robby's revelation that Fritz was near the grisly scene where the archaeologist's body was found seemed to hit him like the kick of a mule. Wirt's voice was angry.

"It's just speculation right now, what we have on Müller. But it looks like he was the one that parked Harrison Howdy's truck on slickrock, threw his body over the cliff to make it look like an accident, then caught a ride with Belva to get back to his camp. If Herb Thompson figured out that Fritz was digging up cactus, well... it would be just like that tough old geezer to go right up to his camper, pound on the door, and cuss him out. Ever the gentleman, Fritz probably offered Herb a cup of Mormon tea and just happened to add a little water hemlock to the cup. Must have been an excruciating way to die. This man is dangerous."

* * *

Andy's nonchalant whistling to the tune of "*I'm an old cowhand from the Rio Grande,*" announced his arrival. Fritz yawned as he stepped out of the camper, giving Andy the impression that he had been taking an afternoon siesta.

Andy dismounted, led Dunnie a short distance from the camper, and dropped the reins on the cleared surface of the well pad, where there was no vegetation to tempt the horse to drift, forgetting his ground tie manners.

Fritz yawned again as Cowboy approached, but recovered quickly, greeted his guest, and suggested a cup of tea. Cowboy plopped in the one chair under the canopy and threw up his hands. "No, no tea. But a glass of cold water would be mighty welcome."

Fritz disappeared back into the camper, pulling the door closed behind him, not allowing Andy a glimpse of the inside. He returned with a second chair in one hand, two glass mugs dangling from his other hand and two brown bottles tucked under an arm. When Fritz leaned down to place glasses and bottles on the table between them, a cell phone dropped out of his shirt pocket and landed on the ground. With a disgusted grunt, he picked it up, blowing on it and wiping it with a handkerchief until every speck of sand was gone. He gave it one last inspection and laid it on the table.

Meanwhile, Cowboy picked up the offered bottle and turned it slowly, as if inspecting the label. "*Negra Modelo.* Brewed in Mexico.*" He twisted the cap, feeling its firm resistance and hearing a reassuring pop. The bottle had not been tampered with.

Tossing back a big swallow right from the bottle, he said, "Fritz, you know how to treat a fellow."

Fritz opened his bottle and followed suit, leaving the two frosted mugs dripping moisture on the table. "To what do I owe the honor of your visit?" Fritz said, and mirrored Cowboy's gesture of swiping his shirtsleeve across his lips.

Keeping his voice casual and taking his time to answer, Cowboy began with, "Regarding our little arrangement, Fritz, I need to get a better handle on just when you expect those tourists. Hay is expensive, you know. I don't want to be feeding those mustangs any longer than necessary."

From this, the mustang expert went into a lengthy explanation of how he'd lure the horses to the designated clearing and how he'd need to lay out enough hay for all members of the band to get a share, not just the most dominant animals. Cowboy's discourse on a wild herd's hierarchy held the fascinated German's total attention.

"So you see, Fritz, for me to do a top-notch job of putting genuine wild horses in front of your photographers, I need you to tell me just when you want those cayuses there."

"You're going to be a big help with my business," Fritz lifted his bottle in salute to his partner. "The mustangs need to be in the right spot the afternoon that my group arrives. I will be picking them up at the Wellstown airport at 9:30 on..."

The cell phone on the table rang and vibrated simultaneously. Fritz put it to his ear. "Good afternoon, my friend." Cowboy grabbed his beer and tossed back the last few drops, to conceal his frustration at the interruption just as Fritz was about to give a vital piece of information.

Fritz listened intently, keeping his eyes directed at the rivulets of water that were creeping along the table from condensation on the chilled glasses. Fritz said nothing more to the caller until concluding with, "Thank you, my friend. You will be well rewarded for this."

Fritz's voice was tense, "I apologize. I must end our visit. I have important business to attend to." He gathered up the glasses and empty bottles and rushed into the camper.

Agent Anderson snatched the cell phone, hit the recent calls button, and committed to memory the phone number that appeared on the screen.

The door opened just as Cowboy was pulling his arm back from replacing the phone in the same spot Fritz had left it. He had to get Fritz back on track. "I thought our business was important. When did you say your clients would arrive?"

A distracted Fritz collapsed the table and began taking down the canopy, making Cowboy back out of its shade. "They come two days from now. The mustangs must be in place Saturday morning."

Agent Anderson casually draped an arm over Dunnie's saddle as he watched the green camper spray gravel when Fritz pulled away.

As soon as he believed Fritz could no longer see him, the Special Agent punched the phone number into his own cell phone.

"Piñon Resource Area. How may I direct your call?" Cowboy pulled the phone away from his ear and looked at the screen to check whether he had dialed correctly. It was Momma Agnes's voice.

"This is Special Agent Anderson. Put me through to Wirt."

Andy's rushed words to the area manager made Dunnie restless. Andy gave the reins a firm jerk downward, and the horse stood still long enough for him step into the saddle.

Atop Dunnie, Andy reined the anxious horse in tight circles while dividing his attention between keeping an eye on the green camper as it bumped away from the well site and alerting Wirt to his worst fears.

When the camper reached the main road and turned, not toward Wellstown, but in the direction of the T-two plot, Cowboy Andy tucked the phone into his pocket and urged the horse into a gallop.

* * *

The area manager slammed the phone down. "That's crazy. Who would be making a call to Fritz Müller from this office?"

Momma Agnes rushed into Wirt's office. "If Andy had gotten the extension number off that cell, I could tell you in a New York minute whose office it came from. What are we going to do, Wirt?"

He didn't bother acknowledging her pesky habit of neglecting to hang up her phone after transferring a call to his office. He lost that battle with Momma Agnes long ago. He knew she had listened to every word the Special Agent said.

"Call Robby on the radio, and if she doesn't answer, try her mobile, then Millie's. I just hope they're in cell tower range. Then check the sign-out board. See if any of our range cons or petroleum techs are on that side of the Resource Area today."

Reaching for his phone, Wirt said, "I'm calling 911 emergency dispatch to see if they can contact anyone in that vicinity. They can put the word out to report any sightings of a green camper. There's got to be oil and gas field hands out there."

Before he pushed the numbers, he saw the anguish on Momma Agnes's face and prodded her to action. "Make those calls, then tell TJ to bring my vehicle around front—and have it gassed up."

33. Keep Talking

When you take a dig at someone, make sure that they don't
have a bigger shovel.
—*Anthony T. Hincks*

Millie slowed, leaned closer to the windshield, and
looked up toward the petroglyph boulder. She would
like nothing more than to stop and check on her favorite
San Juan cactus plot. The delicate fuchsia blossoms of late
spring would now be round nubbins containing nearly
mature seeds.

She repressed the dark thoughts that if she had never found this unrecorded population, she would not be
accompanying law enforcement officers to catch a murderer. And Herb Thompson would still be alive.

Robby pulled next to the Suburban and glowered
through the window. Millie pressed the accelerator,
resuming normal speed. Robby dropped back a couple car
lengths.

The Lejos Canyon Road looped away from the wash
where runoff from heavy rainstorms produced steep
banks along the waterway. Millie focused on the road
ahead where it ran close to the canyon wall. The Suburban's
ancient radio crackled. She turned it off. No hope of receiving any radio signal for the next several miles.

Robby's Chevy Tahoe was right on her back bumper again. Millie speeded up.

On the narrow spur road leading to the T-two plot, rabbitbrush crowded among the sagebrush and both pushed their new summer growth over the road's edge. No longer did Millie perceive the landscape as sparse. She knew the gray-green swale of sagebrush concealed colorful orange and red lichens clinging to rocks and prickly pear cactus flaunting maroon seedpods.

Millie parked near the same spot where she had picked up the d-CON package. Robby pulled in behind her. The two women headed in opposite directions to begin their assignments.

Millie twirled a roll of orange marker tape around her thumb and stopped at the first San Juan cactus plant. She took ten steps back and looked for a palm-sized stone or heavy stick. The plan was to put short lengths of marker tape at ground level, in widely spaced intervals, such that they would be inconspicuous to someone casually viewing the plot.

When Robby jogged up, Millie took a last look around. "I've got the three sides facing the road marked. Follow me and I'll point out where they are."

As they walked the marked perimeter, Robby reported on her efforts. "I've got a pretty good handle on where we can park at least three vehicles so they can't be seen by someone coming in on this road. Someone that—let's say—might pretend to be a photographer, leading not very innocent tourists around to see mustangs. There's a very faint, old track about a tenth of a mile back. You wouldn't notice it if you weren't looking for it. Might even go back to horse and wagon times. It follows around a big boulder where there are traces of a fallen down corral. I think it's the remains of an old homestead. I bet there's a foundation somewhere beyond that corral."

Halfway to the vehicles, Millie stopped, waited until Robby was by her side, and turned back to face the cactus plot. "Now, can you tell exactly where those markers are, so you can keep anybody from stepping on the cactus?"

Robby let her voice take on a quiver and dropped a troubled expression over her face. "I don't know, Millie, these cactus are mighty small, easy to step on, and not feel anything but a squish."

Millie's mouth dropped open, speechless.

Robby bumped her shoulder against Millie's, laughing at her companion's intensity, "Come on, let's get a granola bar, and I'll show you that old corral. Then you head back to the office. I'll wait for Andy, um, maybe Cowboy. No telling which role he'll show up as."

Millie had to be content with hoping Robby's keen observation skills would suffice in recognizing the low markers she had put out. After dark, anyone on the stakeout focused on watching for Fritz Müller wouldn't be watching where they stepped. She wanted to stay, regardless of the plan and Wirt's order to return to the office.

Robby poked her toe against a half-buried object in the middle of what had been a corral. She pulled out a two-foot length of rope, grimy and weather-beaten. "Look, it's rawhide. Probably from a long reata they used to break horses. The stories this place could tell."

Robby cocked her head as they rounded the boulder on the way back. "Thought I might have heard my radio." She finished crumpling the granola bar wrapper and stuffed it in the upper pocket of her tan shirt. "Guess it was just this."

The crackling came again as they were halfway to the vehicles. Robby sprinted ahead and was fiddling with the radio knobs when Millie caught up.

"Can't get anything but static between these canyon walls. Probably just the usual 'where you at' police chatter. But I should check in with Momma Agnes in case it was her calling. I'll try my cell."

Millie waited by the open driver's side door. Robby shook her head. "No bars. Try yours."

"No luck on mine, either."

Robby glanced at her watch. "I'll just run back to Lejos Canyon Road and drive up to where it tops out on the mesa and try again. I'll be back by the time Andy the Cowboy gets here. And you'll be well on your way back to the office, right?"

Millie took the not-so-subtle hint that she was dismissed, gave a goodbye wave, and went to the Suburban. The rear hatch was still open from their snack foray. She flipped up the lid of a cooler and pulled out a fresh water bottle, closed the hatch, and walked a few yards toward the T-two plot. Satisfied that no orange tape was visible from the road, she turned back.

Caught between concern for the cactus and orders to return to the office, Millie paused next to the Suburban. Engine noise made Millie glance down the road. She assumed Robby was returning.

Millie froze. Fritz made direct eye contact with her as he passed. He wrenched the camper over and backed up until he bumped the Suburban, blocking her vehicle from making any escape forward.

Immediately, Fritz was standing in front of her. The side mirror protruded on her right, his gray eyes just inches away bored into hers, and the shovel he banged on the ground prevented her from moving to the left. She was trapped against the door.

"Get away from me, Fritz."

"A little cuckoo bird informed me that you are here

with a law enforcement officer. Where is he?"

"I'm just surveying plants, like I told you I was the other day. It's nothing that concerns you." Millie could smell the scent of pipe tobacco on his clothes. *Where was Robby? He doesn't know the BLM ranger is a 'she.' Or else he is on to Agent Anderson.*

"Do not act like a child with me, Madam Millie, or harm will come to you."

"Back off, Fritz Müller. Any harm to me will result in your never getting back into this country."

"I can make it look like an accident, like those two others."

He seemed to be enjoying this cat-and-mouse game. He took a step back, moved his hand to the top of the shovel, tipping it back and forth. Daring her to run.

Keep talking. Keep him talking, Robby's got to return any minute.

"What do you mean, accidents like those others?"

"I know what you were looking for in the canyon, the water hemlock. You're a smart girl. You figured out that Mr. Herb drank poison, didn't you?"

Millie pressed her lips together. If she spoke, he'd hear her teeth chatter.

"It is too bad. Mr. Herb and I had many interesting conversations. He told me all about the plants, the geology, even the stars we see here. He told me about the little San Juan cactus, how happy he was to discover it. He showed me where they live."

Millie was transfixed, she could not pull away from his eyes, impenetrable and callous. She had to understand how this barbarian could befriend a man, then poison him.

"Why did you put water hemlock in Herb's tea?" She tried to put an admiring tone in her voice, hoping he would think she was impressed with his cunning.

"I had to. He came to my camp at a very inconvenient time. I was preparing my little treasures to send to my country, where they are loved and protected. Mr. Herb saw them. He became angry. He was panting, holding a hand over his heart."

"You knew he had a bad heart, didn't you?"

"Of course. He always made me laugh when he talked about his 'ticker.' I couldn't let him go back to Wellstown, now, could I? I made him sit in a chair and prepared his favorite tea.

"That other man, he called himself an archaeologist. Ha, he was just snooping around. I was cleaning shovels. I did not want them dirtying my camper. He said I must be digging up ancient artifacts illegally. He went into my camper without my permission. That is not right."

Fritz's face twisted in anger. "He was a very naughty man. I hit him with the tripod. He moved, so I hit him again. I could not have his truck there. I put him into it and drove it away."

Millie forced herself to ask, "Was he dead when you rolled him over the cliff?"

"What does that matter?"

There is no reasoning with this man. Millie broke eye contact, looking for a way to escape. *Keep him talking.*

"Why did you want my map, Fritz, that day you nearly ran me off the road?"

"I must know where you found more San Juan cactus, Miss Millie. If that oaf, Buddy, had not arrived..."

"How do you know about the cactus, Fritz?"

"I told you—your colleague botanist came for tea one day. That fine gentleman liked that I make tea the way the pioneers did. He explained to me all about the giant trees he saw in Oregon. He had pictures of the ocean. He had a seashell in his pocket. He said to me that you, Miss

Millie, told him about another collection of San Juan cactus somewhere nearby."

Millie weighed this statement. Why would Herb tell anyone about the location of an endangered species?

"It was TJ who was showing you maps. I saw you with him at the BLM. Did TJ tell you?"

A raspy, disparaging sound came from deep within Fritz's throat. "Ha. That man knows nothing. He is, I believe your expression is, all hat and no cattle."

"Herb told you? I don't believe it."

"He trusted me. Why else would he show me places where cactus grow. One time, he'd show me claret cup in blossom, another year those delightful yellow prickly pear flowers. I made pictures of them. He liked to put them in his office. It is too bad that Mr. Herb came the day I was putting the little cactus in boxes to mail." Fritz was pounding the shovel up and down, barely able to control his anger. "He should not have come that day.

"Now, suppose you slip and fall, and hit your head on a rock." He slipped his hands down the shovel's handle and turned the blade upward, holding it like a baseball bat.

"But no. You will come with me, madam." He rested the shovel handle against his right shoulder, pulled the keys to his camper from his left jacket pocket and dangled them before her face. "I have clients arriving in two days. I will bring them here. We mustn't have them find vultures circling over a dead body." He smiled, seeming to enjoy his vision created from TV westerns.

Robby, where are you. She grasped for her only weapon, knowledge.

"Don't, Fritz. You'll never know where I found the third cactus plot. I can show you. You can follow me to it." She eased aside one step and moved a hand toward the door handle.

He considered this option for a moment, then glanced at the roll of maps on the back seat. "I'll have your map anyway." He raised the shovel.

Millie threw up her arms to protect her head.

34. Missed Catch

A lasso... is a loop of rope designed as a restraint to be thrown around a target and tightened when pulled. It is a well-known tool of the American cowboy.
—Wikipedia

No blow came. Instead, Millie heard the shovel smash against glass and clatter to the ground.

"You all right, Miss Whitehall?"

Millie lowered her arms. All she could see was a pink nose, blowing and splattering snot over her face.

She looked up through Dunnie's ears and nodded to Andy. Sweat dripped from the horse's neck; white lather curled out from under the saddle blanket. Fritz was nowhere within sight.

Andy stepped down from the saddle and Millie felt his steadying hand on her arm, then a gentle shake. He asked again, "Are you all right?"

"I... I'm okay. He said he did it," she managed to get out. "Fritz murdered those two men."

"He admitted it? That's what we figured." Andy bent down and grabbed the shovel. He used both hands to disentangle his rope from the handle, propped the shovel against the back door, and worked the rope back into a coil, keeping a fair-sized loop in his right hand. He stepped back into the saddle and appraised Millie's condition with one last look. Andy turned his body in the direction Fritz had sprinted away back down the road. The exhausted horse responded immediately, breaking into a gallop.

Millie leaned against the Suburban, pressing one palm against the BLM logo and the other against the back door to steady herself. From this stance, she watched chaos unfold.

Even though Dunnie's rump blocked her view of Fritz, Millie could tell Andy was closing in on his prey. The cowboy was swinging the rope over his head, letting the loop elongate with each swing.

Millie felt a drop of liquid run into her eye. She wiped it away and almost staggered when she saw her hand covered in blood. She touched her forehead and for the first time realized she stood among shards of glass from the window smashed by the shovel. If Andy's lasso had not accurately caught the shovel, deflecting Fritz's aim, her skull would have taken the blow.

Feeling her knees about to buckle, Millie put both hands on the side mirror, steadying herself. A streak of blood colored the mirror's edge. Millie leaned closer and groaned. There was a splinter of glass in her cheek and one in her chin. Most of the blood came from a gash above her eye.

The sound of an engine jerked her attention back to the fracas. Fritz was trapped between the oncoming horse and Robby returning in her Chevy Tahoe.

Fritz stumbled, but recovered. He dodged to the right, with the speed of a rabbit pursued by a coyote. Millie heard Andy's rope clunk against the Tahoe's front bumper, landing just beyond its target.

She heard running steps and crunching gravel before she saw the reflection of Fritz's approaching figure. She swung around and grabbed the shovel. Fritz dove toward her feet, grabbing for the keys to the camper, dropped there when Cowboy's lasso yanked the shovel aside. Millie kicked out, hitting Fritz's shoulder, nearly toppling him sideways. He reached again for the keys. Millie slammed the shovel's blade onto the back of his hand. She heard bones crack.

Fritz uttered a primal growl. He staggered upright, gaping wide-mouthed at one angry botanist. Millie drove the shovel down again inches from his feet and simultaneously dug her heeled boot in the dirt, giving a hard kick backwards. The keys landed somewhere under the vehicle.

Robbie shouted, "Move, goddammit."

Fritz heard Robbie's command. He ran, cradling his right hand against his stomach.

Holding onto the side mirror for support, Millie twisted toward Robby, who was waving her arms and aiming curses at the big horse in front of her. "Move, move, move, damn it."

Andy was hunched over the saddle, trying to yank the rope loose from where it was caught around the bumper. The more Robby tried to wave horse and rider out of her way, the more Dunnie twirled and fussed. Robby darted around them and trotted toward Millie, buckling her gun belt around her waist as she went.

As Robby neared the Suburban, Millie saw Andy dismount, work at the tangled rope for a moment, and swing back up on the prancing mustang.

"Jesus, you're a bloody mess. What happened to you, girl?"

"I'm all right—I think. Fritz tried to kill me." Millie still held tight to the mirror.

"Millie, we need to get an ambulance here for you."

Dunnie came up at a fast trot and stopped beside them. Andy laid a hand on his mane. The horse, accepting the signal to rest, lowered his head, still breathing hard.

"It's just little cuts." Millie stepped away from the mirror and pointed in the direction Fritz had gone. "We've got to stop him."

Fritz, now forced to a slow jog by rough ground, had reached the T-two plot.

"He's probably heading there because it's familiar ground. He's been there before. But he'll keep going, that's for certain." Robby said.

"We need back-up." Andy pulled a cell phone out of his pocket, frowned at the no bars icon, and put it away. "It wasn't supposed to go down this way."

"Even if you could get through, it'll take at least an hour for anybody from the sheriff's office to get here." Robby looked at Millie's bleeding face. "We can't wait. That bastard's not getting away."

Dunnie was the first to hear the heavy footsteps behind them. He swung his head around, nearly pushing Robby aside. The white truck with its orange flag was parked behind Robby's vehicle. Buddy Maddox was approaching at a jog.

"What's going on here? I heard the alert on my radio. Came as fast as I could." He puffed out, not used to covering distance on his own two feet. "What happened to you!"

"I'm all right, okay?" Millie didn't like being the focus of any more remarks on her appearance, even if she couldn't bring herself to look in the mirror again.

"Buddy, will you do me a favor?" With some slight-of-hand, Andy flipped open a case that put a sturdy metal badge in front of Buddy's startled face. "We've got a murderer on the run. Call the sheriff's office. Tell them Special Agent Andrew Anderson needs them *now* at the location they were to meet me. And no sirens."

"I'm on it," Buddy managed to say, although his mouth still hung open. "I'll get help for Miss Millie, too."

"Robby, ease up to that clump of junipers on this side of the cactus and make yourself invisible. I'm going to ride a wide circle and herd our friend back toward you. You ready?"

Robby was already moving, right hand resting on her holster.

* * *

Millie leaned her head back against the headrest. The silence was eerie. The Suburban felt like a sanctuary after enduring Buddy's tender, albeit clumsy, administration of first aid. The glass shards were small and she barely felt it as Buddy extracted them with tweezers.

"That's the best I can do. I got to drive out to where I can get a radio signal and do what Cowboy said. You put these on those bad cuts."

"Go Buddy, call the sheriff's office."

"Like I told you, we help each other out, here in the gas patch. Stay here and keep your doors locked."

She still held the first aid kit and a half-dozen Band Aids he had pushed into her hand.

She watched in the rear view mirror as he trotted back to his truck. She was safe, for the time being. His well-meant "keep your doors locked" made her smile, even though it caused a small cut on her upper lip to exude another drop of blood. The window behind her head was a gaping hole.

35. Whoa Dunnie

Scientists busy themselves with making descriptions of the natural world, and at some point they notice that behavior is a natural phenomenon, so turning their spotlight on it, out comes a relatively humble set of observations about how animals learn.

—Patricia Barlow-Irick, *How 2 Train A* _____

Millie's head shot forward when she heard Robby's distant shout. She stepped out of the vehicle, still pressing a square of gauze against her forehead. Buddy's truck was gone. Robby's Tahoe blocked the road about half a football field from where she stood. The green camper loomed in front of the Suburban.

Concerned that she heard nothing further from Robby, only a cicada complaining about summer ending, Millie pushed her way into the sagebrush. Then Millie heard Robby's voice in a sharp command. "Stop, Müller. Let me see both your hands."

On the far side of the T-two plot, Fritz was bent in a crouch, heaving like a runner finishing a marathon.

Fritz pulled the same rabbit-like move, sprinting in the opposite direction from the ranger's voice.

A raven's scream drowned out the sound of Dunnie crashing out of the junipers. The raven made a steep dive, passing inches in front of Fritz's face. Fritz did not notice the lasso until it tightened against his chest.

"Get up, Müller." Andy gathered the rope, keeping it taut, as Dunnie moved forward.

Fritz grunted, rolled over onto his knees, and thrust his body upright. The unforgiving rope almost toppled him backwards again.

Cowboy urged Dunnie forward, allowing enough slack for Fritz to turn and face him.

Millie stepped out of the sagebrush, the toes of her boots resting on one of the orange markers she had placed not more than two hours earlier. This time, she was not about to chastise the cowboy for riding across the cactus. The US Fish and Wildlife Special Agent was putting a halt to cactus rustling.

Fritz struggled against the rope, cursing in his native language. When Dunnie stepped forward, Fritz stumbled back, his eyes wide. He yelled, "Get it away. Don't let that beast hurt me."

Fritz's focus was only on keeping a distance between himself and the mustang. Robby appeared thirty feet beyond him, arms out straight, hands gripping the Glock. She edged sideways, matching Fritz's movement. He continued stepping back.

Cowboy gave a soft, "Whoa Dunnie," made another wrap of the rope around the saddle horn, and dismounted. He approached his captive, running one hand along the rope while flipping his badge open with the other.

Andy barked out his name and title. Fritz's body stiffened with rage. The full ramification of Cowboy turned cop hit him. Fritz snarled, "You… you betrayed me." He emitted the same primal growl as he gave out when Millie crushed his hand with the shovel.

Fritz looked left toward Robby, now only a few feet

away. He wiggled enough to be able to place his left hand on the rope, but it still held his injured right arm tight to his chest. Andy was now ten feet in front of him.

"What are you doing here, Fritz?" Andy said with a genial smile, removing his hat.

Fritz spat on the ground and clamped his mouth shut.

Dunnie took a step back, jerking a surprised Fritz into taking a giant step forward, almost losing his balance. Robby and Andy took a step sideways, staying even with their captive.

"You must untie this rope."

Dunnie took another step back. The friendly voice came again, "Why did you come here?"

"That animal is going to run away. You must remove this rope. I will do what you want."

"That's right. Wild mustangs can be unpredictable. Are you giving me permission to look inside your camper, Fritz?"

Fritz did not respond. Dunnie stepped back.

Millie's jaw dropped. This time she was looking at Andy as he morphed between Special Agent and Cowboy. His right hand hovered by his ear and each time his index finger bobbed up and down, Dunnie took a step, responding to his master's signal.

"Ja, I will take you to my camper," Fritz grumbled in resignation.

* * *

Millie saw Buddy's white truck down the road, parked behind Robby's Tahoe. Buddy had one foot propped on the Tahoe's bumper. Another vehicle was angled behind his truck, blocking the road.

Two men were walking in their direction. The men wore the brown slacks and tan shirts of sheriff's officers.

Alert, but not interfering with the bizarre scene playing out at the camper, they stood ready to provide back-up.

Fritz yanked open the door of the camper and growled something unintelligible toward Andy. Andy loosened the rope enough for it drop to the ground. Fritz rubbed his arms, scanning the stony-faced officers encircling him. Robby spoke. Fritz raised his arms over his head and placed his palms against the camper.

Andy stepped into the dark interior.

36. Buddy's Tale

A friend in need, is a friend indeed.
—*Latin Proverb, 3rd Century BC*

"I'm telling you, Wirt. It was like a scene from the wild west." Millie knew she was about to suffer through another of Buddy's rendition of the nightmarish episode.

He had the story down pat. He'd refined it during the ride to Wellstown when he twice waved down a passing field hand and gave them a blow-by-blow account of his dramatic rescue. Millie was pretty sure the story would reach every rancher and oil field worker in the San Juan Basin by noon the next day. When Buddy slowed as he approached the third white truck, she had tapped his arm and pointed to the blotch of blood seeping through the bandage on her forehead. Buddy gasped and apologized profusely for delaying getting her to the hospital.

She didn't mind now. She was next in line to be called into an examining room. Buddy's voice blended in with the emergency room's surrounding noise. At Momma Agnes's call, Wirt had detoured back to Wellstown to meet them at the hospital. He assured the intake administrator about insurance coverage and held the clipboard steady as Millie signed one form after another, too weak to give her customary scrutiny to the fine print.

Buddy was coming to his favorite part of the story. "Here comes this German fellow, stumbling along with a rope tied around him. Cowboy's on his horse, walking this guy along like a pet cow. That BLM ranger has a gun on him. Millie, here, looking like she's been hit by a tornado, goes trotting in the opposite direction. I had to go get her. Know what she was doing? She was pushing dirt back over those little cactus where all that ruckus turned some of them up."

The ride to Wellstown Regional Hospital was mostly a blur in Millie's mind. She remembered Buddy placing her in his truck and clicking the seatbelt over her shoulder. She wanted to erase the images of how the faces of the truck drivers Buddy talked to changed from curiosity to incredulity to compassion.

She did not remember seeing the lights of Wellstown or arriving at the hospital's emergency entrance. Perhaps she had drifted in and out of consciousness. She touched her lip, checking to see if the cut might have started bleeding again. She did recall that it hurt to smile when Buddy, trying to keep her preoccupied, spotted a plastic grocery bag flapping from a fencepost. "Know what I call those? I call them desert seagulls. Just like Edward Abby wrote about tourists tossing out Kleenex when he worked at Arches National Park. 'Sagebrush flowers,' is what he called them."

A tall figure dressed in white appeared in front of her. "Millicent Whitehall? We're ready for you now."

* * *

It was nearly midnight when the doctor guided Millie back out to the lobby. "I want to see you in three days to check those stitches on your forehead. The other cuts will probably heal okay, but that deeper one on your forehead may leave a scar. If you see any redness, any sign of infection, come in immediately." He pushed two pill bottles into her hand. "And begin taking these pain and antibiotic tablets as soon as you get home."

The lobby's bright lights made Millie blink. She blinked again. Ben Benallee stood in front of her, replacing the doctor's hand on her arm with his own. For once, his face did not reveal a wide grin and flashing white teeth, but only sympathetic eyes under furrowed brows.

"Momma Agnes told me you were here. I've been waiting for ages for you to come out. Well, since Wirt left an hour ago. I promised him I'd take you home, safe and sound." He glanced at her pale face and bandaged forehead and added, "Maybe not so sound."

As Ben walked her through the parking lot to the Miata, he explained that he had stopped by the BLM office a little before quitting time to pick up a map of deer habitat that he needed. "As soon as I walked in I heard Momma Agnes yakking on the radio. She was fielding calls like crazy. When this Buddy guy called and said he was bringing you into the hospital, well, I thought she was going to blow a gasket. When he couldn't tell her where the BLM ranger was and somebody she called 'Andy,' she said something in Spanish—it didn't sound friendly."

Ben held the door open while Millie eased into the passenger seat. "Momma Agnes sent me here to pick you up. Wirt had to go to the sheriff's office. She made me promise to call her as soon as I saw you." Ben started the engine and reached for his cell phone.

Millie touched his arm. "No, just take me home. You can call her later."

Ben gave her a sideways glance. "Sure thing, *ayoo ani-inish'ni.*"

37. Collectors' Syndrome

In the United States, cactus poachers from foreign countries have detailed directions published by their local clubs and societies to populations of rare cacti in the United States. As tourists they dig plants, package them, and ship them home via first class airmail. The packages are infrequently opened and inspected by customs officials.

—Richard Spellenberg, in *William A. Dick-Peddie, New Mexico Vegetation*

Belva Banks planted her elbows on the BLM conference room table. "Sure, I'll testify. Fritz waved me down on Lejos Canyon Road and I drove him back to his camper. That S.O.B.—stealing our cactus, pretending to be such a gentleman." She seemed to be having the time of her life, gratified to have the chance to contribute to protecting a natural resource.

Agent Andy nodded, "Thanks, Belva, that will help." The US Fish and Wildlife Special Agent sat at the head of the table.

Belva elbowed the yawning sheriff's deputy sitting next her, then made sure she had the full attention of Wirt, Robby, Millie, and TJ. "I know I filled up with gas that morning before I drove out to go hiking. I can get the exact date off my credit card statement."

Andy continued, "That is just the piece we need to link Müller to the vicinity where the archaeologist's body was found. Once we get the forensics back on the few hairs we found caught in an expansion joint in the leg of his tripod, we'll have enough evidence to charge him with Harrison Howdy's death.

"We might have missed examining that tripod if Müller hadn't made the mistake of bragging to Millie about how clever he was. He was getting bold. He'd gotten away with stealing cactus on his pseudo-photography tours in the past. He wasn't going to let anyone break up a lucrative business."

Robby poked Millie's arm. "Cowboy, if you weren't so good with that lasso, Müller might have added Millie to his victims."

Millie tried to spread her hair a little lower over her forehead. Momma Agnes had looked so doleful this morning, not because Millie arrived late after returning from the hospital, but because of the angry-looking scab that marred the young woman's face. The doctor reported the laceration was healing satisfactorily. But for Millie, it would have been better to keep the black-and-blue wound hidden under a bandage.

The sheriff's deputy spoke up. "Don't worry about Müller. We charged him for assault on Miss Whitehall and resisting arrest. He spent the night in our county jail. Then first thing the next morning we got him before the Federal Magistrate for charges under the Endangered Species Act, with attempt to transport San Juan cactus out of the country. US Marshals showed up at noon to escort him to the federal holding facility in Albuquerque. He's locked up tight. We've got enough evidence to hold him as long as it takes to build a case to bring charges for the two murders."

The deputy looked at the Special Agent, "I guess maybe we have that horse, Dunnie—I think you call him—to thank for convincing the guy to let us search his camper." He added with a smirk, "Can't imagine why a photographer would need all those shovels and digging trowels that we found."

A smile briefly invaded Andy's serious demeanor at this acknowledgment of his mustang. "We found a box of San Juan cactus stashed under the bed. Each one stuck in a paper cup with a little sand thrown in. One had five stems nearly three inches long—a real grandfather. The rest were smaller."

"That big one would be at least fifteen to twenty years old, the smaller ones at least three or four years old," Millie said.

Andy was working his leather case around and around in his hands. "That's probably what Herb Thompson saw at Müller's camp, and confronted him about it. The really sick thing is, we found a banged-up BLM cap under the driver's seat of Mueller's camper. It probably belonged to Mr. Thompson."

"That bastard," Wirt slammed both hands on the table. "What kind of a man would kill to make money off selling a cactus?"

"I'm guessing that after the tripod incident, Müller made preparations in case someone else got too curious. We found a plastic container inside the freezer section of the camper's refrigerator. It looked suspicious, with a couple of wraps of duct tape around it. All it had inside was an ice cube tray. The slots had a small amount of a yellowish liquid. I'm betting he collected it from water hemlock root. We just put the whole kit-n-caboodle into a cooler and sent it to the Dallas lab."

The Special Agent leaned back, seeming relieved to

be past the worst part of his report. "There's no telling what greed will make a person do. But it goes beyond just greed, it's the collector's syndrome. Buyers of illegally collected cactus, or stolen Native American artifacts, are driven to take risks beyond what seem normal to us. They may be competitive, engaging in one-upmanship with rival collectors. They may be compulsive—not satisfied until they have one of every species, especially rare species. An obsessive collector may be ego-dystonic, knowing they are engaging in destructive behavior but unable to stop themselves."

Andy unzipped his case and flipped through notes. "I think Müller falls into that last category. In his confession statement, he never admitted to wrongdoing. He justified his actions every which way. This is part of what he said," Andy assumed a raspy accent. "'People in my country love the little cactus. They keep them in greenhouses—no hot summer winds to shrivel them up, no freezing snow. How can you say I commit a crime? We take much better care of the little cactus. You Americans just leave them in the wilderness at nature's mercy. You Americans have so much, so much space, so many cactus. You Americans do not appreciate what you have.'"

"But, but..." Millie spluttered in indignation, "they're adapted to high desert seasonal extremes. And they're rare. Did he think digging them up was going to save them?"

"He did, Miss Whitehall. He believed he knew better than Mother Nature. He bragged about his 'gardening' techniques. Seems on his visits here every couple of years, he not only dug up cactus, but prepared for future collecting trips. In between taking his fellow photographer-collectors around, he spent time removing stones and sticks where they might cause a cactus to grow misshapen."

Andy looked at Robby and Millie, pausing for effect. "Remember that package of rodent poison you found?"

"Don't tell me he was poisoning mice, so he could come back later and dig up prettier cactus," Robby said.

"That's what he was doing, all right." Andy let that statement hang in the air for a moment. "He'd gotten away with it for a dozen years, alternating between Arizona and New Mexico. Having his thieves take just enough cactus along the outer edges not to be noticed. In between times, he was tidying up locations of rare cactus so they could dig up perfect specimens on future trips."

Millie couldn't contain herself. "I knew it! I knew there was something different that made those two plots look so, so… tidy. Remember, Robby, you said that one looked like it had been swept clean? That wasn't natural."

"I figured you'd be glad to hear that part of Müller's story," Andy said. "But we couldn't get him to say who called from this office and alerted him about law enforcement heading to the T-two plot. He would not reveal his informant."

"I can help you with that." All eyes turned to the area manager. "After I got your call, Agent Anderson, I told our Motor Pool clerk to bring my vehicle around. TJ, I'll let you take it from here."

At Wirt's nod, TJ cleared his throat and began in a low voice. "I called Fritz. He asked me to let him know whenever any of the BLM crew was going to the north unit. He told me he'd invite them to have lunch with him or something. I figured he was just lonely. So I'd give him a call. Every so often, he came by the office. Didn't even check in up front. Just came right to see me back in the shop, 'cause he'd have a bottle of Jim Beam or a box of cigars under his jacket."

TJ steadied the head of his cane leaning against the

table, perhaps to reassure himself that support was close. "I always thought he was a real stand-up fellow, the way he dressed and that accent and all. He made me feel like I was important around here." TJ raised his head and looked at the incredulous faces around him.

So that explains why TJ is here. Millie leaned forward to see past the others. She had the chair farthest from where he sat. *It wasn't just that one day I saw them at the copy machine. Fritz was pumping TJ for information all along.*

The Special Agent was blunt, "What did you know about his stealing cactus?"

TJ crossed his arms. "I swear, I didn't know Fritz was involved with anything like that. You think I'd be working for BLM and let something like that go...?"

"I believe TJ," Wirt broke the tension. "I've got to write him up for accepting gifts on the job, but I wouldn't want to see his involvement in this matter taken any further."

Agent Andy gave a long look in Wirt's direction, then nodded. "I can live with that, given the Piñon Resource Area was the linchpin for busting a decade of this guy's thumbing his nose at us."

Turning to TJ, he said, "I'll still need a sworn statement from you, Mister...?"

"Theodore Jackson, but I go by TJ. Yeah, okay. I'll put my hand on a stack of bibles, take a lie detector test, anything you want. I didn't have nothin' to do with cactus rustling."

TJ pushed himself up and limped to Millie's end of the table. "And I'm sure sorry, girlie, about what happened to you."

"TJ, I'll forgive you, if you just stop calling me girlie."

38. Shiny Reward

I believe that there is a subtle magnetism in Nature, which, if
we unconsciously yield to it, will direct us aright.
—*Henry David Thoreau*

"Green," Millie had to shout to be heard over laughter
filling the Devil's Claw Café. The waitress nodded,
scribbled the order, and pushed her pad in Ben Benallee's
direction.

"Add a *Dos Equis* to that. My treat. We're celebrating.
I'll have your Navajo Taco, but I bet it's not as good as my
grandma's."

"Coming right up," the waitress beamed. She could
anticipate a better than usual haul of tips from this crew,
for a Friday night. She scurried to the kitchen. The chips
and salsa on every table would soon need replenishing.

Piñon Resource Area staff, many wearing tan shirts
with triangular arm patches, dominated the majority of
the café's tables. This annual end of season gathering was
occasion to celebrate the winding down of field work and
say farewell to the seasonal staff.

Wirt motioned to Millie, then Ben. Like dominoes, they
wiggled out of their booth so he could slide out. He took
a few steps to the center of the room, causing the noisy
gathering to hush.

"Folks, I won't take much of your time tonight, I just want to thank everybody for all your hard work this summer." He waited until the cheers and clinking of glasses died down. "I can't say it was all fun and games. We lost a couple of good friends and I hope I never see another situation like that for the rest of my career. But we'll just keep doing our job, and with the help of our friends, we'll hold the line and protect the resource." He nodded to Belva, crammed into their booth next to Robby. Then Wirt made his way over to shake hands with Buddy Maddox and Special Agent Andy Anderson, who sat at a table near the kitchen, along with Linda and Momma Agnes.

The cook and two waitresses pushed through the kitchen's swinging doors, each balancing trays laden with oval platters. Every platter contained beans and rice, regardless of whether the order was for burritos, tamales, chimichangas, or enchiladas. The room quieted as the celebrants tucked into their meals.

A waitress distributing sopaipillas maneuvered a basket onto their crowded table and rushed on to the next booth. Buddy's blocky figure took her place. "Miss Millie, I found something in my truck after I took you to the hospital. I wasn't sure, but Momma Agnes said I should give it to you."

He glanced across the café to where Momma Agnes was squeezing honey into a sopaipilla. She waved a hand, signaling go ahead, give it to her.

"I kind of polished it up as a souvenir." Buddy placed a half-dollar sized crystal on the table. It was crazed with a network of fine silvery lines. Millie picked it up and held it up to the light. A network of cracks formed the startling outline of a bird's head.

Robby sucked in her breath and whispered, "You know what that is, don't you? You were standing in a pile of broken glass. A piece must have caught in your clothes and dropped off in Buddy's truck."

Millie sat the piece back on the table. She had the scar on her forehead, and sometimes dreams resounding with crashing glass, as souvenirs of that terrifying day.

"Thanks, Buddy. I'll never forget your kindness."

Ben snatched up the proffered gift and held it to the light, eyeing Buddy's hopeful face. "This sure is—ah—a one-of-a-kind thing."

Ben reached behind Millie's shoulders. "Here Wirt, take a look at this. Oh, Buddy, Momma Agnes is waving you over."

As Buddy made his way back across the room, the unorthodox souvenir passed from hand to hand, until Robby slipped it back to Ben, who shoved it into his jeans pocket.

Wirt steered the conversation away from the past. "So, Millie, when are you heading back East?"

Well-meaning as it was, this didn't lift Millie's spirits either. "I'll spend a day packing, and I want to take one last visit to Split Lip Canyon Overlook and my favorite cactus plot." She was leaving the land she had come to know and love, trading wide-open spaces for a three-day road trip with a meowing Ragged Ear. "I plan to be on the road by Monday." Worst of all, she was taking leave of friends, good friends.

"I hope we'll be seeing you back next summer. There's still the west unit canyon country to inventory," Wirt said.

Millie started to giggle. "Seriously? What if I find another endangered plant on the Resource Area? I thought I caused you enough trouble."

"No trouble at all. Seems the company was about to pull their application to drill anyway. Their regional headquarters out of Dallas wants to shift focus downstate. They're keeping the lease, of course. But any future drilling plans will need to assure no impact on the Millie plot."

Belva's arm shot up—meeting Millie's in a high-five, then slapping hands all around the table.

* * *

The moon was riding high by the time numerous good byes, *hasta luegos,* and *buen viajes* were exchanged. Ben darted ahead and had Rust Bucket's door open. "Sure I can't stop by your place tomorrow? We can go out to Split Lip together."

He held the door pushed open with one arm, corralling Millie between himself and the front seat. His hair glistened in the moonlight. She made no move to slide behind the steering wheel.

"No, Ben. I have to do this on my own. I know I can do it now."

He steadied the door and eased both arms around her. They stood embraced like this for some time, sharing a warmth that kept the night's chill at bay.

Finally, Millie stirred. "That piece of glass Buddy gave me. Where is it?"

Ben took a step back and dug in his pocket. "I didn't think you wanted a reminder of what happened."

She curled her fingers around the crystal in his outstretched palm. "I know a very special raven to give this to. She likes shiny things."

Millie slid into the Explorer. Neither could give voice to that lonely word, goodbye.

Ben resumed his unquenchable optimism. Gently closing the door, he said, "You know what we Navajos say, once you live in the shadow of Ship Rock, you'll always return."

Author's Notes

The characters in this story are fictional, although they are drawn from the many remarkable people I have encountered while living in western states. Wellstown and Devil's Claw Café do not exist but may seem familiar to those who have traveled in the Southwest.

Plant species occurring in northwest New Mexico are accurately described to the best of my ability. An important exception to this is the San Juan cactus. There is no recognized species by this name; instead, it represents concerns typically associated with threatened and endangered species.

Very real are the complexities of managing Bureau of Land Management public lands—which historically nobody wanted but now, it seems, everybody wants.

I relied on the *Flora of the Four Corners Region* taxonomy guide for many of the species accounts. I did take some liberty with the yucca species. Occurrence at higher versus lower elevation is not clear cut for banana yucca and narrowleaf yucca, as the ranges of these two species overlap. However, from personal observation, banana yucca is more often found at higher elevations.

I often gleaned interesting facts from *New Mexico Vegetation: Past, Present, and Future*; *Wild Plants and Native Peoples of the Four Corners*; and the Southwest Colorado Wild Flowers website. In addition to these, I incorporated much outdoor lore gathered from many field trips with knowledgeable people and through my own interests.

Writing an entire novel is a lengthy process. There were many people involved with getting me to the finish line.

Artemesia Press editor Geoff Habiger helped make the characters real, resulting in a much better story. My friend, Elaine Benally, San Juan College West Campus Director, kindly reviewed the manuscript for cultural concerns. Dr. Linda Mary Reeves, botanist, kept the plant information on the straight and narrow. Dr. Stu Wilson, retired pathologist, helped with medical terminology.

I am indebted to Anne Hillerman, Elaine Benally, and Jonathan Thompson for kindly reading the manuscript and providing a cover testimonial. The work of each of these individuals represent the best of their professions.

I also want to thank my writing groups, the Persistence Club and the San Juan Writers, for their practical, incredibly helpful critiquing, mixed with continuous encouragement. The crew at San Juan College Copy Services produced the many versions of the manuscript with patience and good cheer. I also appreciate all the organizers and presenters who have shared their knowledge at the Tony Hillerman Writers Conferences, the Women Writing the West conferences, New Mexico Press Women conferences and other gatherings, where I learned a bit of the craft. Lastly, I acknowledge the men and woman, past, present and future, employed by public lands agencies who hold the line.

Most important of all, I thank my husband, technical advisor, and best friend, Jim Ramakka, retired BLM biologist, for continuous support and a wonderful life.

Resources:

Heil, K. D., S. L. O'Kane, Jr., L. M. Reeves, A. Clifford. 2013. *Flora of the Four Corners Region: Vascular Plants of the San Juan River Drainage: Arizona, Colorado, New Mexico, and Utah.* Missouri Botanical Garden Press, St. Louis.
https://www.mbgpress.org/product-p/msb-124.htm

Dick-Peddie, W. A. 1993. *New Mexico Vegetation: Past, Present, and Future.* University of New Mexico Press, Albuquerque.
https://unmpress.com/search?keywords=nm+vegetation

Dunmire, W. W. and G. D. Tierney. 1997. *Wild Plants and Native Peoples of the Four Corners.* Museum of New Mexico Press, Santa Fe.
http://mnmpress.org/?p=allBooks&id=183

Southwest Colorado Wild Flowers website, operated by Al Schneider.
http://www.swcoloradowildflowers.com

About the Author

Vicky Ramakka grew up on a farm in upstate New York which sparked an early interest in plants and animals. She has spent most of her career in higher education in the western US while her husband worked as a wildlife biologist for the Bureau of Land Management. During her career, she published in academic journals, wrote numerous grant applications and reports and a variety of marketing materials.  She now she writes about the Four Corners region, where she claims she meets the most fascinating people, who are always willing to share their stories. Her publications have won awards from the New Mexico Press Women. She currently lives in northwest New Mexico with her husband, where Vicky writes and enjoys photographing the flora and fauna that reside in her "back yard" which she considers any place within a mile walk.